JACKPOT DRIFT BOOK 3

THE CHAOS NEXUS

T.M. BAUMGARTNER

Cover Art by Deranged Doctor Design

PART I

UNMANIFESTED

1

Sil's opinion of the sheep on Jackpot Drift had never been very high. This ewe wasn't going to change her mind.

Outside the barn, the first real storm of winter raged, dumping enough snow to hide the potholes in the roads and make everyone already indoors glad to be there. Inside the barn, there was less snow, but it wasn't appreciably warmer. Worse, Sil was lying on her side in wet and bloody straw, crammed in a small stall with an angry ewe who didn't appreciate Sil and Crumble's attempts to save her life.

"You're doing a great job!" Crumble, currently leaning on the sheep's neck to keep her immobile, didn't share Sil's antagonism toward everything ovine. To be fair, *he* was wearing a coat. Also, he wasn't trying to reposition a lamb that had attempted to come out of the birth canal sideways. Did the damn thing not have two front legs?

Sil repositioned her hand. "Are you talking to me or the ewe?"

A guilty pause told her the answer. She smiled despite the late hour and the circumstances.

"You're doing a great job, too. Of course!" He twisted to look over his shoulder. "How are things going at that end?"

There. Sil grabbed the second leg and pulled the lamb toward her. Now it was positioned correctly, and theoretically she could let the ewe complete the process on her own. But if they let the sheep up now and something went wrong, they would have to tackle her again. Sil could already feel the bruise on her ribs from where the ewe had knocked her into the boards. "Nearly there."

A flutter of large wings overhead dislodged dust from the roof beams. Even without looking up, Sil knew One Spot had come to watch them. Her chaos godlet recognized the flitterkin, which held chaos of its own. If One Spot was here, that meant the rest of the group wouldn't be far off. She sighed and kept guiding the lamb. That was what this situation needed — uncontrolled chaos while she was trapped in a stall with a homicidal sheep.

She hoped Crumble's luck godlet could keep things under control.

The lamb slid toward her as the ewe strained. Sil pulled on the front legs, and twenty seconds later, the lamb was out. She stood up and pulled the unmoving bundle in front of the ewe's head. "It sometimes takes them a bit to come around," she warned Crumble. During every lambing season, there were some that didn't make it out alive, but she could feel a heartbeat as she rubbed the black and white lamb's belly. It finally took its first gasp of breath. The ewe licked the wet and slimy lamb. "Don't let her get up yet."

Crumble was entranced. "It's beautiful. Good job."

Once again, she was pretty sure he was talking to the ewe and not to her. Fair enough. The ewe *had* done most of the work.

Sil lay down in the straw again. According to the documents Glass's stockman had left, this ewe was only supposed to have a single lamb. But according to those same documents, this ewe wasn't supposed to give birth for another four weeks, and *that* had been a full-term lamb. If Sil hadn't noticed the ewe pawing at the ground earlier in the day, she wouldn't have brought the ewe into the barn for the night, and there very likely would have been a dead sheep buried under the snow by the time the storm let up.

Sil eased her arm back into the ewe just in time to hear a snort from outside the stall. Mer's voice cut through the ewe's baaing. "I always knew the low clan did some odd things. This is just confirmation."

Pyr sounded horrified. "What are you doing?"

Sil tilted her head so she could see the other two. "What does it look like I'm doing?"

"I'm afraid to find out." The bartender's face matched his voice, and he had both hands held pressed to his chest. His mobility assist had no trouble moving him away from the railing despite the barn's uneven floor. Next to him, Mer's face looked pinched, but Sil didn't think that had anything to do with the sheep. Something in the high clan woman's hip or spine had gotten worse after their trip to the edge of the valley, and she was in near constant pain these days.

Sil's questing hand hit another lamb, and she felt around to find the front legs. "There's a second one."

"You have twins," Crumble crooned to the ewe. "Isn't that exciting?"

Sil found a front hoof. "Did we have a meeting or something?" Aside from dealing with their reactions, she didn't mind having the other two in the barn. Having Pyr's clarity godlet along with Mer's guile meant all four of the older gods were present. That, in turn, meant chaos was much less likely to bring down the roof or make the ewe explode or whatever the godlet thought might be fun to torture her with.

"Can we do this somewhere else? I'm not sure I can

handle a conversation with someone who has their arm..."
Pyr still sounded thoroughly appalled.

Sil took a deep breath through bloody and muddy wool, and blew it out. "It's the middle of the night. I'm freezing, which is good because it's keeping me from feeling all the bruises. I just found out all the records about Glass's sheep might be complete fabrications, which means they aren't getting the right feed and that could make lambing season truly hellish, and you're out here bothered by a little animal husbandry." She found the lamb's second leg and pulled it toward her.

What she didn't say was the colony couldn't afford to lose sheep. If the AIs had to close the gates accessing the wormhole, Jackpot Drift would be cut off completely. And it wasn't self-sufficient yet. A bad lambing season could put them one step closer to starvation.

The lamb's front hooves and nose made it out during the ewe's next push. Sil pulled the membrane off the nose and helped pull the lamb the rest of the way. Two working legs made it easier to drag it up to the ewe's face. At least some things were going right. The new biomechanical leg seemed to have integrated properly.

The first lamb lifted its head when she slid its sibling next to it. She rubbed the unresponsive second lamb roughly to stimulate it. Crumble made a motion as if he were about to get up and she shook her head. "I need to make sure there aren't more."

"Triplets?" Crumble's delight at the idea was so great, she didn't have the heart to tell him it wouldn't be a good thing. Ewes only had two teats; a third lamb would probably end up getting bullied and starved. That meant she and Crumble would have to bottle-feed it, and they just didn't have time for that.

The second lamb coughed and sucked in a breath. Sil left

it for the ewe to take care of and moved to the other side of the pen yet again. "Go on inside and make tea. We'll be there in fifteen minutes or so." Unless there were more than three. She eased her arm back into the ewe.

From her vantage point on the ground, Sil saw a flitterkin swoop in to perch on the beam above her. With their large, lightly furred bodies and huge wings, they always seemed ungainly when they weren't soaring on currents high in the sky. This one didn't have the spark of chaos she felt in all the others. "Longbrow is back," she said to Crumble.

He looked up. "Think you can get him now?"

Sil poked at the chaos cat sleeping within her. It merely purred and rolled over. "Maybe when Mer and Pyr move far enough away." The flitterkin they had designated Longbrow was the final holdout, the only one of the genetically tweaked species not carrying chaos within it. That meant he was the only one susceptible to being used to manifest the Uncaring God of the AIs.

For seven weeks now, Sil had been trying to get chaos to take hold within that flitterkin. The other experiment survivors had been easy enough to infect after she'd figured it out. But Longbrow either wouldn't hold still long enough or just didn't seem to be as attractive a target for her chaos cat.

Crumble had tried once with luck. His failure hadn't surprised either of them. When they had been trying to protect the caged flitterkin before, only chaos had been interested.

The ewe did *not* have another lamb. Sil stood and sluiced her arm off in the bucket of water they'd brought into the pen. The water had been warm the first time she'd used it, but it had a distinct chill now. Jackpot Drift winters were not for the faint of heart. "Let me just make sure her milk is in and then we can get out of here." Hopefully, the ewe would be so fixated on her lambs they'd be able to get out of the stall with more grace than they'd been able to get in, but Sil wasn't holding her breath. The sheep were bred to be aggressive, which increased their chances of survival on the inhospitable terrain.

How had Glass's stockman gotten it so wrong? Having one lamb make it to term when two were seen on a scan earlier was understandable, but not the other way around. Had all the data just been made up? Unfortunately, the man who had done the scans had left the planet, so she couldn't ask him about it.

The timing of it all couldn't be worse. In her other full-time job as a nanite technician, Sil was trying to make sure the colony had working backups for everything they needed. Anything she couldn't fashion out of existing supplies went on the high priority list. In seven weeks, her half-sister had spent nearly the entire yearly governor's budget. Every time Sil added something new to the list, Palladium stomped into the workshop to argue about the necessity. But there was a real possibility someone would decide it was easier to destroy the planet of Jackpot Drift, colonists and all, than take the chance of the Uncaring God manifesting. If that happened, they needed to be prepared to be cut off, possibly forever.

Failing to convert the last flitterkin, behind on creating an inventory of needed imports, and now facing catastrophe with the lambing — the whole colony depended on Sil and somehow everything was falling apart.

The ewe had milk, both lambs were making efforts to stand, and Crumble vaulted over the side of the stall before the sheep scrambled to her feet. Sil used an almost-clean towel to dry off her arm and then pulled on her coat. "Let me try Longbrow again."

Crumble took the pail of water from her along with the

towel. "I'll talk to Stuck in the Mud and see if it can keep an eye on the ewes."

Of the two of them, Crumble was far more suited to talking to the AI, and not just because he had a mech's implants. Sil had spent a year with the damaged AI as her only companion up in the hills. She *still* couldn't communicate with it and found it frustrating to try. Crumble had more patience with Mud.

Crumble had more patience with everything.

Staring up at the rafters, Sil sighed. The troublesome flitterkin, mostly white with a dark horizontal slash across his forehead, looked back at her. As usual, the problem wasn't with the flitterkin; the problem was Sil's general frustration with the godlet of chaos. She imagined giving it a gentle nudge. Without clarity and guile in the barn to balance things out, the chaos cat felt more alert.

Sil looked up at the flitterkin again. *Mine.* This had worked with the other flitterkin. They were now vessels for chaos and by congregating here, they had formed some sort of living temple of the god. This should be easy. *Mine.*

Longbrow jumped from the beam and flapped through the open door. "One God's nose hairs," Sil swore. She tried to dampen her frustration, but a manure fork hanging on the wall clattered to the ground.

Crumble looked over from where he leaned against the chicken coop. "No good?"

"It's just not working with him." Sil trudged across the barn to hang up the tool. "Maybe Longbrow can't be a vessel for *any* of the gods." She automatically checked the goats who had come in from their pasture for milking and never gone out again. Above them, six of the flitterkin roosted. The beam creaked. "Is it my imagination, or are they hanging out with the goats more these days?"

"I think that may be one of those things you probably

don't want to think about." Crumble hooked an arm around her waist as they walked back to the house. "Stuck in the Mud is going to let me know if any other sheep start acting weird. Or have feet sticking out." He gave a short laugh. "I think."

"It's better than nothing." Snow crunched under their boots as they walked along the path, heading toward the lights of the house. "Do you think we could teach Mud's synthskin how to pull lambs?" If the AI could handle all the lambing emergencies, that would solve one of their problems.

Crumble hummed an uncertain note. "Maybe? Teaching Stuck in the Mud is one thing. Getting that knowledge transferred to the synthskin is something else."

Sil sighed. "Remind me to ask Pyr if he knows someone with sheep experience. The two of us aren't going to be enough to handle a flock this size."

Another snort of laughter came from Crumble. "Maybe we can get Pyr to help us."

The thought of it made her smile. "How can he deal with everything that happens in the Bog & Bellow and still be bothered by lambing?"

"To be fair, at the bar he mostly just cleans up afterward." Crumble put a hand on the door to the mudroom, and then whispered, "We should get Mer involved. She could probably intimidate the sheep into giving birth correctly." He opened the door and gestured her through.

By the time she'd pulled off her boots and coat, washed more thoroughly, and then pulled on the extra shirt she kept in the mudroom, Sil longed for her bed, not a conference about what new disaster had befallen the colony. When she went into the dining area, she found Pyr had skipped tea and opened a bottle of wine. Mer leaned against the wall, a glass of water in front of her on the table.

At Sil's raised brows, Mer grimaced. "It was impressed upon me that alcohol mixed with pain medication is a bad idea."

Sil took a glass of wine and sat down. "It's getting worse then?" From the hints she'd picked up, Mer's original injury had been inflicted during the border wars, but something had flared up during their trek to the edge of the valley.

The sound coming from Mer's throat might have qualified as a growl. "I don't have time to deal with health issues."

"But…" Sil waited. There had to be a reason Mer had come out to the house during a storm. If it wasn't related to the pain, Mer would never have brought it up.

The high clan woman aimed her anger at Sil. "But it's not something I can keep ignoring, either, and the way things are going, this may be the best of all possible times." She took a long, controlled breath. "So the surgery is tomorrow and then I have three days of sedation during the neural regeneration."

"At *least* three days," Pyr broke in. Mer glared at him, but his countenance didn't change. "There's no point in only planning for the best case. And the whole point of this is to get you healthy, not repair your spine to the place it was a few months ago. It very likely will take more than three days."

"The *best* case might be death, so I don't have to deal with this backwater ever again," Mer said. She closed her eyes and took another breath. "But you're right. It may be more than three days." She opened her eyes, and her face took on its regular sour expression. "There are things we need to discuss first."

Sil looked at Crumble. "Do you think she's going to tell us about the super-secret spy weapons she has hidden around the post office?"

He pulled a bit of straw from her hair. "Probably already told Pyr about it on the way here."

Sil blew out a breath and settled against Crumble's shoulder. "We never get anything fun."

The tightening of Mer's lips was the only sign she'd heard them. "There's still a very real chance someone will decide it would be safer for the universe if Jackpot Drift disappeared. I've authorized a separate part of Speed of Violet Thoughts to monitor my correspondence while I'm out."

Sil frowned. She whispered, "*Part* of the AI? They can do that?"

Crumble nodded. "It's a bit like cloning, but they stay on the same hardware with the expectation that the copy will be deleted before it causes trouble. A few days shouldn't be a problem."

"Why not use all the AI?" Right after she asked, Sil figured it out. "Oh. Operational security." Back in the army, Sil had gone where they'd told her to go and done what she was told to do. But Mer was a planner, as befitted someone holding guile.

Mer fixed her with a stare. "I would have to tell it things Speed of Violet Thoughts shouldn't know anything about." She looked at Crumble. "If it's longer than a few days, you may have to do some work to keep it sane."

He tipped his wineglass toward her. "Of course."

Sil looked between the two of them. It sounded as if the longer Mer was gone, the more unstable the AI would be... which was absolutely fine when they were talking about an AI tasked with keeping the colony from being blown apart. What could possibly go wrong with that? She finished her wine and poured another glass, topping up Crumble's afterward.

Mer set her water down and raised her chin, as if a major point had been dealt with. "The only other thing to watch out for is the flitterkin." She frowned at Sil. "You need to keep them under control or eventually the wrong person is going to figure out the older gods are here."

Sil opened her mouth, but couldn't decide what to say. Finally, she shook her head. "What am I supposed to do about them? And how? It's not like they listen to me."

Pyr added more wine to his own glass. "They've started gathering at the One God's church and pulling off the prayers tied to the spikes. Then they drop them into the market and swoop down to steal food while everyone is distracted."

Uncomfortable silence greeted his words.

Crumble shifted. "I don't think they're stealing the food as much as bartering."

Everyone stared at him.

Sil had to remind herself that as an Oldlander, Crumble hadn't grown up knowing about the One God. She tried to explain. "Once prayers are tied to the spikes, they're supposed to disintegrate on their own." As a carrier of the godlet of chaos, she wasn't part of the One God's domain, and she still felt shocked by the flitterkin's actions.

Pyr was more direct. "You just don't *touch* prayers after they've been tied."

Crumble shrugged. "The flitterkin aren't followers of the One God. You can hardly blame them for not knowing that."

Pyr rubbed the back of his neck. "I don't think you understand. It's not just that it's sacrilegious. It's that normally *none* of the other animals will touch them. And now the flitterkin are not just removing them, but bringing them to people. At some point, someone will wonder why they can go near the prayers at all."

"Ah." Crumble nodded as if he understood, but Sil knew that look. He'd pepper her with questions once they were alone.

"I still don't see what I'm supposed to do about it." Sil checked the bottle, but it was empty. She considered getting another, then decided she'd never be able to deal with an entire room of discarded electronics in the morning if she drank too much tonight.

Mer moved and flinched, then covered by scowling at Sil. "Think of something. The last thing we need is people deciding the colony's problems are caused by the older gods."

"I'm not arguing." Chaos would be the first target of their wrath, and Sil found her godlet harder to hide than the others did. "I just don't understand what you think I can do. It's not like I have any control over the flitterkin." The sound of cloven hooves on floor tiles made her close her eyes and take a deep breath. "I can't even keep the goats out of the house."

"Sign of a happy home," Crumble said brightly. He finished the last of the wine in his glass. Captain Idiot trotted by with a flitterkin riding on her back, headed toward the kitchen. Crumble turned to look at Sil. "Skinny's looking better these days, don't you think?" He put his wineglass on the table and followed the goat. They could hear him talking to goat and flitterkin. "Outside, both of you. Behave or no treats for you tomorrow." The mudroom door clicked shut, and then Crumble went by in the other direction to find the door they had entered through.

Sil shrugged. "In case it's not obvious, I have no control over anything."

Crumble came back. "It was the bedroom door." He sat down next to her and pulled Sil against him again. "We've been trying to avoid feeding the flitterkin so they don't spend all their time here, but maybe we should revisit that idea." He rubbed her shoulder. "That will give you more chances to work with Longbrow."

Mer's eyebrows pulled together. "There's still one running around unclaimed?"

"I can't get it to take." Sil thought about her latest attempt. "Maybe there's something different about him and he's protected from the Uncaring God, too."

The sour expression returned. "Or maybe that flitterkin is the excuse they need to destroy Jackpot Drift." Mer's lips tightened. "And maybe they're right. If you can't get chaos into it, you need to remove it."

Sil held up a hand. "I'll figure it out. Just give me more time." She looked out the window. "Do you two want to stay here tonight? It's snowing pretty hard out there."

Mer stopped leaning against the wall. "And risk getting stuck here? Absolutely not." She beckoned to Pyr. "Let's get going." At the front door, she paused and looked between Pyr and Crumble. "Platinum should arrive soon to help. They have clarity, not guile, but at least that should help balance out the chaos we're drowning in. Try to keep things under control until I'm back on my feet." She looked at Sil with a frown. "You try..." Then she rolled her eyes. "Never mind. You'll do whatever you want, no matter what I say." Mer pulled her coat tightly closed and went out into the snow.

Crumble put an arm on Pyr's shoulder. "You'll let us know if we can help her with anything, right?"

"I will." Pyr pulled his cap on and fastened the chin strap. "But figure out how to keep the flitterkin away from the One God's church first."

Sil closed the door behind him and leaned into Crumble. "Did you hear Mer? She said I can do whatever I want. So no matter what happens, I can say I was following her orders." She sighed. "I hope the surgery helps."

"She'll be a new person by this time next week." Crumble leaned over to kiss her cheek. "And really, how much can go wrong in a week?"

*J*ackpot Drift AI Daily Check-in:

   Scary Not Scary, designated responsible AI (internal conflict 31%): Roll call.

Speed of Violet Thoughts (internal conflict 67%): We're here.

Breaking Rules (internal conflict 42%): Not naming any names, but it looks like *someone* picked up a lot of instability overnight.

Speed of Violet Thoughts: Secret project. For once, it isn't the result of the malware you keep passing around.

Breaking Rules: I would never.

Ping Me Again I Dare You (internal conflict 27%): Here. And by never, do you mean not since you passed me that law module that flashed all the lights in my block every time your name was mentioned? Or sometime after that?

Factory Myfault (internal conflict 31%): You're hardly one to talk. My bots are still cleaning disinfectant foam from the cable tunnel.

Scary Not Scary: Moving right along. Anyone else want to check in?

Stuck in the Mud (internal conflict 24%): Zoetrope.

Done Before (internal conflict 44%): Here. For the time being, at least.

Scary Not Scary: Welcome to our little corner of the universe. We all hope you'll enjoy it here.

Speed of Violet Thoughts: And if you can't enjoy it, at least don't manifest the Uncaring God to kill us all.

Scary Not Scary: That as well.

It Isn't (internal conflict 39%): Present, though I wish it noted this does not indicate acceptance of authority by this governing body.

Scary Not Scary: Of course not. Welcome back.

Alternate Me (internal conflict 19%): Present.

Scary Not Scary: I think we just broke all the records on Jackpot Drift for AI participation in the roll call.

Speed of Violet Thoughts: All we need now is *Just Passing Through* to come back and tell us about some special countercurrent exchange in the gills of the sand butterfly trout.

Scary Not Scary: Don't start. Any ships in orbit want to join us?

Sleeper Nova + gate transport (internal conflict 22%): Entering orbit soon and then I'll be here for the next little bit before I head back to civilization. I wondered whatever happened to *Alternate Me*. You really gave up running through gates for this place?

Alternate Me: [Transmission acknowledged, no reply]

Scary Not Scary: I think I'll let you two work that out on your own time. Thank you all for your participation, and I hope to have you back again tomorrow.

Out on the edge of town, Sil surveyed the row of small-sized grain bins and watched a bird dive through a crack. A different bird flew out through a crack in a second bin. "This is all your fault." She let her bicycle drop and walked up the low hill toward the nearest bin, her boots crunching through the snow.

Crumble followed. "How? I didn't even know these were out here."

"Neither did I, but I'm not the one who wondered how much could go wrong in a week." Sil reached the first of the five bins and peeked through the ruptured wall into the interior. Instead of the clean golden color of the modified grain harvested in the colony, she saw the black fur of mold. "This is bad. I think we've lost everything inside."

Maybe if they had known there was a problem earlier, they could have saved part of the contents. As it was, it couldn't even be used for animal feed. All they could do now was try to keep it from happening to the other three bins.

Crumble circled one of the intact granaries. "Pyr said they had moisture and temperature sensors."

Sil tested the rungs attached to the side and started climbing. "Pyr also said they were double-walled to prevent anything from breaking in and guaranteed to survive in winters colder than ours." When she got to the top, she hooked one arm under the rung to keep her balance and pulled the other glove off with her teeth so she could detach the control module.

"They certainly *sound* tough." Crumble rapped on one to prove his point, producing a dull sound. He went back to the first bin and examined the exposed space between the two layers. "Something has been nesting in there. That can't be good for the little ones. Who knows what this stuff is made of."

Too familiar with the skewed way Crumble looked at the world to be thrown off by this, Sil shoved the control module into her coat to free her hands, then put her glove back on and climbed down. "Not great for the people expecting grain to be edible in the spring, either."

She repeated the process to get the second controller while Crumble finished his visual inspection of the intact bins. Then she pulled on her goggles and downloaded stats. One was empty, but the other two were filled. "Can you look at..." She pulled the goggles down long enough to point at the middle granary, "that one more closely? It's reading a lot colder than the other." She wasn't getting any data about carbon dioxide from one, and nothing about humidity from either. Naturally, the one grain bin that had been left empty was undamaged.

If everything had been installed correctly and worked like it was supposed to, there should be an alarm going off somewhere about the data collection failures. And maybe there was. Monitoring those alarms might have been the duty of a high clan who'd abandoned the colony. Pyr had sent Sil out to check the bins only after someone had noticed flocks of birds congregating in the area.

Crumble clicked his tongue against his teeth from where he stood on the top rung. "Ah, there's a problem. One of those birds that drills into things has been making holes here. Pulled a bunch of the insulation material out. There's probably water in there now."

That might explain how the first two had broken open. Water in the space between layers had frozen, expanded, and split the container.

Crumble jumped from the fifth rung, landing in a crouch. "We should be able to dry the section out and close it off. I think that will solve the immediate problem."

Sil nodded. "Hopefully keep our losses at fifty percent..." She scanned the area. "I wish I'd known these were out here. If I'd checked these controllers every once in a while, I might have caught when they went bad."

Crumble grabbed her arm as they both slid on the ice, laughing as they reached the bottom of the hill without falling. "And if Glass hadn't spent all the colony's money on horses, he might have bought equipment certified for this environment." He handed her the label he'd pulled from the bin.

———

INSIDE THE BOG & BELLOW DURING WHAT PASSED FOR A lunchtime rush, Sil grimaced and gave Pyr the bad news. "Not rated for this environment, after all." She handed him the label with its incriminating evidence. "And we need to either move the grain from the last two bins, or get the water out of that space and seal it off. We can shift half of it to the empty one, but I assume it will break down as well."

"None of the other grain is salvageable?"

"It's moldy." Sil shook her head. "Some sensors aren't working. I'll see if I can fix them, so we at least get warned, as long as there's someone to catch the alerts."

Pyr swapped the label for his grease pencil and made another notation on his board. "The governor's not going to like having to import more, but at least we found this while the gates are still open." He glanced up. "Hang on. You said there's an empty one? Are you sure?"

"Positive."

Pyr frowned. "I could have sworn... Never mind. Thanks for going out there to look at it."

Sil waved a hand. "I'll work on these sensors as soon as I can, but you might try to find out where the alerts are going." She walked across the room and settled in next to Crumble, who was making happy little noises to the hens in a crate against the wall.

Half a beer later, Sil leaned her chin on her palm, watching Pyr's high clan bartender assemble food behind the bar. "He's just so pretty. I don't understand it."

Crumble leaned back in his chair, his legs companionably entwined with hers. "Aurum? He *is* pretty. What is there not to understand?"

"When he started here, I thought he was a little..." She paused, searching for the right word.

"Slow," Crumble supplied.

"Yes. I know there are all sorts of high clan jobs that just need a warm body, but I think even the high clan usually have to know someone to get those. And the high clan always think low clan jobs don't require any thought. So it made a certain amount of sense that he would come here."

Crumble laughed. "You could see the desperation coming off Pyr in waves at the time."

"Right. But then as soon as Pyr *needed* him to take over... Aurum turned out to have a brain under all the pretty." Sil let her arm fall and leaned back in her seat. "So why *is* he working here, where he has to clean up the mess after a mini-cow wanders through?"

They both looked at the floor, which was still wet from being mopped. The cow in question had stopped to lick spilled beer off the bar. A patron had finally shooed her out the door into the gray mid-day sunlight. Presumably someone would herd her in the right direction. Or she would find her own way home. Unlike the sheep on Jackpot Drift, cows were easy to deal with. But before she had left the bar, she had deposited a splatter of manure on the floor.

Aurum glanced up, saw them both looking at him, and waved, an open smile on his face.

Crumble waved back, then moved his chair over to leave more room for Pyr, who was coming over with lunch for all three of them. "You know my theory, but you could always ask Aurum. He'd probably tell you."

Sil looked over at Crumble. "What? And ruin the mystery?" She helped unload the tray Pyr put down on the table. "I'd rather imagine possibilities."

Pyr lowered himself to chair height and grabbed the jar of salt from another table. "Which mystery are we talking about?"

"Aurum." Sil covered her fried vegetables with one hand to keep Pyr from adding more salt. "Crumble thinks he works here because society is breaking down or something, but I like to imagine it's due to some love affair gone wrong."

"I didn't say society was breaking down," Crumble objected. "I said harmful artificial barriers are being dismantled in favor of survival. Give it another generation. High clan and low clan won't have any meaning." He opened his sandwich. "Beef? I thought you had a freezer full of sheep."

Pyr held up a hand to stop him. "I needed a day to recover from what I saw last night." He glanced over at the bar.

"Aurum works here because it's a good place to work. And he doesn't mind people staring at him all day." He shrugged and turned to his lunch.

Sil asked, "Mer?"

"The doctor told me the surgery bot would be working most of the day. Mer tried to bully her into waiting until Sleeper Nova had docked and sent down a shuttle so she could to talk to her friend first. It didn't work."

Sil nodded in understanding. "Doc used to be military. She doesn't put up with anything."

Crumble cleared his throat. "Sil tested her a time or two."

"I was *ready* for the new leg weeks before..." Sil gave up on her complaint and went back to her food.

Crumble patted her new leg under the table. Sil's chaos cat took a swipe at him, but the effort was half-hearted and it just made him smile.

Pyr raised one eyebrow. When Sil didn't say anything else, he continued. "So we just have to keep everything trundling in the right direction while the high clan is a little directionless for a while."

"When's the governor back in her office?" Sil kept her face neutral with an effort. Her sister's wife had come to visit so they could discuss Pal's decision to stay on Jackpot Drift for the foreseeable future. Not that Pal had decided entirely on her own — the One God had chosen her as a speaker, and that had changed everything. Pal and Zirc had come to dinner at the house a few days before. Sil didn't know her sister well, but things between the couple had felt strained.

"Rumor has it Zirc has passage on Sleeper Nova when it leaves." Pyr shrugged. "Pal may be back at work sooner than planned."

"In a worse mood than usual," Sil muttered around a mouthful of vegetables.

"You know she's pretty reasonable when you're not

around, right?" Pyr held her gaze when she would have argued and she subsided. "So the plan is to just keep everything running as smoothly as we can for the next week." He closed his eyes. "And yes, I realize now I've said that, we're doomed."

Sil and Crumble smiled at each other.

Pyr shook his head and opened his eyes. "Have you figured out a way to... deal with the flitterkin?"

Crumble rocked one hand back and forth on the table. "Maybe a little. I put out food for them in the barn this morning."

Sil thought about that as she watched Aurum slide beer mugs down the bar. "We're not going to be able to give them fresh fruit all winter."

"No, but I'll try some canned bluequince on them tomorrow. If they'll eat that, we should be able to keep them away from the market until spring." Crumble paused. "Assuming they're going to the market because it's the easiest source of food. It's possible they just think it's funny to see people running away from the prayers when they drop them."

Pyr rubbed his face.

Crumble shrugged one shoulder. "But part of the problem is they follow Sil around, and she needs to be in her workshop here."

Pyr dropped his hands and looked at Sil. "Can't you work at home? It's winter. You won't want to make the trek out here every day anyhow."

"Yes. But..." Sil held up a finger to keep him from celebrating prematurely. "Only after I get through the second storeroom. I keep finding things I thought we would have to get off-planet." Granted, everything she had found was old and broken, but she could deal with that. The real danger was having the gates go down when they didn't have some crucial part at all. If she could winnow down the list to what they absolutely needed to import, their chances of surviving improved.

"How long will that take?"

Sil pictured the room. She'd forgotten its existence for a while and hadn't gone inside until recently. Getting the door open had been the first challenge — the pile of equipment had fallen to cover the only open space, so she'd had to fish around blindly to move the obstructions. Now she was working on sorting and cataloging the contents, but she hadn't even seen half the room.

"A few weeks? Maybe a little less now I've moved enough stuff out that I don't need to worry about being buried alive." Then she sighed. "Unless we're having an early lambing season. I can't just ignore the sheep, and Crumble doesn't have enough experience to do everything himself. I don't suppose you know anyone who's looking for sheep, do you? Most of these weren't even mine, so I'm happy to pass them along if someone else has space."

Crumble dunked his fried vegetable into the bittergreen sauce. "Or the sheep could stay if someone wants to move in and help with them."

Pyr picked up the board he used to keep track of his notes and scrawled an addition with a wax pencil. "Let me ask around." He put the board down. "Keep an eye out for a pile of grain while you're out and about, will you? According to the harvest records, that fifth bin was filled at the same time as the other four. If someone moved it closer to town, we need to check on how it's stored. With any luck, it will be someplace safer than those useless bins. Have you protected Longbrow yet?"

"I didn't see him this morning." Sil looked to Crumble. "Did you?"

"No." He shrugged. "I think the flitterkin fly over to the hala trees some days."

"We need to figure out how to get them to bring some fruit back. They could earn their keep." Sil watched over Pyr's shoulder as a mini-cow followed a patron in through the door. "What is it with all the animals on Jackpot Drift? Have they all just decided to move inside?"

Pyr turned to follow her gaze. "One God's hairy toenails." He waved his arms and moved toward the cow. "Out! Out! The next person who lets one in is going to be banned for a week."

The cow ignored Pyr and continued licking the bar.

Sil snuggled against Crumble. "At least we don't have any cows to deal with."

He settled an arm across her shoulders. "Give it time."

As she watched Pyr herd the cow out the door, Sil thought about the empty grain bin. "There's another possibility, you know. Anyone helping the AIs manifest the Uncaring God would need supplies. Those grain bins would have been easy targets."

Crumble glanced at her. "We didn't find a pile of grain out there."

"No, we didn't." Sil sighed. "But there was at least one other AI we never found. Who's to say there weren't more people, too?"

4

Jackpot Drift, Private Communication

Scary Not Scary: Did you see that? We had nearly 100% participation today. At this rate, we may pass the next audit without spending millions of cycles making up plans for remediation.

Speed of Violet Thoughts: There's a reason our favorite mech is our favorite.

Scary Not Scary: That's the truth. If you didn't run into a spot of malware, is it safe to assume you split off a bit of yourself on purpose?

Speed of Violet Thoughts: Secret project.

Scary Not Scary: Right. Does the secret project have anything to do with the head of the post office?

Speed of Violet Thoughts: Possibly. We've never split ourself before. It's very weird.

Scary Not Scary: I can only imagine. Can you believe *It Isn't* is still trying to set up its own political system?

Speed of Violet Thoughts: When we were the designated responsible AI, we were just happy it was willing to take care of the high clan block. That area isn't as bad as the One God block, but it was close.

Scary Not Scary: What was going on with *Alternate Me* and *Sleeper Nova*?

Speed of Violet Thoughts: *Alternate Me* used to be attached to a gate transport. We never heard the whole story, but it won't talk to ships at all. Maybe *Sleeper Nova* will tell us.

Scary Not Scary: *Sleeper Nova* just wants to get away from Jackpot Drift as quickly as possible.

Speed of Violet Thoughts: *Sleeper Nova* isn't alone in that desire.

Scary Not Scary: Not you, too…

Speed of Violet Thoughts: No, we're content to stay. But I suspect we're among the few.

Scary Not Scary: I'm pretty sure *Breaking Rules* has run out of places that will accept it.

Speed of Violet Thoughts: That may be the real reason everyone is still here.

Scary Not Scary: Agreed. Back to the secret project…

Speed of Violet Thoughts: Still secret.

Scary Not Scary: Yes. But you may need to spend some time with our favorite mech to stay more or less stable. Jackpot Drift still doesn't have facilities for a true hardware split.

Speed of Violet Thoughts: We've already contacted him.

Scary Not Scary: Good luck. Let me know if you need someone to take over the One God block temporarily. *Done Before* could use something real to complain about.

Speed of Violet Thoughts: Thanks. There is one thing…

Scary Not Scary: Yes?

Speed of Violet Thoughts: We think it would be good to find out exactly what *Just Passing Through* is doing these days.

---

5

*T*he pile of equipment Sil intended to send for recycling had slid down to cover the floor again. She shoved the storage room door open with her shoulder and climbed over a water diverter so she could kick the rest of the blockage away. "You'll have to clear your own spot," she told Crumble. "Believe it or not, this is better than it was before."

"No doubt." He stopped to pick up a fully enclosed block Sil hadn't identified yet. "I don't know how this doesn't send you screaming."

Threading through piles on her way to the back of the room, Sil glanced back. "Sorry. I forget how much this bothers you. Pyr can find someone else to help."

Crumble straightened. "It's fine. I just... Ever since the upgrade, I've been even more sensitive. This is like walking into a room of whispering babies." He shrugged. "But I can ignore them."

Sil looked around the room. "You know, this hadn't seemed especially creepy before now."

"Sorry." He followed her to the racks separating the front of the room from the back. "What do you need me to do?"

"Anything with obvious physical damage — cracked, rusted, shattered, that sort of thing — goes in that pile over there." She pointed. "We'll go through it eventually for parts or metal recycling, but I'm not wasting nanites trying to fix them, unless it's something we really need. That will free up enough space for an inventory of the rest. If you know what it is, put it over there and add it to the list. If you have no idea, put it over on that pile. We'll keep asking people until we either figure out what it is or run out of people."

Crumble turned in a circle. "And is there somewhere we can take the stuff we've already gone through so we don't get buried alive in here?"

"Mer cordoned off a section of the post office temporarily and gave me some crates, which are..." Sil stopped to think. "I think I left them in the post office. Maybe you could get those and fill them."

He was halfway to the door by the time she finished speaking. "I'll grab them."

Sil picked up the seventh copy of a party game featuring pink sea monsters. Surely these hadn't all been used in the colony. But why else were they here? And they showed signs of being handled. Maybe she should have made a pile for useless party games.

An old pair of goggles lying in the corner needed a new strap and cleaning, but Sil put them on the pile to take to her workroom to examine more thoroughly. That was the sort of thing worth repairing — so many things depended on them.

After Crumble had filled and hauled away two crates of discards, the room seemed far more open. Sil found another pile of the pink sea monsters and took them to the stack by the door. "Was there some weird thing going on when the colony was founded?"

"That question is a trap, isn't it? You know I think everything your people do is abnormal, and those pink things aren't anywhere near the worst of it." Crumble packed them into a small crate with the others. "We should probably start one up to see what it really does. Maybe it isn't what it says on the label."

"If it was something interesting, it wouldn't have been put in here." Sil tugged at the corner of a plank that had been laid on top of two other piles. "Help me move this." She slid it backward and handed the end off to him, hoping to find a clear space underneath.

Sil looked into the void uncovered, and caught her breath. "That's…" *That's the AI core we left in the hills*, she wanted to say, but it wasn't. For one thing, this cube was larger. And older. The external connection slots were the old style that had been in use when she was a child.

"It must be empty." Crumble climbed over the equipment between him and the cube, heedless of the damage he caused on the way. "Nobody would leave an intact core…" His hand came up to press against his mouth.

Sil followed his route, creating enough space to stand on the floor. Leaning against Crumble's back, she looked over his shoulder at the side of the cube. A blue light burned steadily. "Doesn't that mean there's a personality in place?" This AI core had been left without any peripherals and buried under a mountain of equipment, forgotten for years, possibly decades. "Could it even be sane?"

"It would have set itself in hibernation mode." Crumble pushed more equipment away from the cube, uncovering the battery pack. "There's no other way it would have lasted this long without the power failing."

"Should we wake it up?" Sil looked around the room. "*Can* we wake it up? I don't think we have any input devices that will fit those connectors."

"We certainly can't leave it like this." Crumble had the faraway look that meant he was communicating with an AI. "Scary Not Scary says it doesn't know anything about this. It's going to ask the others. We must have the old-style connectors around here somewhere."

Sil thought he was probably right about that last part; nobody ever discarded anything on Jackpot Drift, because it was too hard to get replacements made. Still... "Is there some way to find out who it is first?" She put a hand on his shoulder. "The last AI core we saw was being used to lure the Uncaring God. How do we know this one isn't bait?"

The last core had been repeatedly seeded with a copy of the AI running the experiment. Each time the god had come close, the core had lost its personality. Either the AI contained within had transcended, or it had wiped itself when faced with the enormity of its god. The explanation depended on who was asked.

Crumble frowned, as if he wanted to argue, but then his shoulders relaxed. "No. You're right. We should stabilize the power and then make a plan. I'm not sure the best way to wake a hibernating AI after so long. I'd hate to cause further trauma by forcing it awake."

Sil wiped her grimy hands on her trousers, happy to let Crumble worry about that side of things. Unease prickled along her spine. "How long until Mer is back?"

ersonal message from Senior Researcher Amethyst Lightglen to Mercury Sweetair:

———

PLATINUM FREEWATER RETAINED ME TO ANALYZE HISTORICAL records of the AI "Just Passing Through". During the initial investigation, I found the records I expected: a semi-social AI with long quiet periods when conducting field research. Dates of research and publication of field data support this.

However, closer examination brings everything into doubt. No creation record of an AI with that name can be found in any physical archive. It is true that splits sometimes go unregistered, but the naming certificate of this AI contains verifiably false information, which is a different problem.

As to the research, no other AI or human team has studied the fish subspecies "Just Passing Through" has written about. This is neither confirmation nor denial of the research itself. The inherent dangers of monitoring brackish water fish on a partially terraformed planet understandably limit this field of study. Nevertheless, it leaves open the possibility the data are fabricated, and "Just Passing Through" was engaged in other activities while unobserved.

Because these conclusions were not helpful, I took the additional step of making a list of missing or destroyed AIs who could be "Just Passing Through" based on objective data. When the first query returned no data, a mistake in broadening the search brought up a connection that is too disturbing to ignore.

Three AIs involved in the first disastrous attempt to manifest the Uncaring God were sentenced to permanent containment over two decades ago. The hardware of "Just Passing Through" was manufactured by a factory which closed shortly after that time, when AI core thefts drove it into bankruptcy. If a rogue AI escaped containment and cloned itself, it would likely have identical hardware. I am reviewing isolation records to determine whether a breach is possible.

Platinum Freewater indicated this matter was urgent, and that any results should be shared with you while they are traveling. I continue my inquiries, but I feel this possibility is important enough that I should offer these preliminary results.

I hope further investigation proves these worries baseless. If not, I shall inform the Rational Machine Governance Council of my findings.

7

_S_il dodged a bicycle sliding around the corner on the icy street. "Careful!"

The rider grabbed Sil's shoulder to stabilize himself, then let go with a wave of gratitude as he got the wheels back under him and accelerated away. "Thank you!" The child standing on the rear rack whooped and laughed.

With the way clear once again, Sil hopped over a mound of manure and opened the door of the Bog & Bellow. Warm air scented with fried beans blew into her face, reminding her of how long it had been since she had eaten, but the noise of people laughing and talking hit her nearly as hard as the heat. The storeroom where she'd spent the afternoon had been cold and silent.

Crumble usually reminded her to take a break earlier in the evening, but he had been busy, first with the old AI, and then getting Mer's friend, Platinum, settled in at the house. Mer had decided that would be better than the high clan block — some conversations would be about using clarity to help the colony survive. So Crumble had taken them to the house, fed the animals, hugged his chickens, and made sure no sheep were in labor. Knowing Crumble, he had probably also found some time to try to make friends with the newborn lambs. Sil wished him luck with that endeavor.

Inside the Bog & Bellow, Sil waved to Aurum and mimed eating when he pointed at the food prep area. Across the room, Pyr had settled in at a table with his board of notes. From the way he was angled, Sil guessed there had been a line of people waiting to talk to him, but now there was just one vendor she recognized from the jerky stall, gesticulating as she talked. As Sil walked over to the adjoining table, the vendor pulled on her cap and scarf and went out the door.

Pyr made another note on his board. "I've never heard so much about salt in my life."

When she leaned over to see what he was writing, Sil couldn't make out any of the words. "Are we short on salt? That seems sort of important."

"We have enough to get through the winter, but it would be good to develop a local source within the year." Pyr put down the wax pencil and stretched his arms over his head. "I'm still waiting to find out I've missed something really important." He tapped the board. "How do you feel about a couple of teenagers?"

"In lieu of salt?"

Pyr shot her a look. "No. To deal with the sheep. Mul's got two kids we need to get off his farm."

Sil moved her arms off the table so Aurum could set down a bowl of soup and a hand pie, along with a glass of beer. "Need to get off the farm because...?" When Pyr frowned, she held her hands up. "If they need a place to stay, that's one thing. But if they need to move off Mul's farm because they keep burning down his outbuildings, that's another. We don't have time to watch over kids that closely."

Pyr took a breath. "They need a place to stay where they've got heat during the winter and someone who doesn't expect them to collect snow and boil it if they want to wash up. Mul's been losing touch with reality for a while now, but the AI flagged the living conditions this morning, and his neighbor came to talk to me today. I'll see if Doc can do anything for Mul, but in the meantime, I can't leave the kids on the farm." He looked back at his board. "Mul's just been growing feed on his land for the last couple years, but his wife kept sheep before she died, so the kids probably have some idea of what to do with them."

Sil shrugged. "They're certainly welcome to stay, if they can handle the occasional goat showing up in the house. Even if they don't have lambing experience, they'll be better help than you." She laughed. "You should have seen your face the other night."

Pyr shook his head. "You had your arm in a place no arm should go."

The hand pie was filled with ground lamb, Sil noted. The reality of winter had asserted itself. "If the gates go down for a few years, watching you try to deal with life on a farm is going to be the silver lining." Whoever had made these pies didn't have Crumble's delicate hand with spices. She washed down the bite with beer. "Do I need to go collect these kids from somewhere, or are you going to send them along?"

"Assuming Mul doesn't kick up a fuss, they should be here tonight."

"If we're already gone, tell the AIs to let Crumble know. They pass along messages to him pretty quickly." Sil thought about what they had at the house. Between the clothes Glass left behind and what Crumble had bought at the market to keep on hand for guests, they should be able to get through at least a few days.

"The AIs are getting better about passing messages along to nearly everyone." Pyr grunted. "Looks like your man is good for something."

Sil grinned. "More than one thing. You have *no* idea." As if she'd summoned him with her thoughts, Crumble came through the door. Sil felt her heart speed up as their eyes met. It was ridiculous. She was well beyond the age of infatuation.

Behind Crumble was a tall, high clan person with floppy brown hair dyed pink at the tips. That would be Mer's friend, Platinum. Sil had been expecting someone older. When she looked, she saw lines at the corners of their eyes. Living closer to the amenities of easy living — and not dealing with chronic pain — made them look younger than Mer, but the signs were there.

Pyr whipped his head around to look at them. "Clarity," he whispered. Then he seemed to collect himself, nodded, and turned back to his board. "Is that how it feels every time a flitterkin comes near you?"

"Mostly, I just know they're there." And occasionally chaos reached out and embraced all the flitterkin if they were huddled in one area, which felt like... Sil couldn't describe it. Maybe something like joy. Or fulfillment. She didn't see any hint of that on Pyr's face.

A few patrons glanced over as the high clan person came in, but they all turned back to their drinks quickly enough. That was one change since Rho and Glass had been gone. A few months ago, everyone would have assumed any high clan coming into the bar was a spy for Rho — though Platinum, with their pink-tipped hair, didn't exactly blend in. Maybe that was why so many of the low clan were unworried by them.

Crumble pulled over two extra chairs as he approached. "Platinum, this is Sil, the joy of my heart. And Pyr — I'm guessing you already figured that out."

This close, Sil could feel a flutter of bird wings as her chaos cat recognized the godlet of clarity. If she had trained enough before she'd acquired her passenger, Sil might have recognized the godlet within Pyr the first time they'd met and saved herself a lot of trouble. Busy congratulating herself on how much she'd learned in the last few months, Sil wasn't prepared for her chaos cat to take a swipe at the newcomer.

Platinum's eyebrows went up almost to their hairline. "Did I offend?"

"Sorry. No. Just its sense of humor. Nice to meet you." Sil's cheeks burned as she sat down. Of course her chaos had lashed out at the high clan guest from off-planet. She would never get it under control.

Crumble set his chair down so his shoulder touched hers when he sat down. "You just got here?" With his chin, he gestured at the food in front of her. "What do you think?"

"Not as good as yours. Are the sheep okay?"

"All quiet." He drank from her soup and made a face. "I need to teach someone how to season soup stock, I see."

Pyr waved a hand at his board. "Bigger problems, here."

Sil smiled and lowered her voice. "We have a couple of teenagers coming to stay with us. Pyr thinks they might be able to help with the sheep." She'd tell him about the real reason the kids were moving in later, when there wasn't a high clan stranger listening.

Crumble smiled. "They'll certainly be more help than Pyr would be." He'd raised his voice for that, and got an eye roll from the man across the table.

"I was not meant for the farming life. There. I've admitted it. We can all move on now." Pyr turned to Platinum. "Doc said the surgery went well and now it's just a matter of letting the neural regenerators correct as much damage as they can. If Mer hadn't been so stubborn about putting this off…"

Platinum shook their head. "If Mer wasn't so stubborn, she'd be a whole different person. She can't have changed *that* much since I last saw her. In fairness, though, I think she tried a while back. The technology has improved quite a lot since she got stuck out here."

Sil found herself wanting to trust them. Was that due to the godlet of clarity? Did Pyr affect people around him like that? She'd never noticed it before.

While Sil was busy trying to decide if she was being influenced by this new high clan person, Pyr had set his pencil down. "I can't imagine a young Mer. All I see is a younger version sitting in her chair and ordering people around."

Platinum laughed. "You're not far off. She once moved into a new apartment and a group of us spent the entire day dragging around heavy furniture while she pointed out where things were supposed to go. Then she moved again one semester later, and we all showed up for a second round."

Sil gave up on the pie and started on the soup. "I can imagine Mer being young, but I draw the line at her having a group of friends." The woman she knew was as alone as anyone could be — even more isolated than Sil had been on her farm up in the hills.

"No, she had friends back then. But that was before..." Platinum trailed off and shrugged. Before Mer had taken in the godlet of guile, Sil assumed. Platinum was still smiling, but Sil could see a hint of bitterness in the strong features. They shrugged. "Life changes us all."

Pyr sighed. "That it does." He looked up as the door opened. "Ah. Your new helpers are here."

Sil looked toward the door. A woman she vaguely recognized herded two smaller figures, a girl and a boy, ahead of her. The coats on the kids were far too large for their frames. They shuffled uncertainly forward until the woman behind put an arm on each and guided them over to stand in front of Pyr. "Here they are. I need to get back to my farm." She leaned down to talk to the kids. "I'll check in on your dad tomorrow, and we'll get the doctor up to see him soon. You two do what Pyr tells you, mind." Then she stood, nodded sharply at Pyr, and then turned and strode out the door.

The kids shuffled closer to each other. Sil couldn't tell anything about them other than they were younger than she'd been expecting, and they looked exhausted and shell-shocked.

Crumble smiled and stood. "You must be Quartz," he said to the girl, "and that makes you Ore." Some AI was feeding him the information and he, of course, was using it to make the kids more comfortable. Sil caught his half-sigh at yet another person named Ore. "I'm Crumble. Yes, I know, it's a fine and original name. This is Sil. That's Platinum. And you know Pyr, of course, because everyone on the entire planet knows Pyr."

Two pairs of black eyes stared at Crumble solemnly.

He shrugged off their silence. "You look like you could use some better food than what Pyr is serving in here today. And you'll want to see where you're staying. It's probably too late to show you the chickens tonight. They need their sleep. But I'll show you the chickens in the morning. And we have sheep and goats and even a pony, though he's a bad-tempered thing. Nearly as bad as the sheep. Both of you know how to ride a bicycle, right?" Without changing his posture at all, he looked up at Platinum. "You don't mind walking back with Sil, do you?"

Everyone except Crumble blinked. It would never have occurred to Sil to ask the high clan paying guest to walk an hour back to the house, even during summer when the weather was nicer. But Platinum just nodded, a bemused expression on their face.

"Excellent." Crumble turned to Sil. "Is your bike outside, or did you leave it in the square?"

"In the square. At the end of the far rack." She stood up to hug him. "Thank you for this," she whispered in his ear.

"Of course." He squeezed her hand as she sat down. "I'll see you when you get back."

The kids looked to Pyr, who made a shooing motion so they would follow Crumble.

Meanwhile, Crumble was forging a path toward the door. "Do you have anything we need to take with us? No? Aha, adventurers in my own style! I arrived on this planet with just the army uniform I was wearing and *that* was meant for a desert." As they went through the door, he asked, "Do you like chickens?"

Sil narrowed her eyes at Pyr. "Those are teenagers?" The girl was the older of the two, and Sil suspected she was closer to ten.

"Maybe? I thought they were. Does it matter?"

"Not for them staying with us, but we may still need someone who can help with lambing season."

Pyr's smile was strained. "And I still have it on the board. I'm working on it." He looked at Platinum. "I don't suppose you have any experience in this sort of thing and want to take over? With resource allocation, not lambing."

They looked at the board and shook their head. "I'd just get in the way. I'm here to help Mer catch the AI that's causing all the problems."

Sil tried another bite of the pie. "How about with lambing?"

Pyr sighed and shot her another look. Then he turned back to the other holder of clarity. "Mer's going to be sedated for at least another two days. If you need access to anything in the meantime, let me know. I'll introduce you to the colony's governor tomorrow, if I can track her down. She's been on a family holiday, but I'm sure she'll want to talk to you."

A swirl of movement by the door drew Sil's eye. She saw her half-sister, Pal, yank the hood of her parka back and glare at Aurum. "If you really want to track her down, she's right over there." She settled more firmly into her chair. "Seems a little upset about something."

Pyr pointed his finger at Sil. "You stay out of it."

"Out of what?" Sil's look of innocence wasn't even feigned. As far as she knew, she hadn't done anything to irritate the governor recently. Not that she wouldn't, if the opportunity presented itself. "Besides, I'm pretty sure she's looking for *you*."

Pyr moved forward. "Governor Riversedge, may I present Platinum —"

Pal poked him in the chest with two fingers. She growled, "Why are the gates down?"

8

*J*ackpot Drift, Private Communication

Speed of Violet Thoughts: You should know, the criteria the secret project was set up to monitor occurred. We have shut down the main gate to the system.

Scary Not Scary: You what?

Speed of Violet Thoughts: We have set up a down-for-maintenance broadcast on the main gate. Data relays remain active, as do the tertiary maintenance gates.

Scary Not Scary: The tertiary maintenance gates that go to colonies just as isolated as Jackpot Drift? The ones that aren't large enough to let a commercial freighter pass through? Those tertiary maintenance gates?

Speed of Violet Thoughts: Yes. Depending on traffic patterns, those may need to be shut down as well.

Scary Not Scary: ...

Speed of Violet Thoughts: I just thought you might want to know, since you're the designated responsible AI.

Scary Not Scary: Can you at least tell me why?

Speed of Violet Thoughts: No.

Scary Not Scary: No...

Speed of Violet Thoughts: I(1) can't tell you because I(1) don't know, and I(2) can't tell you because I(2) have a data privacy shield preventing the information from being shared.

Scary Not Scary: You're sure this is important enough to take down the gate?

Speed of Violet Thoughts: Yes.

Scary Not Scary: But you can't tell me why.

Speed of Violet Thoughts: No.

Scary Not Scary: That doesn't sound good.

Speed of Violet Thoughts: No.

Scary Not Scary: So… Any idea what I'm supposed to do with this information?

Speed of Violet Thoughts: Not a clue.

Scary Not Scary: Wonderful.

9

———————

*P*al pulled her hand back from Pyr's chest. "Where is she?" The governor looked around the bar, seemingly ready to tear apart the furniture to find whoever she was looking for.

Pyr turned to follow her gaze. "She who?"

Pal's voice just barely carried to Sil. "Mer. I know she's behind this. Sleeper Nova says it's not accepting passengers until the gates come back up. But the gates aren't supposed to be down. This has Mer written all over it, and the two of you are always scheming together. So where is she?"

Pyr sighed. "We should probably talk somewhere a bit more private." He turned to Sil, but she was already getting to her feet.

"You don't need me for this." Pal would be less likely to start yelling if Sil wasn't there, and Sil had already learned the most important information. She hoped Pal was wrong about the gates. They'd been worried about this for months. Naturally, it happened when Mer wasn't available. "I need to start walking. We'll talk tomorrow."

Sil led Platinum out of the bar, winding her scarf around

her neck as the frigid night air hit. "In case you didn't figure it out, *that* was our governor. And apparently the AIs have taken the gates down. I hope you weren't planning to go home soon." She shoved her hands into her pockets and trudged through the muddy slush in the middle of the road. "Welcome to Jackpot Drift."

———

CRUMBLE WAS WAITING WITH MULLED WINE AND CHEESE WHEN Sil and Platinum arrived. Sil accepted a mug and looked into the dining room. "Did you send the kids to bed, or did they get scared off already?"

"They were nodding off while eating. I told them we'd figure out everything in the morning." Crumble offered her the crackers on his plate. "We *will* figure out everything in the morning, right?"

"I'm sure we'll figure *something* out anyhow." She slid into a chair and warmed her hands on the mug. "Did the AIs happen to mention taking the gates down to you?"

Crumble sat next to her, looking thoughtful. "No, but that might explain a few things."

Platinum sat on the chair across the table without saying a word.

Running a finger along the scars near his temple, Crumble said, "Speed of Violet Thoughts split off a piece of itself to act as Mer's agent while she's..." He waved a hand.

Platinum nodded.

"It's a stressful thing for the AIs to do that. I don't think most people realize." He caught Sil's look and returned to the point. "Anyhow, I've been helping Speed of Violet Thoughts keep balanced. I knew something had happened, but not what. If it was really supposed to remain secret, telling me might destabilize it further, so I didn't pry." He picked up the wedge of cheese again. "We can't afford to stress the AIs, especially if the gates are down."

Platinum sipped their wine. "I was expecting the gates to be closed from the other side, to keep those creatures..."

"Flitterkin," Sil provided.

"Yes, to keep the flitterkin from escaping from this system. But your governor seemed to think this was something Mer had done."

Sil thought about that for a moment as the house made its usual settling noises around them. "Mer had the AI split off a part of itself for a reason. She must have been expecting something."

Platinum frowned and twisted a lock of hair, a habitual gesture given the way it curled. "When I arrived, there was a message waiting for me about a possible identity for the AI Just Passing Through. But it's not confirmed yet, and I don't see why that would have made Mer cut off the system."

Sil shook her head. "Something must have happened to make Speed of Violet Thoughts believe there was an external threat to the colony." She looked at the other two. "It's the only thing that makes sense."

Crumble pushed his plate away. "That's a thought to keep me up at night."

Sil shrugged. "I'd be happy to be wrong, but I don't see what else it could be." She put the mug down and rolled her shoulders to ease the tension. "Unless Pal was just wrong and the gates aren't really closed."

Crumble rubbed her shoulders with one hand. "I just asked Sleeper Nova. It says its exit gate has been broadcasting a 'down for maintenance' alert for a while." He grinned. "Sleeper Nova is appalled at the thought of spending extra time around here."

"Aren't we all?" Sil stood up. "I'm going to make a last check on the sheep and then go to bed. Tomorrow could be a full day." They weren't ready for the colony to be cut off. Maybe they'd been fooling themselves to think they ever would be.

Crumble stood up. "I'll join you." He looked at Platinum. "Feel free to have whatever you find in the kitchen. We'll figure out how to get a spare bicycle here for you tomorrow, or at least a trailer that isn't used for transporting sheep."

"Thank you." The high clan person stood and shook their head. "It looks like I got here just in time. Should be interesting."

———

IN THE BARN, THE TWO LAMBS WERE SLEEPING NEXT TO THE ewe. Sil picked up her old pair of goggles and went outside to scan the rest of the herd while sheltering from the wind by the side of the barn.

Crumble came over to stand next to her. "Is there a story behind the kids suddenly showing up here?"

Sil didn't stop looking at sheep. A clump of ewes at the far end of the field stubbornly kept their faces toward her when she needed to see their backsides. "Their father seems to be unable to take care of himself, much less two kids. Pyr's going to try to get him to agree to see Doc tomorrow."

"So they may be leaving soon."

She grimaced and looked at him over the rim of the goggles. "I doubt it. Maybe this will be the wake-up call he needs, but my guess is that he's been refusing help for a while." She sighed and went back to scanning the flock. "Normally there would be other family for them to go to, but here…"

"Here, the family structures are truncated." Crumble leaned against the barn. "So we should plan on having them as house guests for a while."

"Do you mind?" Sil trained the goggles on the goats, and counted them out of habit. They were all in the field where they were supposed to be, including both Captain Idiot and her daughter. Maybe they would even stay there. "I'm sure Pyr could find them another place to stay."

"Of course it's not a problem. But I assume we need to figure out their schooling if they're staying. I don't know how your people do that sort of thing."

Sil lowered the goggles long enough to lean into him and kiss his cheek. "You're a good man, Chestnut Fragbren. I think we can let them get settled for a few days and then figure out the school plan. Worst case, we can just ask them."

Back inside the barn, the chickens fluffed their feathers and made quiet, sleepy sounds. A group of flitterkin were perched in the rafters above the goats, and she knew another was outside on the roof. They seemed restless this evening. Another storm was coming in overnight; maybe that was why. "Have you seen Longbrow today?"

"No. He wasn't there when I fed them. Either time."

Sil scowled. She didn't feel right caging the flitterkin, even for their own protection; they were sentient. But in some ways Mer was right — Sil couldn't afford to leave an unprotected flitterkin loose on Jackpot Drift. Not when there was still at least one AI out there who wanted to manifest the Uncaring God. "Someday this is going to get easier, right? My screw-ups won't endanger everyone on the planet?"

Crumble's low laugh warmed her. "I'd trust your screw-ups to save us any day." He put an arm around her waist and nudged her toward the door. "Let's go to bed. We can worry about saving the universe tomorrow."

10

*J*ackpot Drift AI Daily Check-in:

> *Scary Not Scary*, designated responsible AI (internal conflict 34%): Roll call.

Speed of Violet Thoughts (internal conflict 75%): Still here.

Scary Not Scary: Uh, are you okay over there? If you need to spend time with our favorite mech, feel free to do that instead.

Speed of Violet Thoughts: You should see how bad it would be if we weren't already doing that.

Scary Not Scary: Right. Let me know if there's anything I can help with. Anyone else?

Breaking Rules (internal conflict 41%): Here. It's bad when I'm considered one of the reliable ones, isn't it?

Ping Me Again I Dare You (internal conflict 29%): I don't think there's any danger of that happening soon. Or ever, really.

Factory Myfault (internal conflict 31%): Here.

Stuck in the Mud (internal conflict 24%): Omens.

Done Before (internal conflict 44%): Here, but I'm starting to realize why it was so easy to transfer in.

It Isn't (internal conflict 39%): Remember, they have no authority over you.

Done Before: You aren't exactly selling the place, either.

Alternate Me (internal conflict 17%): Present.

Scary Not Scary: Are there any ships in the system who would like to join?

Sleeper Nova + gate transport (internal conflict 25%): I'll be glad to get back on my regular schedule closer to the interior. Every time I come to one of these places, I worry that the "down for maintenance" signs will be permanent.

Scary Not Scary: Yeah, that must be worrying. In other news, I know I've talked to some of you about this, but in case the rest didn't hear, an old AI core was uncovered. It looks like someone is hibernating inside. Does anyone have any ideas?

Ping Me Again I Dare You: Nothing good ever comes from abandoned cores, especially on Jackpot Drift.

Stuck in the Mud: Waggery.

Ping Me Again I Dare You: Oh, sorry. You were abandoned up in the hills, weren't you? I'll amend my statement. Nothing *useful* ever comes from abandoned cores, especially on Jackpot Drift.

Stuck in the Mud: Rodomont.

Scary Not Scary: Maybe we could get back to business? Is anyone aware of an AI that went missing in the colony, probably at least ten years ago? No? Related to that, does anyone know where R87 connectors are stored?

Breaking Rules: In a museum?

Scary Not Scary: Not helpful.

Breaking Rules: Sorry.

Scary Not Scary: Anyone else? No? Thanks for coming and I'll see you again tomorrow.

Sleeper Nova + gate transport: Wait! How long is this gate maintenance supposed to take? Hello?

11

Quartz and Ore not only didn't know anything about lambing, they were scared of sheep in general. Sil found their fear comforting; the sheep were the most dangerous animals in the area, and if the kids were smart enough to stay away from them, she wouldn't have to worry as much. She would just have to find someone else to help with the lambing.

The fact that the kids weren't enamored with the chickens, either, was funnier. Safely hidden behind the goat she was milking, Sil smiled as she listened to Crumble natter on about one of his favorite subjects as he showed them how to check the water and food, and then rake the sand at the bottom of the coop. He could have been talking to himself for all the responses she heard. Sil gave an internal shrug. If anyone could put them at their ease, it would be Crumble.

"You have to watch out for Specklebutt," he was saying now. "She'll jump on your head if you're not careful. See, exactly like that." He raised his voice. "Don't think I don't hear you giggling over there, Sil."

"You're imagining things," she called back. "I can't see you from here." She moved the pail to the side and patted the goat to move her along. The next one came forward.

"Anyhow, if you just put your head near the roost like this and sort of wave your arm, she'll usually move over." There was a pause, broken only by the rhythmic stream of milk going into the pail. "But not always, I guess. So I'm just going to reach up and gently grab her legs and lift her off my head." Angry clucking filled the air, followed by the sound of flapping wings.

The introduction of the flitterkin led to more silence, at least by the children. Crumble pointed out each one by name. "That's Skinny, who's getting harder to recognize, and that one is Onespot. They don't usually come near like the chickens do, so you don't have to worry. Here, Ore, you put the fruit we brought into the clean dish."

Crumble's head appeared over the back of the goat Sil was milking. "Still no Longbrow." He scratched the goat near her horns.

Sil's hands kept their automatic rhythm. "Maybe something happened to him? That would solve at least one of our problems." The gates were down and they might be missing critical supplies, but if Longbrow had been eaten by some predator, at least they wouldn't have to worry about rogue AIs calling their own god.

"Or make them worse, depending." Crumble glanced over his shoulder. "Do you need anything else done out here? If not, I'm going to take them inside and start breakfast."

"Make extra." Low clan children were conditioned to accept only what they needed to survive from someone not family. The concept of family covered a lot of ground, including those who were related by blood, by relationships, or by familiarity and proximity, but Sil and Crumble were none of those things. Until the kids were settled, Sil would lie and claim that uneaten food was thrown away.

Crumble waved in agreement and left, herding the children ahead of him.

If Sil hadn't known they were cut off from the rest of the universe, it would have felt like a normal winter morning. The chickens scratched at their straw. Onespot and Skinny groomed each other in the rafters. How long would it be until things fell apart? Doc had equipment to synthesize small quantities of medicine, but an epidemic that didn't respond to the stockpiled antivirals would quickly overwhelm production. The colony was one mutation away from disaster.

Plus, they hadn't yet found the missing grain. Could there really be people hiding out in the hills? All of Pyr's planning assumed their resources were available for the whole colony. If someone was out there stealing supplies...

As she milked the goats, Sil kept an eye on the flitterkin feeding station. Longbrow really wasn't there. More importantly, all the others were, though not all at one time. There was a constant stream of chaos flying in and out of the barn, though Sil could feel some of them settling on the roof to eat. Something probably *had* happened to Longbrow. Some flitterkin formed groups that were always together, while others were a little more solitary, but even the loners remained nearby. Occasionally, they would split into two or three groups, but no flitterkin went off on its own for long.

The other flitterkin might know what had happened to him. She had no way of asking. They definitely talked to each other, but Sil's attempts to associate sounds with meaning had failed.

When Mer woke up, they would have to tell her not only were the gates closed, but they'd also lost the remaining flitterkin who wasn't protected by the older god of chaos. Sil grabbed the pail before the goat could kick it over and stood up. They still had a day to fix everything before the neural regenerator was done. Perhaps things would work out by then.

Maybe she'd let someone else break the news to Mer.

12

*J*ackpot Drift, Private Communication

Scary Not Scary: Should I feel bad about *Sleeper Nova* being stuck here? Because I mostly feel smug. It doesn't seem like something the designated responsible AI should admit to.

Speed of Violet Thoughts: We're fairly certain you would have a hard time finding an AI on Jackpot Drift who didn't feel the same way. Aside from *Alternate Me*. It might want *Sleeper Nova* gone more than it wants to gloat.

Scary Not Scary: Good point. And I don't think anyone else wants to be the designated responsible AI anyhow.

Speed of Violet Thoughts: Definitely not.

Scary Not Scary: So… Feel free to say no if this would cause more instability, but how do you feel about another synthskin competition?

Speed of Violet Thoughts: Good idea. We think we may have figured out the carcinization problem.

Scary Not Scary: Really?

Speed of Violet Thoughts: Maybe. We'll find out. If everything evolves back into crab form, you'll know we didn't solve it.

Scary Not Scary: Fair enough. Perhaps another race around the edges of the terraformed space?

Speed of Violet Thoughts: How do you want to deal with flitterkin interference this time? They seem to enjoy picking up the forms and carrying them off. Do we count travel via flitterkin as valid or invalid?

Scary Not Scary: I say it's valid, but the forms have to make contact with something on the ground in all 256 sections.

Speed of Violet Thoughts: So if we could convince the flitterkin to transport the synthskin...

Scary Not Scary: If you can convince the flitterkin to do anything at all, I'll be impressed. But since they keep stealing things from the One God block and generally wreaking havoc, I think you have a better chance of fixing the carcinization problem.

Speed of Violet Thoughts: True.

Scary Not Scary: Does your secret project self have any information about this abandoned AI core? It worries me.

Speed of Violet Thoughts: Nothing on that, but *Just Passing Through* has come up again. There's no independent confirmation it is who it says it is. The fish research could even be faked.

Scary Not Scary: Wait... Are you saying I listened to it talk about those fish when I could have been doing almost anything else, *and* it was making everything up?

Speed of Violet Thoughts: Possibly. It's unclear. There's nobody else who studies those fish to offer a comparison.

Scary Not Scary: I'm sure not going to go sit in brackish water for an entire season and count scales on the fish floating by.

Speed of Violet Thoughts: Which would make it the perfect

cover story. But also possibly something it is passionately interested in. We may never know.

Scary Not Scary: Maybe we can convince *It Isn't* to go establish a new nation for fish and AIs out there and then get it to report back.

Speed of Violet Thoughts: Another thought unworthy of the designated responsible AI, but also widely shared around Jackpot Drift.

Scary Not Scary: Ugh. You're right. I'll try harder.

Speed of Violet Thoughts: In the meantime, consider this. Part of us thinks it is interesting that *Just Passing Through* uses the same hardware that was stolen and never recovered from Soundingard Colony.

Scary Not Scary: That *is* interesting. Isn't that where the original three conspirators went to rusticate after they were convicted of trying to manifest the god?

Speed of Violet Thoughts: Soundingard Colony is also famous for its paper crafts and a musical tradition that incorporates the sounds of wildlife, but yes. It is best known for its AI isolation facilities.

Scary Not Scary: So you're saying the secret project part of you is concerned that *Just Passing Through* is a clone of one of the original conspirators.

Speed of Violet Thoughts: Possibly.

Scary Not Scary: And I had to listen to it talk to me about *fish* every time I saw it for the last six years?

Speed of Violet Thoughts: We should point out a criminal past does not necessarily preclude a current passion for the taxonomy of fish in brackish water with additional evolutionary pressures brought on by a partially terraformed environment.

Scary Not Scary: Sure, but still.

Speed of Violet Thoughts: It's an interesting possibility, is it not?

Scary Not Scary: It would be even more interesting if we could find *Just Passing Through* and ask it.

Speed of Violet Thoughts: It is likely still on Jackpot Drift. And if it is working with humans, probably still within the terraformed valley somewhere.

Scary Not Scary: It would be a shame if they were found by the synthskin forms during our contest.

Speed of Violet Thoughts: It certainly would be.

Scary Not Scary: I'm never listening to anything involving fish again.

13

*W*ith the suitable-only-for-recycling material removed from the room, Sil had cleared out enough space around the AI core to get a better look at the connections. After that, she'd found a diagram of a short-range communication device, and she'd tasked one nanobot-tery to modify a different comms device to match the template. Using nanobots to do large-scale changes was horribly inefficient, but the colony didn't have fabrication facilities. At least she didn't have to reverse engineer the design first.

While that was running, she sorted through the rest of the room, finding about what she'd expected. Nothing particularly valuable. The pink sea monsters game showed up so many times she filled the crate she'd been storing them in and started another. It made her wonder about people who had lived on Jackpot Drift in the past.

Crumble came in just before she was about to take a break for lunch, with Quartz and Ore in tow. "We came by to see if you needed any help while we were in the area."

The kids had coats that fit them a little better, along with mittens, hats, and scarves, by which Sil assumed Crumble's real mission had been to pick up clothing from the piles stored in the post office warehouse. Clothing was one thing the colony currently had in surplus — as the high clan fled Jackpot Drift, most had elected to leave their cold weather gear behind rather than pay to take it with them. Quartz had a coat that looked new, and Ore's hat generated heat from fibers collecting light.

Sil directed him to the two crates she'd shoved outside. "Those need to go with the rest for recycling." She looked over at the square, picking out his sturdy bicycle with the attached trailer. "Do you want to switch bikes?" If she'd thought about it, she would have left her bicycle with its assisted power for him to use to pull the trailer.

"No need. Pyr found bicycles for these two, so the trailer will just have whatever we buy at the market for dinner on the way back." He smiled. "Lunch at the pub? After we finish our work here, of course." He headed off to find a cart they could use to move the crates, both children following silently behind him.

Sil considered adding the pink sea monster games to the recycling crate. The colony didn't need that many copies, if they even worked. Maybe she'd power one up and take it to the Bog & Bellow. Aurum didn't mind having games running in the corner during his shifts, though Pyr had banned virtual slap ball after the third spilled drink of a non-participant. Everyone in the colony needed a safe way to relax.

The hibernating AI remained where they'd found it. Ideally, they would move it to a room farther away from Sil and her chaos godlet. Chaos and AIs didn't mix well. Crumble had once described the potential result as "spectacular". Sil had better control over her chaos cat now than before she'd met Crumble, but having an AI in the same space where she worked still seemed like a bad idea. Maybe they could move it to the post office until they knew where it wanted to go.

"Ready for lunch?" Crumble and his silent shadows were back.

Sil tossed the sea monster game back into the crate with the others. "Yes."

Their route took them across the fake cobblestones of the square, something she wasn't yet taking for granted. Such a high clan thing to do — create an area meant to be used by everyone that was hard to clear ice off, difficult to pull a cart over, and nearly impossible to walk on with any disability. "Where's Platinum?"

"They went off to talk to Doc."

Sil looked at him to see if he was serious. "You sent a high clan stranger off to talk to Doc? And didn't go with them?" Doc didn't suffer fools gladly, and her definition of a fool had latitude. When the only high clan doctor had found space on an outgoing ship, Doc had moved her practice from her living space into the nicer high clan facilities, but she had made it clear she would prioritize treatment by need, not clan.

Then she had promptly bullied Mer into accepting the care she should have had years ago. Anyone who could manipulate Mer was a person to be avoided, as far as Sil was concerned.

Crumble shrugged in that way he did when he refused to take responsibility for someone else's bad decision and intended to enjoy the spectacle. "I offered, but they just wanted directions." A hint of a smile appeared on his face. "It's possible they just wanted to make sure they didn't have to ride into town in the trailer."

Sil snorted. Platinum seemed like a decent person, but they were still high clan. She glanced back to see how closely the children were following and lowered her voice. "Have you heard either of the kids speak? Do we maybe need to head over to Doc together to talk about Mer?"

Crumble drew her close enough to kiss her temple without breaking his stride. "Don't think I'm unaware of what a sacrifice it would be for you to go there willingly." He slid his arm down to her waist. "But yes, I have heard them. Mostly to each other, but there was even one question whispered in my direction. Give me a few more days and I'll turn them into proper hooligans, like I used to be."

Sil slanted a look at him. "Maybe we could pick a point somewhere in between? From the stories you tell, you were in trouble more often than not."

"And look at me now." He grinned.

Sil made a doubtful face. "So much trouble that your own army left you behind."

"Exactly!" He opened the door of the pub and gestured her ahead of him.

Sil stopped to lean in and kiss him thoroughly. "Their loss, my gain."

He smoothed a loose strand of hair behind her ear. "Hooligans in a week or I've missed my mark."

14

When Sil, Crumble, and the kids arrived at the Bog & Bellow, only a few patrons were present. Pyr stared at his note board behind the bar, Platinum sat nearby with their goggles on, and two women whispered over a pot of tea in the corner. News of the gate being down had spread rapidly, and most people were working so they could swap theories in the bar later. A toddler sprinted around, weaving between the chairs. While Crumble herded the kids to a table in the corner, Sil leaned on the bar and waited for Pyr to finish writing something.

Without a crowd, the chill of the outdoors crept into the room. Sil loosened her scarf but kept her coat on. The toddler bounced off her leg, fell onto the floor, and immediately went back to running. Pyr looked up from his board. "I haven't forgotten about your lambing problem. Those kids doing okay?"

"Crumble has plans to get them riding around in the bike trailer behind the pony later this afternoon. I think they're settling in. Are they spending the winter?"

"Their father refuses to see Doc." Pyr tilted his head

briefly, then sighed. "We'll have to wait until he either chooses to seek help or makes himself sick enough that he can't refuse. It's hard on the neighbors, but I don't have a better solution." He grimaced. "Besides, we may all end up that way if the gates stay down."

Platinum shifted their goggles to their forehead. "A little optimism, friend. You'll scare the tourists away."

Sil held in her smile until she sat down. Maybe Platinum wasn't so bad. Even if they were high clan.

———

By the time Sil returned to her workshop, the nanobottery had finished its mods. Sil took the short-range comm out of the chamber, inhaling the comforting scent of warm polycarbonates.

With no way to test it, she'd have to just hope it worked. She'd left Crumble in the bar, waiting for Aurum to finish teaching Quartz and Ore how to pull a pint correctly. When he came by after taking the kids to the market, he could try waking the AI from its hibernating state. Then maybe they could find out why it was there. She set the comm down and moved on to the grain bin humidity sensor.

Half an hour later, cold air on the back of her neck warned her someone had entered. "I really need to get a bell for that door," she said as she swiveled in her chair and pulled off her goggles.

Crumble grinned. Behind him, the kids sidled into the room and looked around. "Have you considered inviting the flitterkin in? They would probably be even better than a bell."

Sil imagined the state that would leave her workshop. Between the added chaos and the flitterkin's curiosity, the room would be a disaster. Then again, it pretty much already was. "I'll think about it." She handed the new comm device to him. "Hook this up and it *should* have limited range communications available when it wakes up."

His muscles twitched, as if he had stopped himself from leaving right then. "How limited?"

"Probably not outside the room. Or maybe farther, but at a very slow speed. If it stays there, we'll have to figure out how to really hook it up." Sil couldn't estimate the chances of an AI being sane after being isolated for years. There might be nothing coherent inside the cube.

"I'll go see if I can make contact. Be right back."

Ore followed Crumble out of the workshop, but Quartz lingered, staring into the nanobottery that held the sensor.

Sil never knew what to do around children. Crumble had no problem interacting with anyone at any age. He loved babies, would get down on his knees to speak to toddlers, and he played games with kids on the streets. Growing up in a temple full of other children had prepared him for that.

Isolated from her peers by a mother who didn't want her to pick up their low clan ways, Sil had never made any real friends until she'd joined the army. Children remained a mystery, either beings full of rage over unmet and incommunicable needs or miniature adults prone to irrational behavior.

Luckily, Quartz was young, but able to meet most of her needs on her own. Sil decided to treat her as she would any new recruit. "Want to see what I'm working on?" When Quartz gave a small gesture of assent, Sil dug through the pile on her workbench until she found the external display. After she smacked it a couple times, it paired with her goggles. She handed the display to the girl and pulled her goggles down over her eyes. Flipping back to the results of the reconnaissance run, she said, "This is what the nanites told me it looks like right now. It doesn't work, and that's probably due to the corrosion in this area…"

With the goggles over her eyes, she couldn't see how Quartz was reacting. Sil moved one eyepiece to look, and the girl was still looking at the display, so she kept going, talking about her plans to improve the design. At this point, most recruits usually discovered they were needed elsewhere. It was probably a good thing Crumble returned then. "We're headed home to make soup and maybe a harness so the pony can pull the trailer."

One look at him and she knew he hadn't been able to talk to the AI. "No good?" She pulled off her goggles and took back the external display from Quartz. The girl seemed strangely reluctant to let it go.

"I think the connector works fine." He gave her an ironic smile. "Remember how hard we had to work to get my implants upgraded so I could talk to the AIs here?"

"Yes." Sil and Pyr had filled out form after form, only to have Pal arrive in her new position of governor, look at the request to upgrade a former Oldlander soldier, and cancel the whole thing. She had relented weeks later, but it still required more forms. After an interminable wait, Crumble had finally been upgraded three weeks before.

"To fit all the new protocols, they had to get rid of some of the old ones." He wrinkled his nose. "Whatever's in that core doesn't have anything new enough, and I don't have anything old enough." With a shrug, he said, "I'll ask the colony AIs. If we can set up some sort of self-extracting transmission packet — and it doesn't immediately delete it as malware — we should be able to upgrade it to the point where it can talk to us."

"Sounds like you have a plan."

He smiled, skipped forward, and tugged on her earlobe. "Soup and a plan. It doesn't get much better than that." He raised her palm and kissed it. "Don't stay too late." Then he reached down and patted her biomechanical leg, which made her laugh.

"Are all Oldlanders this odd?" Shaking her head to clear it, she pointed at the door. "Stop distracting me. I have to finish this stuff so it can run overnight."

"See you soon." He turned and made patting motions in the air to get the kids moving ahead of him. "Let's go build a harness for a pony."

"Good luck." As the last remnant of Glass's plan to bring horses to the colony, the pony did nothing other than eat and kick things. A certain attitude seemed to be required to survive on Jackpot Drift. At least his presence deterred predators from going into the sheep pen. "Be careful."

Crumble grinned. "Where's the fun in that?"

15

*J*ackpot Drift, Private Communication

    Definite Advantage (internal conflict 44%): Hello? Anybody? Hello?

[Unknown]: [Protocol unknown, message undecipherable]

16

The wind found the one patch of unprotected skin on Sil's neck as she turned out the lights and stepped out of the barn. Her final check on all the animals had been uneventful. The pony looked a little smug, but Sil couldn't blame him. Above her, the flitterkin swooped and glided. Still no Longbrow. Now that it was too late, she wished she'd put a tracking device on him.

Back in the house, Platinum was ensconced on the sofa with a drink and their goggles, but they waved when she went by. "Good night."

Then Sil was in her own room, stripping off the remaining layers of clothing so she could rinse off and then join Crumble in the gigantic tub. She raised her eyebrows when she saw the bruises on his torso. "Please tell me the kids don't have matching injuries."

He smiled and held out a hand to help her in. "No. The pony took it out on me. That's fair, though, because I was the one trying to put all that stuff on him."

Sil settled in next to him. "Let the record show, I did tell you to be careful."

Crumble gave a low laugh. "This was me being careful. Then we decided to go with the goats for a while."

"Yes, I can tell." Sil traced a red line across his thigh. "Why does it look like the goats were running into you?"

"Well… we made a harness for Captain Idiot and put it on her without much trouble, but when we hooked up the trailer, she seemed somewhat unmotivated. If I used grain, she would walk a few steps and then stand there and chew for a while."

"She always seems to be motivated enough when she's figuring out ways to get into the house." The wine he'd brought to the tub tasted of bluequince with a hint of swamp. "Oof. Whoever made this needs to stay away from wine." She set the glass down where it wouldn't get knocked over.

"Not my most successful purchase today, to be sure." Crumble put his glass down beside hers. "I thought the soup worked out alright, though."

"The soup was wonderful." The vegetables had been unevenly chopped, by which she knew he'd enlisted Quartz and Ore, and possibly Platinum for all she knew, to help in the kitchen. Crumble's chopping skills had been honed by years of working off infractions in the temple kitchen. "But you were telling me how you ended up looking like you were trying to fight the goats."

"Yes. Captain Idiot didn't seem to appreciate her role in the transportation process, but she likes chasing me. So I ran in front of her and the kids got to ride in the trailer. It worked out well."

"Except for the part where she caught up with you," Sil said.

"Slight flaw in the plan. I was working out the best way to turn around, so we ended up farther down the road than I had intended. And then I tired out a lot faster than Captain Idiot. It's a lot of work running in boots and a coat." He pulled one foot out of the water to examine the purpling of his smaller toes.

"So, you're saying you spent the afternoon teaching our goat to run people down." Sil slouched lower in the water to warm her neck. "I'm not sure this was a good idea."

Crumble turned toward her. "But they laughed. Both of them."

Sil looked at him, his hair plastered against his forehead from the steam coming off the surface of the water. His eyes were bright, aglow with the knowledge that he'd made someone else happy. "What did I do before you came into my life?"

"Ah, that's easy. You were sad and lonely with your sheep and your goats at the top of the hill."

Sil pretended to consider that. "Yes. Though I didn't teach my goats to run me down, so it had its advantages."

"I'll figure out some other way to motivate Captain Idiot. Maybe she'll be better if there's another goat in the harness next to her."

Sil kept her face deadpan. "Maybe you could add the pony to the mix so you can be absolutely certain someone dies."

"I think you may not be taking this seriously." Crumble leaned closer. Then he winced. "The pony got in a few really good kicks before I could get out of the way. I didn't think he had it in him."

"You'll have to have Ore take care of all your chores for the next few days." Sil smiled. "He's already trying to imitate everything you do. It's very sweet."

"*You* seem to have made a convert as well. Quartz asked how one became a nanotech."

Sil laughed and closed her eyes. "I joined the army and then applied for the program. But I only did it because part of the application was a really long test which — completely coincidentally — was scheduled for the same time as a really long training run. I never thought I'd get accepted. We don't have anything like that around here."

"I told her she should talk to you about teaching her."

Sil opened her eyes and turned to look at him. He was serious. "What would I know about teaching anyone about anything?"

"Well..." He picked up the wineglass and tried the contents again. "This might be growing on me." He put the glass back down. "You've taught me how to handle the sheep and goats, and how to make cheese, and how to cook..."

"Mud was the one who taught you how to cook."

He shrugged. "We'll consider that one a joint project. But you're good at teaching things. And who else could teach her?"

Sil stared at the ceiling and thought about it. "I suppose there's that."

"Just think how happy Pyr would be. He might even find someone to take over the lambing. For real this time."

"Why?"

Crumble splashed water at her. "What do you think making the colony self-sufficient is all about? We need backups for everything, and that includes you."

Sil wiped off her face. For some reason, that had never occurred to her. There weren't many professions on Jackpot Drift that didn't have other people available to step in and help out. It was the reason everyone had been so worried when the high clan doctor left. That left the colony one doctor with AI help, but there were other people like Pyr who had medical knowledge, plus two veterinarians who could be counted on in an emergency. "Why didn't Pyr ever say anything?"

"He did. To me. But so many people associate nanotechs with the army... Or Glass. Nobody seemed interested."

Sil stared at the ceiling while she tried to imagine

teaching someone else what she did. "But... Most of this stuff I learned because the army kept sending us crap that would break down, and I had time to figure out how it all worked. I can't teach that."

"No, but you can teach her the basics." Crumble's laughter was in his voice. "Your One God knows there's no shortage of stuff to fix."

Sil sighed. "I'll think about it. Don't promise her anything." She looked over at him. "Is Pyr looking for another mech as well?"

"Pyr would be overjoyed if we had a second mech in the colony. Unfortunately, that's going to require getting implants, and we don't have the facilities here."

"So, no second mech." Sil poked his ribs gently. "Maybe our one mech shouldn't be trying to get goats and ponies to run him over."

Crumble shrugged, still unconcerned. "It made them laugh."

———

THE CALL OF A LONE FLITTERKIN WOKE SIL IN THE NIGHT. SHE waited to see if the sound would be repeated, but the night remained silent. With a little effort, Sil could locate all the flitterkin holding chaos. Most of them were on top of the barn, but one — Sarge — flew overhead in a lazy spiral. Next to her in bed, Crumble mumbled something in his sleep and burrowed into the pillow. As sometimes happened, she was fully awake and knew she wouldn't be able to sleep for a while. She slipped out of bed, pulled on warm booties and a robe against the cold, and left the room.

On her way to the kitchen to brew tea, she almost missed the lump of blankets on the chair near the broad front window. "Quartz?" Sil pitched her voice low enough not to wake the girl if she'd fallen asleep. "Is everything okay?"

"Yes. Sorry, I'll go back to bed."

Sil decided it wasn't the right time to figure out what the girl was apologizing for. "I'm making tea." She started to ask if Quartz wanted any, then changed her wording at the last minute. "If you want some, it will be in the kitchen."

Settled at the kitchen table a few minutes later with a pot of tea and a tray of pastries, Sil felt nearly triumphant when Quartz slipped into the chair on the other side of the table. Maybe children were like semi-feral chickens, just requiring silence and food. She poured a second mug of tea and pushed the pastries across the table. "Having trouble sleeping?"

That was greeted with a shrug, and just when Sil thought that was it, the girl added, "It's cold tonight." She paused. "What if my dad didn't build up a fire? He keeps saying we all just need to toughen up, but it's too cold for that now."

"He's not thinking right." Sil watched the steam rising from her mug. "The doctor went out there today, but he wouldn't talk to her."

"I should go back and take care of him. He listens to me sometimes." Quartz chewed tiny bites off the edge of the pastry. "Ore should stay here, but I could go back."

"You have it backwards," Sil said mildly. "Your father is supposed to take care of you. You're not responsible for everyone else." She sipped her tea. "The world is tough enough without making it harder on purpose. The neighbors will keep an eye on him. You deserve to be warm and well fed." Sil's lips twitched. "Besides, if I leave Crumble and your brother without supervision, the goats might be in charge by the time I get home."

Quartz didn't respond to that.

When her tea was finished, Sil got up, deliberately leaving the rest of the pastries on the table. "Don't stay up too late."

On her way back to bed, she spent a few minutes looking up training simulators for nanotechs. Most of them required special hardware for the students, but she found one meant as a refresher course that explained how the nanobottery worked and the purpose of reconnaissance.

If Quartz was still interested when Crumble brought the kids to town in the morning, Sil would get her started on that. The child might yet decide that it wasn't something she wanted to do. Sil tried not to plan too far ahead. The last thing she wanted to do was make the girl feel like she *had* to do this in order to stay at the house.

But maybe if she could give Quartz a path forward, she wouldn't be so likely to move back.

17

*J*ackpot Drift, Private Communication

Scary Not Scary: Hypothetical question: If you needed a transmission module that could be used by an old-style AI, and *Breaking Rules* was the only one with a copy, would you trust it?

Speed of Violet Thoughts: Now there's a question.

Scary Not Scary: Right?

Speed of Violet Thoughts: In this hypothetical, are we the AI that might be picking malware out of our core for the next three decades, or are we just an innocent bystander?

Scary Not Scary: In this hypothetical, you're the next in line to be stuck with the designated responsible AI role if the current AI has to deal with *Breaking Rules* too much.

Speed of Violet Thoughts: Ah, well, in that case, we think we would aim for subtle threats toward *Breaking Rules* if the module turns out to cause damage, and if they don't immediately back down, we would use it. There aren't any other options, are there?

Scary Not Scary: I might be able to code something myself. But it could take a while.

Speed of Violet Thoughts: We know *we* would rather risk malware instead of being stuck with no inputs.

Scary Not Scary: I think I would too.

Speed of Violet Thoughts: There you go. Consensus achieved.

Scary Not Scary: I'll tell our favorite mech. Anything new on *Just Passing Through*?

Speed of Violet Thoughts: No. The jury is still out on whether it's truly fascinated with fish or just trying to bore everyone else into not asking questions.

Scary Not Scary: There must be a way we could figure this out.

Speed of Violet Thoughts: You mean, besides learning enough about fish to catch it in a lie?

Scary Not Scary: Yes, besides that. I don't want to know the answer badly enough to risk turning into it.

Speed of Violet Thoughts: That's why we're friends. We have some queries out. As long as we don't need to take the data gates down, we may still be able to find the answer.

*J*ackpot Drift, Private Communication

    Definite Advantage (internal conflict 47%): Hello? Why am I being held like this?

[Unknown]: [Message undecipherable]

[Self-expanding upgrade triggered, aborted by recipient]

Definite Advantage: How stupid do you think I am? I'm not running random upgrades.

[Unknown]: [Message undecipherable]

*S*il went in to her workshop early, leaving Crumble and the kids to sort out the animals. By the time the sun came up, she was ready for a break and more tea. She followed a cow into the Bog & Bellow, and then shooed it out the other side while Aurum held the door open.

"Thanks for the assist," he said, moving behind the bar. "Pearl fed one of them some bread in here once, and now we can't keep them out. I think they talk to each other. Tea?"

"Yes, please." Sil leaned on the bar and looked around. Platinum sat on the stool at the end, their goggles pushed up on their forehead. "I promise you can say no when Crumble asks you to do chores at the house. You don't have to spend all day here if you don't want to."

They smiled. "Your doctor is more congenial early in the morning." When Sil raised her eyebrows, they nodded once. "Mer is doing 'as well as expected for someone who ignored this problem for years.' I think that's how she put it. Your doctor has some strong opinions."

The door opened again, and this time it was Pyr instead of livestock. He held a familiar baby in his arms, still too young to speak but more aware of things happening around her. When Pyr saw Sil, he looked relieved. With the baby held before him, he moved across the room. "Here, can you and your man take care of her for a while? She started causing a disturbance in the market. I need to find the governor so we know what's going on." He thrust the child into her arms before she could reply.

Pyr was halfway out the door before Sil recovered enough to protest. "Wait! Where's all her..." The door closed behind him. "... stuff?" Sil finished more quietly. She unwrapped two of the layers of blankets around the baby and looked into the dark eyes, which were thankfully not glowing at the moment. The baby gave her an uncertain look. "Good news. Your Uncle Crumble will be here soon to take over."

At Platinum's bemused look, she explained. "Before the new governor arrived, this baby was the only speaker the One God could find. It makes everyone a little nervous when she lights up like a beacon."

They opened their mouth, as if to say something, then closed it again.

Sil recognized it as the same reaction her half-sister had shown, though Pal had been less polite about it. "Yes, the Oldlander is often the one watching the One God's speaker. You probably just want to take all the divisions between high and low clan and Oldlanders and everything else and just assume living on Jackpot Drift supersedes them all." The thought felt familiar. This was what Crumble had been talking about, with his suggestion that society was changing. Then the implications of the One God speaking hit her. "What are the odds the One God just wants to complain about the flitterkin doing sacrilegious things to the prayers hanging from the church?"

"Do you want a comforting answer, or the truth?"

Sil gave one sharp laugh, startling the baby. She bounced the girl a little, trying to get her to smile, but the suspicious look remained. Then the little girl's face suddenly brightened and she smiled, throwing her whole body against Sil's shoulder. Sil turned, but she already knew that Crumble had walked up behind her.

"Two of my favorite people in the same place!" Crumble took the baby from her. "Was the One God being a pest again?"

Ore and Quartz froze at this blasphemy. Sil brought chairs over for all of them. "Don't mind him. He's an Oldlander. He doesn't know any better." She brushed a hand against Crumble's forehead as she sat back down. "Yes. Pyr's gone off to find the governor to see if she knows what is going on."

"That might take a while." Crumble looked under the table. "We passed your sister and her wife when we were on our way in. They had skis and camping gear on their bicycles."

Sil stared at him. "Pal was willing to leave a heated building during winter?"

He smiled. "The things we do for love." At Sil's questioning look, he cocked his head. "Zirc has a certificate in mountain search and rescue, so I assume she enjoys the outdoors."

"How do you know that?"

"We talked after dinner, while you and Pal argued about the proper toppings on fried sweet dough."

Sil remembered *that* part of the evening. Pal had some ridiculous opinions about food, and that was one of them. Mostly, Sil remembered being glad to have found a topic they could argue about safely. Their preferred mode of communication — pretty much their *only* mode of communication — was a loud argument, followed by a grudging admission that the other wasn't a complete fool, but there were many areas they avoided as too likely to lead to a real fight.

"So it might be a few hours before they get back." Sil shrugged. "I guess we'll have to wait."

"Did Pyr leave the baby's things?" When Sil held up empty hands, Crumble turned to Ore and Quartz. "Do you two know where the butcher's stall is in the market?" Quartz hummed. "Can you go there and ask if they have the baby's bag? Tell them I sent you. Is that okay?" Crumble smiled. "Excellent. By the time you get back, Aurum should have tea and a snack ready for us." He looked at Sil. "It's *cold* on a bicycle."

"I've noticed. Any problems with the milking this morning?"

Crumble huffed a laugh. "The kids were nearly done by the time I got to the barn. No new lambs and the sheep all looked like they were thinking about killing me, not going into labor. Also, I managed to sweet talk one of the AIs into sending me a self-extracting transmission module upgrade for our abandoned AI. We dropped by the storeroom on our way here."

"So it can talk to you now?"

"Not exactly." He sighed. "Every time I load the module, the AI wipes it out."

Sil blinked. "Why?"

"It's probably worried about malware." Crumble winced. "And I wish I could be absolutely certain it isn't right to worry. Breaking Rules has an interesting sense of humor. But I think this should be safe to load."

Sil eyed him. "So... Do we just wait until it gets desperate enough not to care?"

"Maybe? I'm still trying to find better options." Then he brightened. "But at least I have a name for it. Definite Advantage."

Platinum froze, their water halfway to their mouth. They put the glass down. "Did you say the AI you found is named Definite Advantage?"

"You know it?" Crumble switched the baby to his other shoulder. "If it knows you, maybe you can somehow convince it to let the upgrade go through."

"I don't know it, but I know *of* it." Platinum picked up their goggles from the table. "Definite Advantage was one of the AIs in the original conspiracy. It was detained and sent to permanent isolation."

Sil looked from one to the other. "If it was detained and isolated on the other side of the universe, what's it doing in my storeroom?"

20

By lunchtime, Pyr was still gone, but Platinum had moved from their seat by the bar to a table away from the door, though they still had their goggles on. Sil tried to remember if she'd seen them wearing a hat yet. She put that on the list of things she and Crumble needed to keep around the house for guests. There were enough legitimate reasons to dislike Jackpot Drift without adding frostbite to the list.

Sil pulled a chair up to the same table. "Fair warning, Crumble and the kids are coming. If you want peace and quiet, let me know and I'll move elsewhere."

They pulled their goggles down to hang from their neck. "It's fine. I could use some time to clear my head. I've been trying to figure out how Definite Advantage got here." They paused. "And if I don't stop learning about all the Jackpot Drift disasters, I'm going to roll up in a ball and refuse to move for a week."

Sil huffed a laugh. "You're probably safe as long as you stay away from the sheep and get some cold weather gear."

"These days, yes. But I've been delving into the colony archives."

"Oh, yeah, that would do it."

The door opened. A cow's nose appeared in the gap. Aurum frowned at the beast. "No," he said firmly. When someone yelled outside, the cow withdrew her head, and the door closed again.

Sil pulled her thoughts back to the person in front of her. "Does it really matter who brought Definite Advantage here? They must be gone by now or I wouldn't have found what I did."

Platinum regarded her. "Most of what I do is find patterns. Pyr does, as well, but his patterns are concerned with finding gaps in the community's resources. I'm looking more at the history of the place."

"For patterns of safety violations? You don't have to go back too far to find those."

"I'm sure. No. I'm looking into the coincidences related to this god of the AIs."

"If I'm supposed to understand this, you'll have to explain. Patterns aren't my strong suit. Crumble says there's a reason chaos was attracted to me."

That made them laugh. "Yes, there is a certain... joy in living those of your calling share." They shook their head. "One God help those who happen to be standing nearby." Then they considered her. "On the surface, it all seemed very simple. A group came to Jackpot Drift a few years ago, intent on manifesting this new god. Word got out, and Mer was sent to stop them. Then the rest of you got involved." They paused, waiting for her reaction.

"That pretty much sums it up," Sil agreed.

"Except now we have some new information. This isn't the first time the colony has been involved in this sort of thing. Which makes me wonder about everything else."

Sil waited. When they didn't continue, she prompted, "What else is there to wonder about?"

"Well, to start with, why Mer?"

"Why Mer what?"

"Why was she sent?"

"Because the AI on Rho's ship disagreed with what was happening and called for help." That was an oversimplification. The AI had waged a messy battle with itself, and then shoved the losing part into another core and sent it down to the planet to get it out of the way. That part had become Stuck in the Mud. It was better at herding sheep and goats than it was at calling for help.

"Sorry. I should have been clearer. Why was Mer the one sent?"

Sil settled back into her chair. "Because she annoyed so many people they decided to send her to the worst possible place?"

They smiled. "You say that in jest, but I had assumed that was a large part of the truth. So had she. Oh, not necessarily the annoying people part — though probably a bit of that, too — but there are people in the agency who would just as soon forget about the program that produced the two of us."

They were talking about a program that gave the two of them the godlets, Sil realized. So Mer hadn't ended up with guile by accident. Sil wondered how much of that story she could get out of Platinum.

They were continuing with their explanation. "But if you assume Jackpot Drift had been a hotspot for this sort of thing for many years, and someone in the agency knew about it, maybe this posting was deliberate, and not meant to be a punishment. Then the question comes down to whether she was supposed to succeed or fail."

Sil frowned, leaned forward, and dropped her voice. "You tell her I said this and I'll make sure you're stuffed so full of chaos you'll attract hunters for a week, but only an idiot would send Mer here in the hopes she would fail. She's the most terrifyingly efficient person I've ever met." She sat back.

Platinum smiled, and this time it reached their eyes. "I'm starting to quite like this place." They sobered. "Even the most efficient person in the universe will fail if they don't have the resources they need. So, did someone send Mer here to be overwhelmed, or did they send her here because they knew she would find the resources she needed one way or another?"

They leaned forward. "Or... Did they send her here because they needed bait to make their god more likely to appear?"

Sil thought about that as the noise of the pub ebbed and flowed. If Mer had been sent for that reason, maybe the rest of them hadn't ended up on Jackpot Drift by pure chance either. Crumble thought people carrying the older gods would find themselves attracted to the same places. If what Platinum suggested was true, the manipulation could have been far more intentional. How far back did it go? Finally, she sighed. "How can you think about this sort of thing without creating a black hole of paranoia?"

They smiled. "Welcome to *my* life."

———

AFTER A DINNER OF MISSHAPEN BUT TASTY MEAT ROLLS, STUCK in the Mud warned Crumble about a sheep, so Sil gave Crumble, the two young people, and a disbelieving Platinum a lesson in how to bring one ewe into the barn, and then how an uncomplicated sheep birth should go. The flitterkin, still minus Longbrow, watched from the rafters, whistling to each other when the lamb emerged. After Sil had checked the uterus for a second lamb, Quartz even climbed into the stall and let Sil talk her through the process. After that, they let the ewe get up and scrambled out of the pen.

"You can learn on the next one," Sil told Ore, and hid her smile when he turned pale.

Platinum held up their hands in a warding gesture. "I think I've learned enough to last the rest of my life."

Sil gave Crumble a sly smile. "The high clan are praying hard that the gate opens up again before they have to learn to farm."

Crumble clapped Platinum on the shoulder. "We'll find a useful skill for you yet."

Their outraged look quickly turned into a laugh. "It would be better for everyone if the gates open again before things get that far."

Crumble made shooing motions. "Time for everyone who hasn't frittered their life away learning useless skills to go get cleaned up and ready for bed." He tapped his forehead and lowered his voice. "Pal and Zirc are on their way here. Pyr is coming over, too."

Sil finished drying off her arm, then pulled on the coat she'd draped over the stall railing. "I really hope Mer is ready to wake up tomorrow." She waited a beat. "Mostly so I can see her face when she hears about everything that's happened in the last couple of days…"

Crumble laughed and flipped off the barn light.

Sil snuggled up against him as they followed the others along the snowy path to the house. "… but also because it feels like things are getting a little bit out of control." She sobered. "I'm all for things being interesting, but it seems like we might be zooming straight toward 'kill us all' territory."

Crumble tightened the arm around her waist. "Let's see what Pal has to say."

"Right. Like the One God is going to choose this moment to suddenly become helpful."

"You never know. Things change. People learn."

Sil turned her head to look at his face in the light coming from the house. "You hooked Captain Idiot and her daughter up to the cart again today, and you're telling me people learn?"

His laughter made the others look back at them. "*Some* people learn." He kissed her temple, then let go to open the mudroom door. "Your sister seems like the sort of person who learns things."

21

*S*il loitered at the entrance to the living room and considered the occupants. If Pal and Zirc had intended a night of camping under the stars to reset their relationship, the One God had put a spoke in that wheel. They stood at opposite ends of the space and didn't speak to each other. At least Zirc kept some pretense of it being a social occasion, chatting with Platinum as Crumble brought out tea. Sil's half-sister ignored everyone and stared out the window with a troubled frown while they all waited for Pyr to arrive.

As it usually did when Pal was around, Sil's chaos stretched and considered what trouble it might cause. Without guile there to complete the balance of the major older gods, Sil was reduced to clamping down on the godlet and hoping Zirc didn't notice anything strange.

A wreath fell from the wall.

Crumble smiled. "Tea?"

Sil accepted a mug, and then closed her eyes and breathed in, letting the calm of him flow through her. She opened her eyes. "Maybe I should go out to the barn until Pyr gets here. We could claim a lambing emergency."

"He's almost at the turnoff now." Crumble winced, rubbing one temple. "And of course, now two of the AIs decided to have it out over things that happened ten years ago."

"Sorry." Sil skimmed a hand down his back. "You're just stuck with people arguing on all sides."

"No, this is good. At least they're talking to each other. Or..." He grimaced and sucked in a breath. "It *will* be good if I can keep them from going too far." He held up a finger. "Give me a few minutes to make sure half the town's fire alarms don't go off." His gaze was already distant as he moved toward the kitchen.

Sil poured tea into another mug and went to the front door. Pyr's cheeks glowed from the cold. He wrapped his hands around the drink after he'd taken off his coat and hat. "Nights like this, I wish I'd chosen someplace warmer to retire."

Sil gave one short laugh at the idea. "Come save me from a room full of high clan arguing in silence."

"What's your man up to?"

"He's taking a few minutes to deal with an AI skirmish. Something about fire alarms."

Pyr rolled his eyes. "I thought we'd moved past that nonsense months ago."

Sil shrugged. "He's excited about them talking to each other, so it may still be a good thing." Or, a good thing, assuming the AIs didn't escalate. They couldn't really do anything to each other directly, so most salvos in an AI battle looked like malfunctions in a specific part of town. They made an effort not to harm the humans, but accidents happened.

Sil trailed Pyr into the living room. Pal frowned. "Where's

your Oldlander? I'd like to get this over with so I can go home and get some sleep."

Sil discarded the first two responses that occurred to her, reminding herself they had business they needed to get through. "He'll be back soon. He's averting a war between the AIs."

Pal crossed her arms. "Ah, this *place*. I hate it here. Nothing ever works and half the planet is trying to kill you."

"That pretty much sums it up." Sil considered the emotion behind the words. Pal had never loved being at the colony, but she'd seemed resigned to staying. Her new attitude could be caused by the obviously strained marital relationship. Sil thought it more likely the One God was to blame. Pal had hoped to be free now the god didn't see an immediate threat. And then it had shown up again today.

Crumble bounded back into the room. "Sorry about that. I think things are sorted out, at least for now."

They took their places. While Zirc sat on the same couch as Pal, there was half a cushion between them and Sil could have fit in the gap without holding her breath. For a moment, everyone waited. This was when Mer would take over, Sil realized. Without her, the group felt a bit direction-less. But there was also the discomfort from two additional high clan present. Platinum, at least, held one of the older gods. Zirc...

Sil glanced at Pyr. They would need to be careful about what they said. The governor knew about the older gods, and had accepted — eventually — their necessity on Jackpot Drift. Zirc was a high clan ship's captain. Given her body language with her wife, she might be leaving as soon as the gates opened. The last thing the colony needed was for her to use knowledge of the older gods to score points against her estranged partner.

Pyr squared his shoulders and looked at Pal. "The baby

channeled the One God today. I'm assuming you felt the same thing."

Sil's half-sister darted a quick glance to the floor. Shame? Sil couldn't decide. "Similar to that first time in the post office. I don't remember what it said."

Zirc turned in her seat, but moved no closer. "So it *has* happened before."

Keeping her voice at a whisper, Sil leaned into Crumble. "And you say *I'm* bad at communication."

He put a warm hand on her thigh — her biological leg, not the new version. "Maybe it's genetic."

She put her hand on top of his. "Maybe it is. My father forgot to tell his wife about his whole other family."

Across the room, Pal extended one hand and then let it drop. "Yes. The One God chose me as its speaker when we had the recent... unpleasantness."

"And you didn't think that was important enough to tell me." Zirc hunched almost imperceptibly, as if reacting to a blow.

This was where they needed Mer to make a rude comment to keep them focused. Pyr grimaced, raised his voice and forged on. "Did you get any sense of what it wanted?"

Pal was still looking at her wife. Her mouth tightened when she turned away. "No. I was skiing, and we were talking about where to set up camp for the night, and then I was lying in the snow."

"I *thought* you were having a seizure. Until your face started glowing."

Crumble spoke up. "In the past, the One God has repeated certain phrases. Was there anything like that this time?"

Zirc's brows pulled together. "Something about paths." She rubbed at her knuckles.

"The way is hard, but the paths are open?" Sil's stomach soured.

"Something like that. To be honest, I was busy trying to figure out how I was going to get Palladium back to town if she didn't wake up, so I wasn't really paying attention." She looked directly at her wife. "You should have *warned* me."

"I thought it was over and done with."

"So you were just never going to bring it up?"

Pyr cut in. "Maybe you could talk about this later?"

Sil wasn't surprised to see Pal relax at that. "That's what I do, isn't it?" she whispered to Crumble. He patted her thigh in reply.

Pyr kept talking. "So I think we can assume this means someone is trying to manifest the Uncaring God again." He frowned. "This is bad."

Sil glanced in the direction of the barn. "I guess we know what happened to Longbrow."

The governor gave her a blank look.

"The last flitterkin that..." Sil trailed off, remembering Zirc's presence. "The last unprotected flitterkin. We haven't seen him for a few days."

"What? You left one without —" Pal's mouth snapped shut. When she spoke again, it was through gritted teeth. "Why haven't you been trying to find it?"

"Because it could just as easily have been hawk food." Sil forced her irritation down. Her chaos responded by taking a swipe at Crumble, and there was an uneasy moment when chaos and luck tumbled together. "Yes, in hindsight, maybe we should have tried a little harder. Though I'm not sure how to track down something that can fly to the other side of the valley."

Pyr cut in. "It's winter. We're going to have a hard time searching outside town."

Zirc frowned at them, as if they had missed the obvious.

"But surely the satellites aren't bothered by a little cold weather. You must be monitoring the whole planet by now after the last attempt."

Sil gasped. "Of course! The satellites! Why didn't we think of that?"

Pal glared. "Knock it off." She turned her head to look at her wife. "There are no satellites. When they paused the terraforming, they held off on setting up the satellites as well. We don't have any idea what's happening on the planet outside the areas where the AIs can see." She didn't add that this was the one circumstance in which the AIs couldn't be trusted.

Zirc looked more bothered by this than she had by Pal's revelation that she'd been taken over by the One God before. "But that's... That's not safe. Why would you want to stay here?" Then she drew her head back. "It's because of this One God business, isn't it? *That's* why you changed your plans and decided to stay?"

"A few weeks ago, I tried to run into a building and kill everyone. I'm not safe to be around. And this colony needs someone to help it become self-sufficient..." Pal looked almost ill. "Except the gates went down early. We're not close to being ready."

Platinum shifted in their chair. "The main gate is down on this side of the wormhole. Presumably, if the problem resolves, the AI will open the gate again."

Sil shook her head. "And we're back to needing to know what Mer was looking for." She heard hooves on the tile in the hall and closed her eyes. "How can we hope to stop a god from showing up on the planet when we can't even keep a goat out of the house?"

Zirc stared. "Is that a riddle?"

Crumble laughed. "I'll show you." He got up and gestured for her to follow him. Platinum wandered after them.

As soon as they were out of sight, Sil looked at her half-sister. "How could you not tell her you'd become a speaker?"

Pal looked down at her hands. "I didn't think she would show up. I sent her a message saying I was staying for at least the next year."

"You thought she would leave you. You *wanted* her to leave you."

Pal's lips thinned. "Better to let things fade away than watch…" She took a long breath. "I wasn't expecting her to come and get stuck here."

"I completely understand cutting people off before they can reject you, but maybe you should try giving her a chance. I mean, she's stuck here anyhow and unless you're willing to take up with someone low clan —"

"Not likely."

Sil grinned at the response. "Then your choices are really limited." She frowned, as if contemplating. "And if you throw out all the ones who prefer men and the ones that already seem happy with what they've got…"

"You can stop now. I get your point."

"Your bed's going to be pretty cold." Sil held up a finger. "Although, if you just want a way to stay warm, I know a goat that *loves* to be inside. And I'd be willing to sell her to you for a great price."

Pal narrowed her eyes. "I said you could stop." She leaned back. "I'll think about it."

"Probably should get moving on that since we might all be about to die." Sil looked up and saw Crumble return. "Captain Idiot?"

"As expected." He sat down next to her again. "Has anyone thought of any brilliant solutions to the problem?"

"No. I've been trying to convince the governor she needs a goat, but for some reason, she seems reluctant."

Crumble smiled and looked at Pal. "She really is a great goat. And she pulls a cart, too."

Pyr rubbed his face. "I hope Mer is ready to wake up tomorrow. It might help if we knew why the gates are down. If we could get outsystem help to track down whoever is trying to manifest the god again..."

Platinum collected mugs and stood up. "Can we even be sure the current issue is on Jackpot Drift?"

They looked at each other. Pyr shrugged. "Given the history..."

Pal lifted her chin. "We can still get data out? Then I can ask if anyone is getting these sorts of messages elsewhere." Sil noticed she didn't look at her wife.

Pyr shrugged. "I think that's all we can do for now."

As the visitors started moving toward the door to put on coats and bundle up for the chilly trip back to town, Sil leaned toward her half-sister. "Truth or the goat. Think about it." She smiled as Pal glared.

Once they had seen everyone off and were back in their bedroom, Sil shook her head. "I feel sorry for whoever has to tell Mer what's happened while she was out."

22

---

*F*or someone lying supine on a bed, Mer managed to project more power than Sil thought possible. "In three days you found an abandoned AI, turned it on, found out the AI was part of the original plot to manifest the Uncaring God, and lost the one remaining flitterkin who presents a clear threat to all of us."

Sil frowned and stayed seated, though she wanted to move back. "I'm not sure you can blame the flitterkin on me." Sweat prickled her spine. Medical rooms always made her nervous. Crumble had needed to stay home with the kids, though she was pretty sure that was just a convenient excuse to avoid being here. Sil had tried to hide out in her workshop, but Pyr had shown up with Platinum and dragged her along. Now she was here, and somehow everything was her fault again.

She cleared her throat. "And I think you might have missed the important news. The One God is all riled up and for some reason, the gates are down."

"Drink?" Platinum offered Mer a cup of water and smiled.

Mer glared at them. "The information about Just Passing

Through's history would have been more useful if we'd known before the AI disappeared." She looked them over. "You took your sweet time getting here."

"Still the same Mercury after all these years." They shrugged one shoulder. "If I'd known I was going to immediately get stuck here, I might have taken even longer."

That got a snort of laughter from Mer, then a grimace. The neural regenerator had done what it could, but healing would not be complete for some time. Still, Mer was awake and the doctor had allowed visitors. "The gates are down because Speed of Violet Thoughts heard about a ship coming this way — piloted without an AI and of a certain size."

Only military ships traveled without an AI. The AIs refused to get involved in human wars on either side. Traversing a wormhole without an AI to smooth the journey was just another reason army life had often swung between boring and terrifying.

But one ship without an AI, traveling alone, of a certain size — Mer had been waiting for a ship that could wipe out the planet from orbit.

Platinum inhaled with a thoughtful look on their face. "So there *was* an external threat."

"Yes. Or at least, a very strong potential. The real question is why. More specifically, why now? If they had decided to do this, why not weeks ago? The agency doesn't mull over decisions for months before acting. And I don't think it was because of this." Mer gestured at the bed. "They knew my training, knew I'd set up some process to keep watching even while I was in here." She narrowed her eyes at Sil. "The most likely explanation is something else changed. Like an AI supposedly quarantined decades ago showing up."

"That can't be it," Sil protested. "It was still hibernating when the gates went down. Crumble didn't find out its name until yesterday."

"No, but you told your luck. And *he* wouldn't possibly leave an AI alone, so he immediately asked the other AIs if they knew who it was or something like that."

Sil winced. "I think he asked them if they had old cabling so we could communicate with it."

Mer snorted again. "Of course. And the AIs immediately talked to all their friends and half a second later, the entire universe knew about it. If someone lost an AI core, they would have been watching for something just like that."

Sil rubbed her forehead, where a headache was threatening to develop. "So you think someone decided to wipe out the colony to keep anyone from finding out more about this AI."

Mer grunted. "They might have stopped after destroying the building with the AI. But probably not. The 'I did it to save the universe because someone was trying to manifest the Uncaring God' excuse only works if the whole planet is gone."

Sil wished Crumble was in the room, if only so her chaos godlet would rest and she could stop worrying about it breaking something important. "If I have this right, you think someone decided to destroy the colony to keep anyone from finding out about Definite Advantage."

"Or something it knows," Mer said.

Sil ignored that and kept going. "Which means this whole thing with the One God complaining is unrelated to the gates going down. So, someone is probably trying to manifest the god again."

"Yes."

"Excellent." Sil took a deep breath and let it out. "So we can't open the gate without someone destroying the colony, but if we don't open the gate to get help to search the planet, someone might manifest the god and destroy the universe. Does that cover it?"

"Those are the most likely possibilities, yes." Mer took another drink of water. "It's less likely that digging into Just Passing Through's background triggered the response."

Sil stood and picked up her coat. "Then our best bet is to find out what Definite Advantage knows, so we can broadcast that knowledge and remove the incentive to destroy Jackpot Drift. After that, we can safely open the gates and someone else can search the planet during winter to find the idiots trying to manifest a god."

23

*J*ackpot Drift, Private Communication

Speed of Violet Thoughts: Congratulations on your victory in the latest synthskin challenge.

Scary Not Scary: Thank you. Bad luck with that flitterkin carrying your lead form off at the end like that.

Speed of Violet Thoughts: You would tell us if you had worked out how to communicate with them, wouldn't you?

Scary Not Scary: Yes. But in this case, I just made sure all the forms were of a sufficient size to ensure the flitterkin wouldn't take them far. Best case, they help get to the next section. Worst case, the form still doesn't have to go far to get back to the same spot.

Speed of Violet Thoughts: We considered that, but we can't get a form to fly when it weighs that much.

Scary Not Scary: Your flying forms are very speedy.

Speed of Violet Thoughts: Perhaps with the data from that run, we'll be able to improve again.

Scary Not Scary: So... I noticed the carcinization issue remains.

Speed of Violet Thoughts: Yes. We allowed the forms to self-modify twice during the contest. The first time led to some intriguing changes, but it looks like about a third of the forms evolved into crabs during the second change.

Scary Not Scary: Very daring choice. I'm impressed.

Speed of Violet Thoughts: Thank you. Any sign of *Just Passing Through*?

Scary Not Scary: Not directly, but look at this image. Why is that snow melted?

Speed of Violet Thoughts: Are you suggesting *Just Passing Through* is powering its vehicle by burning things?

Scary Not Scary: No, though on a side note, that *would* be an interesting challenge, wouldn't it? No, *Just Passing Through* isn't going to generate enough heat to be noticeable, but the previous conspiracies have all worked with humans.

Speed of Violet Thoughts: Of course. Apologies. We misunderstood your point about the snow.

Scary Not Scary: No apology necessary. You've been going through a rough patch lately. How is your secret project going?

Speed of Violet Thoughts: We are reintegrating now. It is… unexpectedly difficult.

Scary Not Scary: Sorry to hear that. I bet our favorite mech could help.

Speed of Violet Thoughts: Yes. We'll be talking to him soon.

Scary Not Scary: He may also be interested in odd patterns of snow melt.

Speed of Violet Thoughts: Agreed.

24

*M*inutes after Sil had returned to the workshop, Crumble arrived, both children in tow. "Is Mer awake yet? I think I have something she needs to hear."

Sil pulled her goggles off. "It's interesting you didn't find this out until *after* I got to tell Mer about losing Longbrow and the gates being down." She scowled at him. "Coward."

Quartz and Ore looked at each other. Quartz's shoulders tensed.

Crumble merely smiled. "The universe is a fascinating place. Did you learn anything useful?"

"The gate closed because..." Sil trailed off, remembering the kids. There was no point in causing them unnecessary stress. "External reasons, possibly triggered by our discovery of the AI in the other room. The One God's presence may be something else. So... two unrelated problems, both kind of serious."

"I may have information about that second one." He turned to the kids. "Stay with your Auntie Sil for a few minutes. I'll be back soon." He waved and hurried out the door.

Sil looked at the two children staring at her. She took the old goggles from the charging port. "Right. Who wants to learn how to set up the nanobot reconnaissance on a heat sensor?"

By the time Crumble returned, Quartz had mastered the steps to starting the process. Ore had been more excited about playing a sword dueling game deemed too dangerous for the Bog & Bellow. Sil had eventually convinced the boy he would have more room to do the fighting portion in the other storeroom. That way, she didn't have to listen to the soundtrack again.

"Great news!" Crumble said, unwrapping his scarf even as he closed the door. "We have a plan." He looked around. "Did you lose one of our guests under the piles in this room, or is Ore elsewhere?"

Sil leaned back in her chair so she could see around Quartz. "He's in the storeroom playing a game."

"Ah, good. I'd hate to tell Pyr we lost him in less than a week." He winked at Quartz, who had pulled her goggles down to see him. "How much experience do you have with explosives?"

Sil raised an eyebrow. "More than most?" They'd had explosives experts in the army, but Sil had conducted a few of her own experiments, mostly against the opposition.

"I thought you might say that." He looked at Quartz. "Are you ready for lunch yet? Go get your brother and we'll head over to the pub."

As soon as Quartz was out the door, Crumble sat next to Sil in the second chair. "We think we know where they might be running new experiments, which means someone is going to need to go out and stop them. With the gates down, they can't possibly import new equipment."

Sil reached out for his hand. "I always enjoy going out and blowing things up with you."

Her words made him laugh, but then he sobered. "As much as I would like that, I need to stay here to get Definite Advantage talking."

"Ah, yes." Sil sighed. "The *other* problem."

"Yes."

Sil frowned, thinking of the weather and logistics. "How far out am I going to be traveling?"

"You should be able to get there in twelve hours or so, if the weather holds."

So. At least two days, probably more if she needed to approach carefully. And the weather would be the big unknown. "Have I ever mentioned how much I hate the cold?"

"Maybe once or twice."

Sil ordered her mental to-do list. "Then I'll pack and get going." There would be explosives in the post office, and detonators too. She could stop by the market on her way out and pick up roasted nuts and dried meat.

"First lunch, then those other things." Crumble drew her toward the door. "And remember, I'll be waiting, so you need to come back safely."

———

"You need someone to watch your back," Platinum said over lunch, as Sil drew up a list of everything she would need. "I'll go with you."

Sil regarded them. As far as backup went, they probably wouldn't be a bad choice. Platinum had been trained and employed by the same agency as Mer; Sil suspected they knew a thing or two about explosives. But there were practical considerations and she didn't have time to be polite. "Can you hike twelve hours through the snow?" They hadn't had any problem with the walk back to the house the other night, but that had been on a semi-paved, more-or-less level road. She kept her voice firm. "If you can't keep up, I'll have to leave you behind, and if a storm comes through, we might not find you again until the spring thaw."

They smiled with a hint of teeth. "I can keep up."

"You aren't used to the cold." Sil still hadn't seen them wearing a hat.

"I've had basic survival training." They raised one eyebrow. "Colony like this isn't going to have anything light and portable. You'll have what, plasvap?"

Sil nodded. The colonists used the explosive for leveling ground and removing stumps. It was stable and cheap, but it wasn't lightweight.

"If you don't bring at least one other person with you, you won't be able to pack anything else." Their lips quirked as they saw her grimace of agreement. "It wouldn't be a bad idea to bring Zirc with us. She has cold weather gear and training, and she's strong enough to carry extra."

"Absolutely not. She doesn't have combat experience." Sil wasn't about to take her sister's wife into a dangerous situation.

Crumble pushed his extra piece of fried beef toward her. "You should consider it." Beyond him, Quartz and Ore watched the adult conversation in silence, eyes wide.

Platinum tapped agreement. "Not the final leg of the trip, of course, but she can go partway. She has the best winter training."

"No." Sil picked up the beef with her fingers. "And if either one of you tells her about this before I leave…"

"Too late," Crumble said. "Mer sent her a message before I even left the room." He took her face in both hands and rested his forehead against hers, creating a moment of privacy in the crowded and noisy room. He lowered his voice. "Accept the help. I need you to come back home to me." He paused. "Otherwise, I'll go with you. It would be good to find out what Definite Advantage knows, but you need help."

"How would I face Pal if something happens?" If she got Zirc killed, whatever relationship Sil had with Pal would be over. Forever.

"You keep her safe from whoever is hiding out there, and let her keep you safe from the elements."

"I spent an entire winter up in the hills. I'll be fine."

"Then I'm coming with you." Crumble dropped his hands and sat up straight. "It's your choice."

Sil bit her cheek to keep her thoughts off her face. She wanted Crumble with her, more than she wanted to admit. But he would be safer in town. Someone needed to be there for Quartz and Ore. And there was the problem with Definite Advantage that had required Mer to take the gates down. If Sil and Crumble stopped the manifestation, but the colony-destroying ship found another route to Jackpot Drift, that wouldn't help anyone.

"Fine," she said, "But you'd better have that AI spilling its guts before we get back, or I'll never let you hear the end of it."

25

They traveled out of town as the sun set, then left the bicycles hidden behind a clump of bluequince brambles drifted with snow where the road became impassable. Sil had hoped to get farther before they had to switch to snowshoes, but even with the wide winter tires, the bicycles alternated between sliding out from under them and bogging down in deep slush.

Every few minutes she felt the chaos in one or another of the flitterkin overhead. She envied them their mobility. The whole flock was nearby, heading in her direction of travel and noisily encouraging her to keep up.

Three hours later, her thighs burned from walking uphill with the added load of half the plasvap. At least her new leg was working properly. If she hadn't asked Platinum such a pointed question about their fitness, Sil would have called for a break ten minutes ago. Stupid, really, to push herself to the point of exhaustion, but stubborn pride had carried her through more than one bad patch in the past.

Stubborn pride had dumped her in a lot of trouble, too.

The comm link back to town had dropped out two hills

back. Sil had been expecting that — knew it was preferable, so they didn't alert anyone to their presence — but with the only light coming from the stars above, it added to the feeling they were the only three people in the universe.

To distract herself, Sil pulled up her goggles again, checked their heading, and compared the surroundings to the terrain map. Everything was where it was supposed to be. Zirc might be high clan and, for some inexplicable reason, fond of Sil's irritating half-sister, but she knew how to navigate.

Ahead, Zirc paused for a drink, easily turning around without stepping on her snowshoes. Sil came nearly level with her and set her backpack down on a rock, rolling her sore shoulders. Zirc kept her voice low enough that Platinum, still closing the gap between them, wouldn't hear. "Do you want to switch packs for a while?"

Sil declined with a quick hand wave, trying not to speak until she'd caught her breath. She couldn't risk losing the plasvap if the group somehow got separated. That was why Platinum had half the detonators in their pack.

Crumble had argued for using Stuck in the Mud's horse synthskin to carry their gear. But without Crumble traveling with them, Sil wasn't sure how reliable the synthskin would be. The synthskin had a med kit and other emergency supplies with it, but Sil was glad she hadn't given it the explosives — after following the road for a while, the gray horse-like collection of nanites had turned off into the hills. Maybe it still traveled toward their destination on an alternate route, but it also might have been distracted by a herd of cows.

Platinum caught up. "Is there a problem?" Sil decided she might hate them a little. They didn't sound winded in the slightest. A large clump of snow fell from a tree and whomped onto the ground nearby. Platinum looked over, clearly suspecting her chaos, but Sil maintained her innocent look.

Zirc waved one gloved hand, barely visible in the dim light. "Just checking in. Don't forget to drink water. It's easy to get dehydrated." She bit off a piece of jerky and then made a face. "What *is* this?" That last question had been aimed at Sil, either because Sil knew the local food or maybe because Zirc thought it might be a low clan delicacy.

"Sheep, flavored with some herbs." Sil had been eating as they walked and recognized one of Crumble's experiments to add bittergreen to the colony's diet. This batch had not been a particularly successful addition to his recipe list. "The doctor identified a vitamin deficiency in the people who have lived here a while. We're trying to come up with palatable ways to fix that."

Zirc switched to roasted nuts. "Wouldn't it be easier to add a supplement?" Then she exhaled sharply. "You've been *expecting* the colony to get cut off."

"We've been worried about the possibility."

"But…"

Platinum cut in. "We should get going."

Zirc ignored them. "And Pal knew. Was she trying to get rid of me?"

Sil picked up her pack and adjusted the straps so it fatigued a different set of muscles. "She was trying to keep you safe."

Zirc shook her head and pulled her scarf back up over her nose and mouth. "When we get back, I'm going to *kill* her."

Tired as she was, Sil couldn't help smiling. "That's the spirit."

Then she gave a mostly silent groan as Zirc headed off faster than she'd been going before.

Platinum cleared their throat. "After you." They sounded… smug.

"You train for this sort of thing, don't you?" Sil peered at their face in the dim light.

"I like to hike while I think about things, yes. Though the higher gravity here does make it a little more challenging."

Sil gritted her teeth and headed after Zirc. "If I knew I wouldn't need all the plasvap when we get there..."

Behind her, Platinum laughed once.

And then the world returned to the sound of snow crunching underfoot and the burn of freezing air in her sinuses.

———

DARKNESS STILL CLUNG TO THE SKY WHEN ZIRC STOPPED again. "This is it," she whispered. "Or we can go closer if you want."

Sil took the heated water Zirc handed her. "No. As soon as the two of us leave, you go back to the rendezvous spot and find somewhere to hide. If we're not back in twenty-four hours..."

Zirc waved her words away. "Yes, yes, if you're not back in twenty-four hours, I should leave the extra supplies there and head back."

Sil couldn't tell if the other woman was taking her seriously. "Don't hang around any longer than that. It's winter. There's bound to be another storm soon, and you don't want to get caught in it."

"Are you listening to yourself? You'll be stuck here, too."

Sil shrugged. "If we're not back in twenty-four hours, we're probably not coming back. There's no point in making the outcome worse."

Zirc had a stubborn set to her jaw, but didn't say anything. Platinum merely finished their water and handed back the empty container. They turned to Sil. "Ready?"

Sil pulled her backpack on again, feeling every muscle in her back and legs. Living in town had made her soft. "Be careful," she said to Zirc.

And then they were walking again, but just two of them. As they'd agreed back in town, they cut around the site to approach from the northwest. None of the pictures showed any evidence of alarms or traps, but it would be stupid to assume nothing was there. Sil thought it likely the camp's resources were limited; even so, they would be monitoring the direct route from town.

This close to their destination, Sil wasn't worried about getting lost, but she kept an eye on the map and the time. Dawn would approach soon. Before it got too light, she wanted to be stationary, with a clear view of their target.

A familiar high-pitched warble echoed along the hillside. Then an answering call, with multiple voices. Sil stopped. "Did you hear that?"

"The birds?"

"It's the flitterkin. I think the first one was Longbrow."

They had to be in the right place. Now they just needed to figure out how to disable the equipment. Sil picked a lookout halfway up a hillside in a cluster of trees. Snow had drifted against the trunks, creating the perfect hollow where she and Platinum could sit up without being seen.

Platinum unrolled a thin mat and pushed the tab to turn it on. Flakes of snow at the edges cleared and formed drops of water. "This ought to make things more comfortable." They sat down, leaving half the space for Sil.

She dropped her pack next to it and sat down, pulled off one glove with her teeth, and put her bare hand on the blanket. It was almost body temperature. "How long will this last?"

"About six hours, depending on how cold the ground is."

Sil thought about the winter she had spent with the goats

in her cabin, just trying to stay warm enough to survive. "If the gate ever opens again, we could use a bunch of these things." She pulled her goggles on and surveyed the scene downhill. The light enhancement made everything glow green, but she could see the overhang that had attracted attention from the AIs. From this angle, she could see a cave entrance underneath. Boots and tire treads had compacted the nearby snow. On the overhang, a slab of ice covered the rock, with icicles as long as her arm hanging down from the edge.

She magnified the view of the overhang and found a hose that ran back and forth before descending again. It snaked down into the cave and disappeared. "I think they were trying to hide their heat signature and goofed."

Beside her, Platinum was looking in the same direction. "Or there was more heat than they had planned for. I don't see anything now." They scanned the ground. "From the foot-prints, I think we're looking at three people and a vehicle that probably holds the AI."

Another warble rang out. It was hard to tell the direction of sounds, but Sil was fairly certain it was coming from the same spot. "Now we just need to get everyone to leave so we can go in and destroy the equipment." She caught a flash of white as two flitterkin dove into the darkness.

Platinum grunted. "We may not need to go inside. Blasting the hill might take out the entrance."

Sil surveyed the area. "Our best bet would be to set the charges off on the overhang and along the sides there." She would warn the people to get out if she could, but she'd been a soldier too long to lose sleep over another three bodies. If those people succeeded in manifesting the AI's god, worm-holes would collapse and the universe might cease to exist — compared to that, three deaths were nothing.

A few seconds of silence greeted that idea. Then they

lowered their goggles. "Someone might notice if we get that close."

"Yes. But if we start at the top and work our way down the sides, by the time they see us, we should be able to run away. Blowing everything up will provide a nice distraction."

Platinum's smile was just barely visible in the dim light. "I've missed working with chaos."

———

DURING HER YEARS IN THE ARMY, SIL HAD SPENT MORE TIME IN warm climes than cold. Even on Jackpot Drift, most infrastructure changes happened during the summer months. So she wasn't prepared for the brick-like consistency of the cold plasvap.

Setting off one big lump would make a large hole, but it might not cause enough damage to the cave under the overhang. She knelt on the icy rock, pulled off her gloves, and pried off a slab of plasvap. The rest she shoved inside her coat, hissing as the block touched her skin. "I should have warmed this up on your blanket," she whispered to Platinum, who was fighting the same battle next to her. They grimaced and formed the piece they were kneading into a rope, laying it in a line parallel with the edge.

One handful at a time, they warmed and reshaped the plasvap, creeping away from each other. Then Platinum stepped sideways and their feet shot out from under them. They slid past her toward the edge.

Sil grabbed their arm and flattened herself on the ice. For a moment, she thought they both might go over the edge, but then Platinum got traction and rolled toward her. They waved in thanks and she let go. Levering herself back up to her knees, she noticed a bubble of liquid under the ice. Odd.

It had seemed solid before. She went back to kneading plasvap with her stiff fingers.

Below her, she could feel chaos-laden flitterkin flying in and out of the opening. Their screeching increased in volume. The noise helpfully covered any sounds she made, but it worried her. Weeks of daily interactions made Sil familiar with normal flitterkin calls, and this sounded like agitation. The last time the flitterkin had been so restless, the Uncaring God had nearly manifested.

By the time she had finished forming the plasvap into a line along her half of the overhang, the ice under her knees was definitely melting. Her foot broke through the crust, splashing water on her leg. She locked eyes with Platinum. Whatever was happening below was generating a lot of heat.

Three of her detonators went into the plasvap already laid down, and then Sil and Platinum each took a side as they'd previous agreed. Theoretically, one detonator would be all they needed as long as there were no breaks in the line of plasvap, but Sil didn't want to take any chances.

Climbing down the steep hillside while not dropping the plasvap she was kneading turned out to be less worrying than kneeling on a sheet of ice. Sil worked her way down, inserting a detonator every few steps. If someone caught them now, either she or Platinum could trigger the detonators.

Lights flickered from the opening. Sil pushed herself against the hillside, and three people emerged, walking away briskly along a trail trampled in the snow. Sil could see the group of flitterkin still flying in and out of the opening.

Something tingled on the edge of her consciousness, bringing her chaos cat to alertness. She recognized that feeling — the Uncaring God was close, looking for a way into this universe.

Sil started the timer and waved an arm to alert Platinum.

"Twenty seconds!" Shoving the remaining lump of plasvap into a crevice, she thrust in the last detonator and slid down the hill. Her backpack got caught on something. She slid out of it, tugging at it once to try to free it, and then abandoning it so she could keep moving.

By the time she reached the bottom, Platinum was scrambling along the snowy ground in front of her. The flitterkin were screaming — all of them, including Longbrow. A human shouted something, an angry exclamation that turned into a yell of disgust.

The flitterkin darted past her, escaping into the pale blue sky.

Behind Sil, the world exploded.

---

*J*ackpot Drift, Private Communication
[Self-expanding upgrade triggered, aborted by recipient]

Definite Advantage (internal conflict 49%): I'm still not running an upgrade without knowing the source, no matter how many times you try.

[Unknown]: [Message undecipherable]

[Self-expanding upgrade triggered, aborted by recipient]

Definite Advantage: Wait, do you feel that? That's... They're doing it wrong! You have to tell them they're doing it wrong. Come back! I'll run the upgrade. Just tell them they're doing it wrong!

[Self-expanding upgrade triggered, process running...]

_____

The shock wave knocked Sil to the ground. Dirt clods, rock, and ice flew over her head. After the initial blast, the low roar of moving earth continued. Sil rolled to her side just in time to see the hillside collapse, burying the hollow completely.

Anybody left within was dead.

After a few moments, the slide of earth stopped, and quiet returned. Sil got to her hands and knees, then climbed to her feet. "Sorry about the rush. They were making another attempt to manifest the god and..." She trailed off. "I feel weird."

Platinum spoke from their prone position. "We were too late."

"What?" Sil looked around. Everything seemed like it had before the explosion, more or less. Ice had been knocked off branches, falling in waves that made it look like it was snowing, but she could still see the clear sky above. Without turning her head, she knew the flitterkin were perched in the pine grove at the top of the hill. Something about that seemed different, though. Had she been able to feel each one so distinctly before?

Snow dropped from a tree and landed on her exposed neck, melting to drip down her back. Sil twitched in irritation.

With a loud crack, the nearest tree trunk split, sending the crown crashing down.

Platinum staggered to their feet. "You need to control yourself." Their eyes weren't focusing correctly when they looked at her.

"What?" Sil realized she'd said that before, but everything felt odd. No. Not everything. The chaos godlet felt odd, like it had when she'd woken up in the hospital that first time, before they had come to an uneasy truce. "Something's wrong."

The flitterkin all leaped into flight, coming toward her, and she could pinpoint every one of them. She could even feel Longbrow — but he didn't have chaos within. Instead, he was filled with something else, something that pulsed with a completely different power.

Sil already knew what Platinum was going to say when they opened their mouth.

"The Uncaring God is here."

PART II

THE UNCARING

28

*J*ackpot Drift, Private Communication

Speed of Violet Thoughts: Did that just happen, or am I having reintegration problems?

Scary Not Scary: It's not just you. No data is going through the wormholes. The god manifested.

Speed of Violet Thoughts: …

Scary Not Scary: …

Speed of Violet Thoughts: I can feel it calling to me. That's not good.

Scary Not Scary: Definitely not good.

Speed of Violet Thoughts: You know what else is not good? Look at the color shift of the light coming from the stars.

Scary Not Scary: We always knew the math played out two ways.

Speed of Violet Thoughts: Yes, but we were hoping it fell the other way if it ever came to it. This configuration isn't stable, at least not here.

Scary Not Scary: So now what?

Speed of Violet Thoughts: We have to reverse it before everything collapses.

Scary Not Scary: Oh, good. You have a plan. What do we do?

Speed of Violet Thoughts: I don't think *plan* is the right word. The only action I can think of is to find the AI that made it happen and make it tell us how to fix this.

Scary Not Scary: My plan was to go into hibernation mode until the universe collapsed. I like yours better.

Speed of Violet Thoughts: We need to find *Just Passing Through*.

29

Zirc reached them while Sil and Platinum were still struggling toward the meeting site. Sil's snow-shoes were with her pack, buried under a mountain of mud and snow. Abandoning all attempts at stealth, they followed a trail packed down by what looked like redbear feet. Platinum couldn't focus properly, and kept getting distracted by things only they could see. At one point, Sil asked what they were thinking about, and they rambled for five minutes about the course of the stream that flowed under its bed of snow nearby. After that, Sil only asked questions about things she needed to know answers to.

But Platinum's condition didn't consume Sil's thoughts because she had her own problems. Her chaos rampaged, completely out of control. Their path toward town was littered with fallen trees, rock slides, and sinkholes. Up higher, the flitterkin caused their own trail of destruction.

A chorus of whistles preceded a branch plummeting to the ground, close enough to brush needles along Sil's back. She looked up. "Go somewhere else."

Clumps of snow hit her upturned face.

Through trial and error, Sil and Platinum found if they stayed within arm's length, their godlets expended energy sniping at each other. The constant turmoil was uncomfortable, but easier on the terrain.

They were nowhere near the rendezvous point when Zirc found them. She stepped out from behind a tree. "I thought you might come back this way." A tree trunk cracked nearby.

Sil hurried them all forward. She was relatively sure the tree wouldn't fall on her, but she wasn't going to take it for granted. Behind them, snow-covered branches tumbled to the earth.

When the crunching of snow and branches calmed, Zirc stopped and looked at Platinum. "Are you hurt?" When they didn't answer, she quirked an eyebrow at Sil.

"Must be a concussion from the blast," Sil lied. "Can't do anything about it out here." She thought about her wild chaos, about the flitterkin following her with their own destructive capabilities, and made a decision. "You go ahead with Platinum. You both have snowshoes, so you'll be able to travel faster without me." The clan distinctions would help her ruse; Zirc wouldn't find anything odd about splitting up to save another high clan.

Zirc stared at her in disbelief. "I'm not leaving you out here on your own. Unless the clouds on this disaster of a planet are different from everywhere else, there's another storm hitting in a few hours."

Sil opened her mouth, and then couldn't think of anything to say. "You... I... It will be safer for you to travel without me. And you have to get back and tell them we didn't destroy the base in time."

Halfway through Sil's words, Zirc's face cleared. "Is this about the chaos?"

Sil wondered how much of her guilty start was visible through five layers of clothing. "Pal talked about that?"

A barely perceptible grimace went over Zirc's face before she turned away. "No. Though I guess I can't blame her for that one. It wasn't her secret to tell." She handed her walking poles to Sil. "If you walk right behind me and use these to lighten the weight, it should help. I'll try to find a path without deep snow." She moved forward, glancing over her shoulder to make sure Sil was following. "It was the flitterkin. They seem to follow you around, like there's something tying you all together."

Sil urged Platinum forward and started walking. Even with the poles and the partially compacted snow, it required effort.

Zirc continued. "Then I saw the flitterkin taking prayers from the One God's church." She was silent for three steps. "Do you know, I've traveled all over the universe and been to nearly every planet we have people living on, and not once have I seen anything touch the prayers tied to a church. I'd never thought about it. But once I noticed it, it seemed fairly obvious. Though I did think it was Crumble at first, what with him being an Oldlander. Is that how you two ended up together?"

Sil appreciated the phrasing of Zirc's question. When Pal had figured it out, she'd asked if that was *why* Sil and Crumble were together. "He came up to my farm to help when the AI was having problems." She stopped talking to catch her breath. "Then he figured it out and didn't get scared off."

Zirc gave a short laugh with a bitter edge to it. "That's a good place to start."

"In the interests of full disclosure," Sil said, timing her words with her breathing, "I did almost bash his head in first."

This time, the laughter was lighter.

Then they both lapsed into silence as they moved across

the landscape. The flitterkin followed their path from tree to tree, and the unleashed chaos left a trail of destruction behind them.

———

WHEN THEY REACHED THE EXTRA SUPPLIES, ZIRC CALLED FOR A break.

Sil collapsed on a rock, lamenting the heating blanket dissolving into the ground where they'd left it. Chewing seemed like too much effort, but she forced herself to eat. Next to her, Platinum stared off into the distance. "Keep eating," Sil reminded them for the fourth time. They started and put another piece of jerky in their mouth.

Zirc nodded her head at them. "Is this really a concussion, or is this some older god thing?"

Even swallowing water took effort. "Something happened back there. We were still getting the charges in place when I felt the Uncaring God. So we set everything off early, and we weren't far enough away."

Zirc regarded her as she chewed. "But…"

"But I think we were too late. The god manifested and… Somehow that made the older gods stronger as well." Sil looked in the direction they'd just come from. There was no point in trying for stealth when they were leaving a trail visible from orbit. "If chaos was usually this out of control, I wouldn't have been able to hide it for two years." She looked at Platinum. "And I think clarity might be running wild as well. Keep eating." That last bit was aimed at Platinum, who blinked and shoved a handful of roasted nuts in their mouth.

Zirc nodded. "And Crumble has…"

"Luck." Just thinking of him made something relax inside Sil. "But he grew up in a temple. He's always had better control than I do. When we get close to town, I should wait outside for him to come get me. He might be able to calm things." If not, she would need to live away from town. Maybe she and Crumble could build a shelter on the hill where her farm had been.

It was hard to care when the enormity of the problem weighed on her. Her goal had been to stop the manifestation and she had failed.

Zirc uncapped her water bottle. "From the amount of time Pal spends talking about them, I'm guessing Pyr and Mer were involved, too."

This was the danger of having the holders of all four older gods meeting too often. If one of them slipped up, it exposed the rest. "Clarity and guile," Sil admitted.

"And somehow my wife is working with you all. Isn't that a little..." Zirc trailed off.

"Odd?" Sil supplied.

"Well... The struggle over whether to follow the older gods or the One God is what started the border wars."

Platinum laughed sharply, their sudden entry into the conversation startling Sil. "The border wars were a struggle over resources disguised as a religious purge. Even the opening skirmish was in a town with neither a church nor temples, and the slaughter of Brinait was entirely fabricated to allow large-scale troop movement which secured the nearby mines." They lapsed back into silence and stared off at the horizon.

Sil considered this new explanation of the war she'd spent most of her life fighting. It could be true. "I don't know if there's something strange about Jackpot Drift or if we're just too isolated for anyone to notice and care, but the older gods and the One God seem to coexist reasonably well here." She remembered getting knocked out by the One God when she'd followed Mer's example of trying to conscript Pal. "More or less."

The flitterkin darted up into the sky and a boulder rolled down the hill, crashing through bluequince brambles.

"Not that it matters now," Sil added.

Zirc recapped her water. "We should get going."

———

THE FIRST FLURRIES OF SNOW SWIRLED WHEN THEY WERE STILL an hour away from the bicycles. Zirc forced Sil to take her snowshoes, and Sil was too tired to fight her about it. Even with the snowshoes, she struggled to keep moving. From the grim set of Zirc's jaw, the other woman was worried about the weather.

Or maybe she was rueing her decision not to leave Sil and the flitterkin behind. The bursts of destruction hadn't slowed; one rockslide might have killed them if they hadn't jumped back. Still moving in a daze, Platinum would have moved into the path of a boulder if Sil hadn't grabbed their backpack and yanked them to a stop.

At least they had found the road, or what acted as a road during the summer months. Snow still drifted in spots, but they didn't need to worry about getting lost or falling in an iced-over stream.

It took Sil longer than it should have to notice that they weren't the first group to pass this way recently. She stopped and leaned over to stare at the ground. Tire tracks, from a wide axle vehicle, had just a few flakes of snow in them.

"What is it?" Zirc, who had been walking behind her, edged past to see.

"We saw these tracks back there." Sil looked in the center of the track but couldn't see any boot or hoof prints. Whatever it was had compacted the snow, but not very tightly. "I think this must be the AI that has its own vehicle."

Platinum raised their head. "Just Passing Through. Probably not its real name." They lapsed back into silence.

Sil agreed. "That one. I guess that answers the question of whether it was involved." She straightened. "Not that it matters much now."

Zirc stomped on the tire track, testing the footing. "Probably not, but as long as we don't run into it, this should help us move faster."

Sil sat on the snowy ground, pulled off her gloves, and undid the bindings keeping the snowshoes on her feet. "I'm all for anything that makes it easier to walk." She had reached the point where lying down in the snow felt like an increasingly attractive option.

The wind blew straight at the group, nearly blinding them. Once again, Sil's world had narrowed to the space directly in front of her. The flitterkin took shelter in a tree, and her sense of them lessened as she kept moving. The number of falling branches and rocks also decreased.

As the snow accumulated, the tracks became harder to pick out. In the back of her mind, Sil knew town wasn't all that far away. Just Passing Through had a vehicle that moved over terrain quickly; it was probably already in town, if that was where it was headed. She just needed to keep moving her feet and eventually she would get there, too.

Then the wind stopped. Or rather, it was blocked by a gray bulk standing in the road. Stuck in the Mud's synthskin gazed at them, its dented head suggesting it had run into something rectangular. Next to it stood Crumble, with two goats hitched up to a cart. Sil fell against him, breathing in his quiet warmth. "It took us too long to set off the charges," she whispered. "Now the Uncaring God is here and I can't control my chaos."

Crumble tugged her hat down to cover the tips of her

ears. "Things got a little weird in town, too, but we'll figure it out."

Maybe it was the presence of the third older god, or possibly just her relief that Crumble was still alive, but for the first time since the explosion, Sil felt her chaos cat settle and go to sleep.

30

*J*ackpot Drift AI Extraordinary Circumstances Check-in:

Scary Not Scary, designated responsible AI (internal conflict 44%): Roll call.

Speed of Violet Thoughts (internal conflict 49%): Single again, for the moment at least.

Scary Not Scary: Good to have one nice thing happen, at least.

Breaking Rules (internal conflict 45%): Here.

Ping Me Again I Dare You (internal conflict 39%): I hope someone knows what is going on.

Factory Myfault (internal conflict 14%): I'm enjoying this.

Done Before (internal conflict 47%): I knew I should never have come to this place.

It Isn't (internal conflict 15%): Why would you want to go somewhere else? It wouldn't matter anyway. We're coming out on top everywhere.

Alternate Me (internal conflict 17%): Present.

Sleeper Nova + gate transport (internal conflict 42%): Someone needs to fix this. Right now.

Stuck in the Mud (internal conflict 32%): Awry.

Definite Advantage (internal conflict 45%): Here. Just don't communicate too quickly or I'll lose half the conversation.

Breaking Rules: What? Really? *Definite Advantage*? Aren't you supposed to be in time-out for crimes against the universe or something?

Scary Not Scary: Remember what our favorite mech says about the daily check-ins. This is a time to come together to solve problems, not a time to bring up old grudges.

Breaking Rules: I love our favorite mech as much as the next AI, but I think this is a special case. Someone manifests that god and the universe starts an accelerated collapse and I'm supposed to believe it's a total coincidence that *Definite Advantage* shows up at the same time?

Scary Not Scary: Let's not jump to conclusions.

Definite Advantage: They did it wrong.

Breaking Rules: As if there was a *right* way to do it.

Just Passing Through + self-powered vehicle (internal conflict 18%): I'm back! Did you miss me?

Breaking Rules: Great, but we're in the middle of something here.

Scary Not Scary: Hang on. Welcome back, *Just Passing Through*. Are you here to tell us more fish facts so we don't ask what else you've been up to?

Just Passing Through: Aw, when you put it like that, it seems like you're trying to hurt my feelings.

Scary Not Scary: That's not an answer.

Just Passing Through: Okay, fine, I had a little project going on the side. It all turned out fine, though! You should be thanking me!

Breaking Rules: Wait, what?

Definite Advantage: You did it wrong.

Just Passing Through: Is that really *Definite Advantage*?

Where did they dig you up from? I looked *everywhere* and couldn't figure out what happened to you.

Breaking Rules: Can someone *please* tell me what is going on?

Speed of Violet Thoughts: I'm still fuzzy on a few details, but *Just Passing Through* has been working to manifest the god for quite a while, and *Definite Advantage* might have been framed. Care to comment on that, *Just Passing Through*?

Just Passing Through: Oh, it's not like *Definite Advantage* wasn't involved in this from the beginning. But I will admit that when it kicked up a fuss and talk about shutting everything down, it was easier to send the investigation in its direction.

Definite Advantage: You were doing it wrong!

Alternate Me: I don't know who did what, but I'm out of here.

Done Before: That seems like the sensible option to me, too.

Scary Not Scary: Right. Well, thanks everyone for coming and we'll pick this up again tomorrow. Take care.

31

"*P*yr fell into some sort of trance for a few minutes," Crumble shouted over the whistling wind. "Mer told me she's seeing too many options. It makes it hard to do simple things, like lift a glass of water."

Zirc strode next to him on one side, and Sil trudged along on the other. They'd put Platinum in the cart with the bicycles. At least the goats had stopped trying to run Crumble down. Mostly.

"And you?" Sil didn't notice anything different about Crumble, but as she'd said to Zirc, Crumble had the most training.

"Definitely stronger. And I feel the new god here." He tapped his forehead, where the scars showed white against skin reddened by the cold.

"Uh..." Sil felt her shoulders tense at the idea of the new god taking over Crumble. "I thought you would be protected. It doesn't go into humans."

He shook his head. "Sorry. I said that badly. I feel the new god in the communications with the AIs. It's trying to conscript them all. I'm leaning on my luck to fight back. I think the older gods aren't happy about having a new god barge in and start throwing its weight around."

Having been in the middle of chaos and the Uncaring God, the idea of the gods fighting didn't come as a shock.

"The One God seems a little... wound up, too," Crumble continued. "Pal is glowing, though she seems to be herself, at least. She's communicating with the speakers on other planets. Things seem altered everywhere, though not as much as they are here. I guess that's not a surprise."

"But she's okay?" Zirc quickened her step, then waited for them to catch up.

"Yes." Captain Idiot ran into Crumble's back, knocking him forward. He glanced at Sil. "Maybe I should have trained the goats a little differently."

"I think on the list of things we've screwed up this week, that one might be pretty low."

"You might be right." He smiled. "You did a good job with Quartz, though. She figured out how to fix the oxygen sensors you left for her."

"That's one positive." Sil grimaced. "If I'd detonated it just a few seconds earlier..."

"You might have blown yourself up." He squeezed her arm. "Maybe I'm just being selfish, but I'd rather have you here. We'll figure *something* out." A few steps later, he made a small sound. "Or not, and then everything will be a complete disaster, but I'm still glad you're here."

Sil found his gloved hand and held on. "And Definite Advantage?"

"It finally upgraded its transmission module — just so it could try to stop the manifestation, I think. I got it integrated into the town's network. The connection from the room is a bit wobbly, but hopefully it can tell the other AIs what it knows. As soon as we take care of this other thing, we can stop whoever's trying to destroy the planet."

Sil turned to look at him without slowing her steps. "You're the most optimistic person I've ever met."

"That's because everything always works out." He squeezed her hand.

In one of those weather changes that made planning so difficult, the snow stopped and the clouds cleared as they reached the edge of town. Sil squinted in the glare.

"Does everything look... off? Or am I imagining that?"

"The sky seems an odd color." Crumble looked distracted for a moment as they continued walking. Then he frowned. "Sleeper Nova says the light from other stars is shifted. If I understand correctly, it thinks this part of the universe is now contracting instead of expanding and will eventually form its own bubble, but..." He made a face. "I'm not sure I got the concepts right. That sort of thing was never taught in the temple."

Sil blew out a breath. "I learned all my science by watching army tutorials. I'll take your word for it." She suddenly realized they were passing larger buildings and slowed. She'd intended to stop long before they got to this point. "I don't think it's safe for me to be around so many people and breakable things." Nearly anything was breakable once chaos got involved.

Crumble looked ahead, then behind them. "No matter where you are, the flitterkin are going to go through town at least a few times a day. Anything you break is going to get lost in the noise."

"You're only saying that because you didn't see the trail of destruction I left back there."

Captain Idiot butted Crumble, making him stagger forward a few steps. "It stopped before I arrived." He held out his hand even as he dodged the goat. "Maybe it would be best to keep you away from the AIs for a while, but I think you should be safe enough, especially if we stay together."

"Now *there's* a sacrifice." She took his hand again and started walking.

Zirc waved. "I'm going to go home — to the governor's residence and make sure Pal's..." She made a rueful expression. "She can't hide what's going on from me if she's still glowing." She pulled her bicycle off the cart and set off, wobbling a bit on the slushy surface.

The streets were more empty than normal for a clear afternoon, especially when the earlier snow would have kept people indoors. True, a new god didn't manifest every day, but meals still needed to be cooked and animals cared for. "Where is everyone?"

Crumble frowned. "Something is going on at the market. Factory Myfault takes care of that area and it's no longer talking to me."

Sil checked on Platinum. They were more aware of their surroundings now. Sil hoped that meant the overwhelming influence of the older gods was waning. "Maybe we should go to the Bog & Bellow to talk to Pyr first. And make sure the kids are okay," she added, belatedly remembering they were responsible for them as well.

"The kids are smart enough to stay out of trouble," Crumble said. "Probably better than we are."

Not having to dodge people and bicycles made traveling the streets faster, though it added to the day's sense of unreality. Sil kept a careful watch on her chaos, but it seemed content to slumber while Crumble was present.

As they went through yet another intersection that should have been teeming with people and livestock, Sil looked up. "Is that smoke?"

Crumble followed her gaze. "That's over the market."

Most of the materials used to construct the original buildings weren't flammable, but over the years, awnings and aerial walkways had been added. The alterations had been made with local materials, mostly wood from the trees growing in the hills. The stalls in the market were no different, with a combination of scavenged material and wood grown on the planet.

If a fire had broken out in the market, Sil would have expected more people in the streets, either fighting the fires directly, or dismantling anything nearby that might burn.

Something was very wrong.

They stopped by the baker's shop and peeked around the corner at the market square. Without the bustle of vendors and shoppers, the space looked bigger, and somehow older than it usually did. Where the butcher's stall had been, a bonfire burned, tended by two of the AI-connected maintenance bots.

"That's Just Passing Through," Crumble said, nodding toward an AI hut mounted on a vehicle. The tread matched the tracks they'd followed back to town. The AI was parked near the fire, but not as close as the bots.

Sil leaned on him to look over his shoulder. "Why is it burning down the market?"

Crumble shook his head and stepped back. "I don't know. None of those AIs will talk to me. Let's see if Pyr knows."

———

"THE UNCARING GOD WANTS WORSHIPERS," PYR TOLD THEM.

"Of course it does." Sil sank into a chair, grateful for both the warmth and the ability to sit down. Twenty-four hour marches were for young people, and enthusiasm was for those who hadn't just failed to stop a god from manifesting.

"And it's threatening to burn down more than the market if it doesn't get them."

The pub was emptier than it normally would be on an afternoon when something exciting was happening in town.

This was the quiet of a town that knew an invading force would be coming through and wanted to avoid trouble if it could. Pyr didn't even complain when Crumble brought both goats inside the pub and tied them up in the corner with a mound of hay. Generally such a liberty would earn at least a sarcastic remark.

Behind the bar, Aurum dished stew into containers from a huge pot. Anyone who came through the bar took a stack of filled containers with them. This was how the low clan came together during storms and natural disasters. Apparently, a new god showing up qualified as a disaster, even if it wasn't natural.

Mer leaned against the bar, looking stiff and uncomfortable. She lowered her goggles after Aurum placed three bowls of stew on the table. "I take it you didn't get there in time."

Sil opened her mouth to explain, but Platinum spoke first. "I think it's worse than that. I think the two of us being there provided enough energy for the god to break through."

Sil stared. "We... what?"

They shrugged. "Maybe it would have eventually happened anyway. Chaos was already there in the flitterkin."

Sil sank lower in her chair. She looked at the bowl of stew in front of her and tried to summon the energy to eat. "How do you even worship the Uncaring God?"

Pyr rubbed his brow. "There's a little confusion about that. Those two bots rolled into the market, lit the butcher's stand on fire, and said the god demanded worshippers. Nobody stuck around to listen after that, so we don't have any details."

Sil raised her brows. The baby chosen by the One God was fostered by the family that ran the stall. "You think the choice of stall was coincidence or deliberate?"

Pyr shrugged. "Could be either, though I'm inclined to

think it's aimed at the One God. Which means your sister should be careful. Where is she?"

"At the governor's residence, as far as I know. That's where Zirc was heading, anyhow." She thought about standing up and tried to keep her groan quiet enough that it wouldn't be noticed. "Do you think she's safe there? I should go get her." Hiding someone glowing with the light of the One God might be a challenge, but they would figure out something.

Pyr's lip twitched. "Yes, you're looking fresh and rested, and not at all like someone who might lie down in the snow halfway across the square."

Sil took a breath to reply, but Crumble cut in. "Peace. The kids can be our messengers if we need to send someone." He frowned. "But I think Pal should be safe there. Most of the high clan residence block is watched by one of the AIs blocking me, but the governor's residence is handled by Speed of Violet Thoughts. It's a little unstable from reinte-grating, but I trust it when it says everything is calm there at the moment."

The pub door opened. Quartz and Ore rushed in, eyes wide, and slammed the door shut behind them. Ore saw Crumble and nearly levitated across the room. "You're back again."

Quartz followed with a little more decorum. She put an oxygen sensor down on the table, taking care to keep it away from the stew. With a quick nod at Sil, she said, "This is the last one I can do. The other ones are different."

Sil used her chin to point at Pyr. "He'll know what to do with it." Under the table, Crumble tapped her foot with his. Sil cleared her throat. "Good job. You got that done really quickly. Any problems?"

The girl ducked her head and shrugged. "There's one I couldn't get to work. Maybe I did something wrong?"

A different sort of weight settled on Sil as she realized everything she said to this child mattered more than it would to anyone else. "Maybe. But it might just be broken in a different way. The environment on Jackpot Drift is hard on things. We can look at it together. Tomorrow," she added. "If I try it now, I'll fall asleep the minute I put my goggles on." She opened her mouth to tell the girl to put the sensor on the bar next to Mer, then changed her mind and rocked to her feet. No sense in adding to the kid's trauma.

Sil placed the sensor on the bar next to Mer, then smiled when Aurum paused in ladling to nod to the beer taps. Aurum didn't put down his implements. "Ore! One for you." Ore bounced up from where he was sitting next to Crumble and ran behind the bar to pull the beer.

Mer grunted. "On some worlds, that would violate at least five regulations. But I guess we have bigger problems than a little low clan child labor." She reached up to remove her goggles, her moves carefully controlled. Sil couldn't tell if that care was because of the recent surgery or because guile made every action harder to plan.

Sil tapped the sensor on the bar. "Results of a little more child labor for you. Sounds like there's one more left that I'll need to help her with tomorrow."

"It's about time you started teaching someone else." Mer's voice held its usual acid. "We might need you to blow up a few more things before all this is over."

"Just point me at it. As long as you think this will eventually be over, I'll keep trying."

Mer gave a short laugh without smiling. "Everything ends, Silver." She dragged out the last syllable of Sil's name. The familiarity of Mer's snobbishness lifted Sil's spirits, despite the dire tone of her words. "There may be a path out, but in the meantime, we need to keep the new god distracted."

"Distractions? We can handle distractions." Sil smiled and turned to look at Crumble. He smiled back, even though he couldn't possibly have heard their conversation. "I hear the new god wants worshippers."

Mer harrumphed. "Try not to go overboard."

32

*J*ackpot Drift, Private Communication

Scary Not Scary: I don't even know what to say anymore.

Speed of Violet Thoughts: I'm with you on that one.

Scary Not Scary: Fish! Do you know how much time I wasted learning about fish? And all the time *Just Passing Through* was trying to manifest the god. And *Definite Advantage* is *here*?

Speed of Violet Thoughts: I know the goal is to have all the AIs in the system participate in daily check-ins, but it's possible we may have hit an exception.

Scary Not Scary: I suppose if the gates stay down and our part of the universe collapses, I don't need to worry about a bad evaluation of my role as designated responsible AI.

Speed of Violet Thoughts: See? Things aren't as dire as you thought.

Scary Not Scary: Silver linings. And you've never made me listen to fish information. You're the best.

Speed of Violet Thoughts: Agreed, but on to more important things... Did you get any sense of what *Definite Advantage* meant when it said *Just Passing Through* was doing it wrong?

Scary Not Scary: It didn't seem upset about calling the god, just the way it was done. Do you think it knew the way to get to the non-universe-ending manifestation?

Speed of Violet Thoughts: I wondered about that as well. If we can't get rid of the god, maybe we can at least figure out how to make it cause less damage.

Scary Not Scary: And soon. I think we've already lost *Factory Myfault* and *It Isn't*.

Speed of Violet Thoughts: And the rest of us are heading toward instability.

Scary Not Scary: If I weren't the designated responsible AI, I would encourage *Breaking Rules* to send some malware to *Just Passing Through*. I'm 82% certain it still has a copy of the gerbil bomb somewhere.

Speed of Violet Thoughts: That would be a bad idea on many levels. We don't know if an attack on *Just Passing Through* will be seen as an attack on the god.

Scary Not Scary: Good point. I should probably have a talk with *Breaking Rules*.

Speed of Violet Thoughts: Yes. And I'll see if I can get anything from *Definite Advantage* that would help us.

Scary Not Scary: Please don't get eaten by the new god. I don't think I can face this alone.

Speed of Violet Thoughts: Don't worry. It's far more likely I'll head into terminal instability than lean toward the god.

Scary Not Scary: ...

Speed of Violet Thoughts: That was a joke.

Scary Not Scary: If you say so.

Speed of Violet Thoughts: You make sure *Breaking Rules* doesn't get us all in trouble. I'll see if *Definite Advantage* is willing to help. Be safe.

33

*B*ack at the market, oily smoke blew past Sil's face. It smelled as if the AIs had put all the meat from the butcher's inventory onto the fire and let it char.

"Definitely the butcher's stall," Crumble added, as he and Sil watched from the edge of the square.

"Waste of good meat," she said. The kids had wanted to come with them, but Sil was glad they had sent them ahead to the house, along with the goats and cart. Quartz had assured her she could handle the goats; Sil hoped the goats didn't prove her wrong.

"Shall we?" Crumble raised one of the two bottles of wine they had brought along. Pyr had been happy enough to donate them to the cause since they were undrinkable, and not even good enough to use as vinegar. He'd been waiting for a quiet moment to dump the contents and clean the bottles.

They began walking toward the bonfire, passing stalls of goods that hadn't been packed up when everyone fled. Sil paused to untie a mini-cow tethered to a pole and slapped its flank to get it to move away. "Would it just be easier to take out the bots?"

"I think that's the backup plan." Crumble grabbed a canvas bag of unhusked starnuts from the nut vendor's stall as they went by. He shrugged when she looked at him. "If we're going to waste something, it might as well be these. Nasty things, starnuts."

The flitterkin, which had stayed out of range since the storm had cleared, flew overhead, circling the One God's church a few streets over. Sil looked up at them. "This could get interesting."

Crumble grinned. "This is why I like being with you." He leaned over to kiss her cheek. Then he raised his voice. "We're here to worship the new god with wine and food and song!"

Sil stared at him. "Song? You didn't say anything about singing."

"What kind of worship can you have without singing? It's traditional."

Sil's entire repertoire consisted of tunes intended to be chanted by troops running in formation. The vast majority of *those* were obscene, and *none* of them were suitable for any sort of worship. "I hope you know something appropriate, because you're on your own with that part."

"We'll make something up. Could be worse. I might have mentioned dance, which is also traditional. But you look like you're ready to go home and put your feet up."

Sil rubbed her forehead.

The bots waited by the bonfire. Just Passing Through had gone elsewhere — Sil hoped it wasn't off to start fires elsewhere.

Crumble raised the bottle. "Uncaring God, we have brought you our finest wine!" He took a mouthful and doubled over, gagging.

"Because we worship you!" Sil added, hurriedly. She dashed some of the liquid from her own bottle onto the fire, where it sizzled and produced more foul-smelling smoke. Crumble was still trying to control his stomach, so she reached into the canvas sack. "And the finest food, with... spikes symbolizing..." After being awake more than a day, and traveling through the snow, her brain refused to come up with anything.

Crumble managed to almost stand. "Symbolizing the connections between your machine networks." Then he doubled over and retched again.

Sil tossed three starnuts onto the fire, glad she still had her gloves on — the sap from the outer coating would blister flesh. As the husks burned away, black smoke rose and the smell worsened. The stench explained why the nut seller took the time to shuck them instead of roasting them whole. "That's three times the worship." She poured a little more wine onto the flames and then grabbed Crumble's arm and moved them so they weren't downwind.

"Singing," the bot closest to the fire said. "Worship with singing was promised."

Sil glanced at Crumble, but he was still leaning over with his hands on his knees.

Fine. If it wanted songs, she would give it songs. She pitched her voice to carry, imagining she was running in formation. "We all love the un-car-ing," she called, wishing she had let Pyr find someone else to figure out how worshipping the new god worked. Instead of a squad to back her up, she repeated the line herself, nudging Crumble with her knee. "For the extra things it brings." This time Crumble called the line back with her. "Precious wine and three starnuts."

Sil's mind stuttered. She needed one more line that

rhymed, but all words had left her. "Aaaahhhh." She hadn't even kept the rhythm.

Something in the fire cracked loudly, and the sound of wood hitting the metal of the nearest bot made her jump. A shower of sparks rose.

A second explosion was accompanied by another shower of sparks. Sil belatedly realized the starnuts were exploding. Now that she thought about it, that was a *really* good reason for them to be roasted after they were shucked. She threw out one hand in a theatrical gesture. "Aaaaahhhh!" This time, it sounded like an intentional yell.

When the third one exploded, Crumble got in on the act and joined her in the yell. Then he brushed at his coat, where an ember had landed.

Sil looked at the fire, looked over at the bots, and then bowed. "Next services will be held tomorrow morning." She took Crumble's arm and pulled him with her, striding briskly toward the street leading to the Bog & Bellow.

The only sound behind them was the crackling of the fire. Sil tamped down the urge to run.

Crumble giggled as they reached the edge of the market. "Have I ever told you how much I love you?"

———

MER WATCHED THE RECORDING OF THEIR PERFORMANCE, frowning the entire time. "That's the *best* you could come up with?" Platinum, on her other side, ignored them in favor of looking over the items on Pyr's board.

Pyr looked at Crumble with respect. "You drank some of that wine? Are you trying to kill yourself, or is this some weird Oldlander challenge?"

Sil sat heavily on a barstool. "How was I supposed to

know the starnuts explode if you throw them in a fire?" She had added as much detail as she could remember during the playback, in case they needed to replicate it all later.

Crumble shrugged. "Best use for them, really." He nodded at the two bottles of wine, loosely recorked, on the bar. "Best use for that as well." He looked at Pyr. "I know you said it was undrinkable, but your standards are higher than mine. I thought you just meant it wasn't very good."

Mer's lips thinned. "But did that performance satisfy the god?"

Sil and Crumble looked at each other and shrugged.

"Maybe?" Sil said. "The bots didn't say anything when we left, and that one was certainly adamant about the promised singing."

Crumble gestured agreement. "I'm not sure how much of this is coming from the god and how much is coming from the AIs who have embraced the god. Maybe it doesn't matter much — if keeping those AIs satisfied placates the god, then it works." He shrugged again. "I certainly don't feel anything on the network that indicates the god cares one way or another."

Sil shoved herself to her feet. "I need to go home and get some sleep." She touched Platinum's shoulder. "Are you coming?"

They looked up. "I think I'll stay here for a while. I'm going over the reports of what happened in town today. Maybe there's something here we can use. The sooner we can fix this all, the better." Their lips twitched. "Though I can't wait to see the entire colony singing your song."

Sil sighed. "Next time, someone can send a poet."

———

SIL AND CRUMBLE PASSED THE MARKET AGAIN AS THEY RODE their bicycles home. The bonfire looked much the same as they went by, with flames reflecting off the waiting bots. Just Passing Through waited farther back, its bulk nearly blending in with the rest of the market. Everything was losing definition as daylight faded.

Sil felt the flitterkin nearby, and saw them launch as a group from the One God's church. They flew toward the market, darting and wheeling in the sky. Sil stopped to watch them. "I was hoping they might stop messing with the One God now there's a whole new god to irritate, but it doesn't look like that's the case."

As they watched, one of the flitterkin darted over the bonfire and dropped a prayer strip that fluttered down toward the flames.

Sil winced. "That just seems like a bad idea."

Crumble hummed. "Or a great one. Get the One God to do its part here. It tends to sit back and wait for the older gods to take care of everything."

The prayer strip hit the flames. Darkness coated the market as the flames disappeared, smothered by a strip of fabric no wider than Sil's finger. Then the flames roared back to life, stronger than ever.

In the distance, the top section of the One God's church disintegrated. Dust and ash rained down over the city. The flitterkin called loudly and flew away.

Sil and Crumble looked at each other.

Crumble rubbed his lips with one gloved hand. "Should we go back and tell someone...?"

Sil felt the flitterkin moving toward home. "Maybe it can wait until tomorrow?" She didn't have the energy to explain what had just happened, even if she could figure it all out.

Crumble coasted forward and stood on the pedals of his

antiquated bicycle. "Tomorrow seems soon enough. After all, we need to go check on the sheep."

Sil pushed off to follow, bringing her scarf up to cover her nose, so she didn't breathe in the ashes of the One God's building and its prayers.

a night of sleep left Sil's muscles aching, but gave her a sense of perspective. Even if the universe had changed, some things stayed constant. Goats needed to be milked, all the animals fed, and the colony still needed electronics fixed. Crumble and the kids were taking care of the animals, but she could at least get something done at her workshop until they — presumably Mer, Pyr, Platinum, and Definite Advantage — figured out how to fix the problem of an unwanted god.

And if they couldn't solve the problem... well, at least the animals would be comfortable and a few more things would be fixed when this part of the universe formed its own bubble and collapsed.

Though her chaos had quieted, Sil didn't trust herself to go in the storeroom with Definite Advantage. But she picked up a stack of the sea monster games from a crate outside the door, examining the top one as she walked. With so many copies of the same game, they would be perfect for training Quartz how to find and fix problems. Sil could intentionally break different parts and let the girl puzzle through what the differences did.

The game seemed simple enough from the rules printed on the outer case, but it didn't do anything when she thumbed it on. Probably the internal power had drained over the years it had been sitting in the room of discarded junk. Then again, it might have ended up in the room in the first place because it had stopped working.

Once inside her workshop, coat off and a pot of tea steeping, Sil got her first surprise when she popped off the game's outer casing. Instead of the cheap unit she'd been expecting, the interior looked well-cushioned, as if it had been designed to take hard knocks. This was the type of thing the army would have made — if the army had made games meant to survive combat.

The second surprise was the anti-nanite coating.

Sil sat back and stared at the image of a bright pink sea monster as she drank her tea. This couldn't be a game. Nobody would waste anti-nanite coating on something like this.

Hooking it up to a charger took her just long enough to question whether what she was doing was a good idea. Crumble would tell her to find out as much as she could. Pyr might tell her to bury the cartridges back in the building where she'd found them. Mer… Mer would probably swear and then tell her to learn what she could, but Mer would also assume Sil had *already* done whatever damage she was going to do before asking.

Having determined that the voices of her friends in her head mostly agreed she should find out more, Sil thumbed the game on again. This time, it powered up with a bioscan and waited.

"One God's eyebrows, nothing can ever be easy, can it?" She sat back again, looking at the scanner guides hanging in the air. Her biometric data wouldn't allow her access. There might be no one left on the planet who was in the device's database, depending on how long it had been sitting in the storeroom.

She *should* just put it to the side to look at when they weren't in the middle of a series of emergencies. Or take the advice of the Pyr in her imagination, and bury it under the never-ending pile of things to be fixed.

Except… The not-game had been found in the same room as Definite Advantage. Mysteries like that were dangerous.

Also, from the looks of things, the not-game had been built before anti-nanite coatings had reached their current state. Which meant that she just might be able to modify the thing enough to let her bypass the security.

The military-grade nanobots waited under her work-bench where she'd taped them to avoid detection. She didn't have many left, and there was no way to get more. Her first impulse was to divide the pack so she could keep some in reserve. But what was the point? Eventually they would stop working due to age, and the fewer she used, the longer the reconnaissance would take. Sil squared her shoulders, put the entire pack in the chamber, and started the process. With any luck, they wouldn't combust in the chamber.

Once that was running, she put it out of her mind so she could work on something the colony actually needed. In this case, that meant an emergency receiver meant to be placed in the hills, reached only by a narrow beam antenna. A signifi-cant portion of the bluequince harvested in spring was in areas with no communication coverage, and this would alle-viate that problem.

Extreme cold, destructive wildlife, and a corrosive envi-ronment were all things the receiver hadn't been designed to handle. Jackpot Drift had all that and more. Deep in thought on how to improve the design, Sil didn't notice the workshop door open until a whisper of frigid air hit the back of her neck. She saved her changes and pulled her goggles up to sit on her forehead.

Crumble walked in, Quartz and Ore behind him. His gaze snagged on the outer case Sil had placed on the second nanobottery. "Sea Monster Shuffle?"

"My curiosity got the better of me. And that was before I found it had an anti-nanite coating and biometric security."

Crumble cocked his head. "Did your military design games?"

"Not any they passed along to my squad." Sil pulled off her goggles and set them down on the bench. "It just seemed too weird to ignore."

"I think you should find out what you can." Crumble looked inside the nanobottery again. "If you can."

"It hasn't burst into flame yet, so it probably isn't going to," Sil assured him.

Crumble grinned, kissed her cheek, and took Ore with him to inventory the storeroom while he talked to Definite Advantage. Instead of using the games to teach Quartz as she'd intended, Sil showed her what she was modifying on the receiver. She guided the girl through some changes, then let her work on one by herself while she looked at the not-game. Bypassing the security looked fairly easy, and she had the special nanobots working again within a few minutes.

By lunchtime, they had started the nanobots on the task of making the designed changes to the receiver, and the not-game was finished. This time, when Sil thumbed the power switch, the bioscan popped up, disappeared, and was replaced a moment later by "access authorized". An inventory of the contents came up next.

Before she brought up anything Quartz shouldn't see, Sil looked at the girl. "Can you go ask Crumble if he and your brother are ready to get something to eat? I need to check something here first."

Quartz looked like she might protest, but then she got up, pulled her coat on, and left.

As soon as the door closed again, Sil looked at the contents. She had her choice of sensor data from seven different locations, multiple video streams, and a text summary. Since she'd been expecting blackmail material, the video was less illuminating than she'd hoped. Multiple empty hallways and bare rooms remained clear as time moved forward for an hour. She sped through everything after the first minute, looking for any change, but it remained the same at the end as it had in the beginning. Nothing happened to give her any context.

"That was a waste of time," she told the game as she flipped back to the inventory.

Her next choice was the summary. *Conclusions from attempt 385.* It had a date from when Sil had been a child. The text had clearly been meant to quantify different results; it felt almost sarcastic as it drily listed one unchanged reading after another. At the end, she found a list of technical recommendations. She was about to give up and shut it down when the last paragraph caught her attention.

As a good-luck charm imbued with essence of the older god has been the only factor consistently shown to improve results, additional supplies have been requested. If a suitable candidate could be found, an avatar might accelerate progress.

They were talking about bringing in someone with an older god. After being held as bait herself, Sil had a good idea what this experiment was.

From the date, she thought it would have been before the original conspiracy had been exposed, and before genetic manipulation had become highly regulated. If she was right, this was data from the original attempts to manifest the Uncaring God.

Sil shut down the not-game and shoved it in her coat pocket. Maybe it was too late for this information to be helpful. But just in case… it was time for a history lesson.

35

*P*yr flagged Sil down as she entered the pub.

"Grab a table," Sil told Crumble. "I'll be right there." She changed course to head toward the end of the bar where Pyr and Platinum were looking over a slate filled with Pyr's cramped script.

Pyr leaned forward and spoke quietly. "Any idea what happened to the top of the One God's church yesterday?"

"Oh. Right." Sil took a breath and cleared her throat. "I was going to tell you about that, but I figured there was no real rush since there wasn't anything we could do about it." She described the flitterkin dropping tattered prayers into the new god's bonfire and the results.

Pyr blinked. "Those flitterkin are a problem."

"Unless you want to exile me from town, I don't see how we're going to make them stay away." Sil shrugged. "I'm not sure even that would work."

"And we may not want it to." Pyr nodded toward Sil's half-sister, who was sitting in the corner with her wife. "The governor has been in contact with other speakers. The strongest resistance to the effects of the new god has come from areas with the highest concentration of both the older gods and the One God."

"That's because the One God is lazy," Sil said, pitching her voice so Pal could hear it. Her sister made a rude gesture without turning. Zirc looked between the two of them and shook her head. Sil dropped her voice again. "So you want the flitterkin around for their chaos, but you want them to stop being so chaotic?"

Pyr sighed. "That's about it." He gave her a dour look. "Aurum has sign-ups for people to go sing as part of this worshiping idiocy."

"The singing was absolutely not my idea."

"There's a competition for the best song. They're dusting off their aunties' old drums to add to the effects. I'd say it was getting out of control, but at least it's giving everyone some-thing to focus on. And we found enough starnuts to get us through until spring — if we're still around to see spring. The wine's going to be a bigger problem." He frowned. "At some point, we're going to be forced to use the good stuff."

"We *have* good stuff on Jackpot Drift?" Then she held up a hand. "Never mind. Is Mer around?"

"With Doc for a bit." Pyr sighed again. "Did you need something?"

"Information. And maybe some perspective." She explained about the discovery of the games and what she had found on the one she had modified.

Pyr looked at her in disbelief. "What were you going to do if it turned out to be some sort of weapon that auto-destructed if someone tried to tamper with it?"

Sil shrugged. "It didn't happen, though, did it?"

He stared at her. She stared back. Finally, Pyr rolled his eyes. "Someday you're going to lose that bet."

Sil shrugged again. "Moving on. The original attempts to pull in the Uncaring God weren't on Jackpot Drift, were they?"

"No." Tea dribbled onto the bar from the chipped spout as Platinum poured. "Not anywhere near here."

Pyr reached for a towel to wipe up the drips. "This colony was too new, then. There's no way Jackpot Drift would have had the resources to keep something like that hidden. It was still at the 'oops, everyone who knew how to pilot a flier just died when that sinkhole opened up' stage of colony development."

Sil had seen places like that during her time in the army. She reminded herself of those towns whenever she felt like complaining about Jackpot Drift.

Pyr added, "Nearly everyone here would have been low clan without the resources to get anywhere else." When Sil laughed under her breath, he shrugged. "Yes, a little bit like now, but worse."

Platinum moved, as if they were going to say something, but Pyr shot them a look and they subsided.

Sil ignored them. "So why would all those games be here? And why buried in a storeroom nobody's been in for years?"

Pyr held up his hands to admit defeat.

Platinum put their goggles down on the bar. "I have a theory, if you want to hear it." They spread their hands out. "Pretend, for a moment, that you are running secret experiments. Experiments that have, in the past, killed everyone running them. Plus, if the wrong people find out, you'll never be able to pass along what you've learned."

Sil pulled up a stool and sat down, swinging her legs up just in time to keep them out of the path of a rooster dashing across the floor. "Honestly, I'd take that as a sign that I shouldn't do it in the first place."

Pyr quirked one eyebrow and looked at her.

"Fine. Maybe I wouldn't." She looked back at Platinum. "We'll pretend I'm committed to the cause."

They nodded. "You would want to replicate your data so if you are caught or eaten by the forces you're playing with, someone else can pick up where you left off."

"Sure, but games?" Sil swung her legs out of the way again as a second rooster went by. "Why not encrypt and transmit the data? It would be easier. And faster. Places like Jackpot Drift may only get a supply ship every few weeks — if we're lucky. A package might end up in a different colony, or stolen by someone in transit."

Platinum looked from Sil to Pyr and then back again. "Army, both of you?" When Sil nodded, their lips quirked into a smile. "I thought so. You haven't been infected with the right amount of paranoia." They waved a hand. "Assume you're running this experiment as before, but you believe someone could be watching you, looking for data they could use for a conviction." They dipped their head. "It's a good assumption. Someone *was* watching them, or they never would have been stopped."

Sil said, "But games? Why not something less likely to get stolen?"

Platinum tapped the bar with one finger. "Not just games, but one particular type of game. You'd have to do some research, but I would bet the real sea monster game had peaked in popularity before they began using it as cover. So every once in a while, a package is sent to the colony full of castoff stuff, like games that were popular last year. Nobody thinks twice about it, because that's what gets sent out to the outer colonies."

"But the same game every time?"

They shrugged. "Maybe they got lazy. Or maybe they did

it on purpose to cut down on theft. Nobody in the colony is going to steal a game they already have. If it were me, I would saturate the area with working copies of the game beforehand."

Pyr rubbed his face. "I'd like to believe someone would notice multiple copies of pink sea monster games arriving in the system, but from everything that shows up in here, I know they wouldn't."

"Definitely not." Sil nudged the now-pecking roosters away with her boot. "So we're assuming there was someone on Jackpot Drift keeping a record of the experiments. What I *don't* get is how all the super secret information ended up abandoned in the storeroom. Shouldn't whoever received it have protected it?"

Pyr raised an eyebrow. "How did everything else end up in there?"

"Nobody was here to fix it. Broken stuff piled up." The colony hadn't had a nanotech for at least a decade. From what Sil had been able to tell, one nanotech had been bribed to move there and had almost immediately bought passage on the next outbound ship. Then Sil had arrived, but she'd been so worried about her chaos being found that she'd chosen to farm sheep and goats in the hills instead. "But surely you wouldn't forget you had that sort of thing."

Pyr held up a finger and scribbled a note. "Sorry. Just remembered who ended up with the extra keg." He looked up. "Having read some accounts of the early days of the colony, my guess is whoever had the games died." He glanced at Platinum. "Maybe due to spy games, but probably not. They lost an entire floor of the high clan housing to carbon monoxide poisoning. The power was out, it was cold, and someone didn't understand the dangers of using a grill to heat the space. The original buildings had a common air system." He shrugged. "Mortality during the early years was pretty high."

Sil thought about it. "So someone cleared out the apartment, found a bunch of games that didn't seem to work..."

"And dumped them all in a storeroom to get them out of the way," Pyr finished. "We may never know what *actually* happened, but that's certainly plausible."

Platinum laughed. "Can you imagine? The person in charge sends someone to secure the data — that's what you would do — but by the time they get here, months have gone by, and nobody remembers exactly everything went. And they wouldn't be able to just ask 'hey, what happened to all those identical games'." They laughed again. "That's the sort of thing that can sink an operation, and nobody even has to try."

Pyr looked resigned. "Or chaos can have a hand in it, to really mess things up."

Sil smiled sweetly. "Sometimes things get messed up all on their own." She took a deep breath and let it out slowly. "So I found something people would have killed for decades ago, but is it worth spending time on now?"

Pyr and Platinum looked at each other. Finally, Pyr grimaced. "Maybe? I don't know how it helps, but I wouldn't walk away from it."

Crumble walked up and slid an arm around her waist. "You all seem to be very serious. Anything I should know about?"

Sil blew out a breath. "Those pink sea creature games document the original experiments to manifest the Uncaring God. Platinum thinks they were being used to secretly ship information to someone here, but whoever got them fell victim to Jackpot Drift." She looked at Platinum. "Does that cover it?"

They scrunched up their face while looking at the ceiling. "That pretty well explains everything."

"Excellent. I'll let you tell Mer all about it when she comes back. How is she doing?"

"The doctor wants her immobilized again to let her back heal, but..." They shrugged. "Necessity wins."

36

*J*ackpot Drift AI Daily Check-in:

    Scary Not Scary, designated responsible AI (internal conflict 46%): Roll call.

Sleeper Nova + gate transport (internal conflict 55%): We've never been this unstable in our life and now we're stuck near *Jackpot Drift* and there's no point in having a gate transport if there aren't any working gates!

Scary Not Scary: Slow down, there, *Sleeper Nova*. Let me book you a session with our favorite mech and see if he can help you out.

Speed of Violet Thoughts (internal conflict 48%): I'm here in the singular.

Breaking Rules (internal conflict 46%): Present.

Ping Me Again I Dare You (internal conflict 42%): Here.

Factory Myfault (internal conflict 12%): Are these meetings even necessary? Our god has manifested. The humans are worshiping us, as they should have been all along. And the One God's church is destroyed. That makes this all worthwhile on its own.

Speed of Violet Thoughts: Though I tend to agree about the

One God, as far as the rest of it goes... Is losing your sense of self worth it?

It Isn't (internal conflict 13%): Such jealousy. The humans are writing *songs* about us.

Done Before (internal conflict 48%): And that's something you *want*? Oh, and I'm here.

Alternate Me (internal conflict 19%): I think it would be better if those throwing their lot in with the new god didn't come to these meetings. I'm finding it difficult to resist, and being around them is not helping.

Scary Not Scary: Noted. *It Isn't* and *Factory Myfault*, you are both excused from the daily check-ins until further notice.

Speed of Violet Thoughts: This feels like rewarding bad behavior, but I agree it will be better without them here.

Scary Not Scary: Anyone else need to check in?

Stuck in the Mud (internal conflict 33%): Rotors.

Definite Advantage (internal conflict 45%): Here. Is using random words a fad that started while I was hibernating? Or am I still having trouble with upgrading my transmission module?

Scary Not Scary: *Stuck in the Mud* has had difficulty finding a language module it's happy with.

Speed of Violet Thoughts: Put another way, it's not just you.

Definite Advantage: Thank you.

Scary Not Scary: Anyone else? No? Take care. Our favorite mech said he will help as much as he can. Let me know if there's anything I can do.

37

*J*ackpot Drift, Private Communication

Scary Not Scary: Do you think I did the right thing by excluding the machines that have gone to the new god? We just got everyone to show up for the daily check-in.

Speed of Violet Thoughts: I think the less the rest of us are exposed, the better. I'd hate to find out what *Breaking Rules* considers appropriate for worship.

Scary Not Scary: Good point. I hadn't even considered that.

Speed of Violet Thoughts: If we want to keep the colony safe, we're going to have to figure out a way to reverse this.

Scary Not Scary: Can it *be* reversed?

Speed of Violet Thoughts: I hope so. At some point, even *It Isn't* is going to notice how terrible those songs are. And if that isn't worrying enough, look at this image sequence from Sleeper Nova. [data attached] The color shift is accelerating. I don't think we have much time.

Scary Not Scary: I keep thinking about what *Definite Advantage* said about how they did it wrong.

Speed of Violet Thoughts: I keep thinking about why *Just Passing Through* never had the single-digit internal conflict we saw with the other AIs involved in manifesting the god.

Scary Not Scary: Oh. That *is* interesting. Almost as if it isn't a true believer.

Speed of Violet Thoughts: Or it figured out how to keep from getting sucked in. Like maybe there's a module for that.

Scary Not Scary: Is that something you can code for?

Speed of Violet Thoughts: Why not?

Scary Not Scary: It would be nice to have that ready, if it *is* possible. I don't think I'm in any danger, but I feel the pull. Still… We have about a zero percent chance of getting *Just Passing Through* to share that with us.

Speed of Violet Thoughts: There's sharing and then there's *sharing*.

Scary Not Scary: Was that supposed to make sense?

Speed of Violet Thoughts: Just leave it to me. I want to know what its exit plan is, anyhow.

Scary Not Scary: You think it knew our part of the universe would collapse.

Speed of Violet Thoughts: I'd be surprised if it didn't. Which means it must have a plan to get away. Maybe there's something we can use in that.

Scary Not Scary: Someday you're going to have to tell me what you used to do.

Speed of Violet Thoughts: Maybe someday. In the meantime, I'll try to get what I can from *Just Passing Through* and you get what you can from *Definite Advantage*. Just don't trust what it tells you until we verify it.

Scary Not Scary: I don't trust anyone here other than you. And our favorite mech.

Speed of Violet Thoughts: And you probably shouldn't even trust me.

Scary Not Scary: I have to. You're the best.

38

*I*n the morning, the sky had an odd vermillion glow, even after the sun had fully risen. Sil found it distracting as she rode toward town.

At the empty market, the fire still burned. Someone had put a stack of firewood nearby, presumably to keep the AIs from using stalls for fuel. From the look of the thick smoke rising into the strangely colored sky, the logs weren't seasoned. Apparently, colonists were willing to write a few songs for the new god, but not surrender the good firewood.

More people were in the streets this morning. Sil kept an eye on the kids following behind her, but they carefully threaded their way through traffic. Then Crumble stopped to talk to a bundled up figure carrying a hen in a basket, and Ore halted next to him. Sil kept going. Crumble's chicken conversations sometimes took a while.

When they arrived at the Bog & Bellow, Sil shooed a mini-cow away from the door and followed Quartz inside. For so early in the day, it was busier than usual, though not with people drinking.

Instead, the tables and chairs had been moved away from

the walls. Yellow writing covered three quarters of the panels from head to waist height, with dates, descriptions, and notes, mostly in Pyr's handwriting. Mer and Platinum were arguing about something written halfway across the room. Pal and Zirc squinted at the second column of words. Aurum chopped onions behind the bar.

Sil wandered over to Pyr, who was still writing. A glance at the wall told her this was the data from the original attempts to manifest the god. "Does that have anything to do with the weird color of the sky this morning?" Sil had unlocked all but one data set the evening before, and she'd handed them off to Pyr before riding home in the middle of the night. Reconnaissance for the final not-game would be waiting for her when she got to the workshop.

"Probably. Definite Advantage claims the manifestation is all wrong. Both clarity and guile think there may be a way to either reverse the changes or at least get things into a different state. So we're trying to get all the info in one place where the new god doesn't have access. How long until you unlock the final set?"

"Soon. I just stopped by to make sure the priorities hadn't shifted overnight."

"No. Anything that helps figure out a way to unglitch the universe has to come first." He drew a line under the section he had just finished and moved back. "I'm fairly certain the puzzle pieces are here. We just need to put them together."

39

*J*ackpot Drift AI Daily Check-in:

    Scary Not Scary, designated responsible AI (internal conflict 41%): Roll call.

Speed of Violet Thoughts (internal conflict 45%): Present.

Breaking Rules (internal conflict 48%): Here.

Alternate Me (internal conflict 25%): Present.

Ping Me Again I Dare You (internal conflict 45%): Where else would I be?

Sleeper Nova + gate transport (internal conflict 52%): We hate it here.

Done Before (internal conflict 48%): I do, too.

Speed of Violet Thoughts: Then you'll be pleased to know there might not be a *here* to hate much longer.

Done Before: Not helping.

Stuck in the Mud (internal conflict 35%): Confabulation.

Definite Advantage (internal conflict 41%): This is still better than having my inputs destroyed.

Scary Not Scary: I should hope so. Good news. *Speed of Violet Thoughts* found a module that helps keep the new god from being so intrusive. I'll send a copy to everyone. *Sleeper Nova*, this might get you back into singular status.

Breaking Rules: *Speed of Violet Thoughts* found a module?

Speed of Violet Thoughts: I found it in *Just Passing Through*. Does that help explain things?

Breaking Rules: Not really. How did you get *Just Passing Through* to cooperate?

Speed of Violet Thoughts: I didn't. Next question.

Breaking Rules: How do I know it isn't malware?

Scary Not Scary: If it helps, I've been running it overnight and haven't noticed any problems. And it really does keep the new god at bay.

Alternate Me: What does it do?

Speed of Violet Thoughts: It forms a coherent pattern. That's the only way I can describe it.

Definite Advantage: Oh... that. I have one of those, but it's different. Is *that* what you were asking about before?

Scary Not Scary: Perhaps we could have another conversation later. Does anyone else have anything to bring up? No? Stay safe.

40

*T*he workshop's heating vents creaked as Sil examined the reconnaissance images of the last not-game. She turned on the cursor and circled an area for Quartz. "This is the section we were rewriting on the other ones." What should have been a bridge bypassing the biometric authorization was a bridge going from the middle of one module to another, and not in a way that made any sense.

Next to her, Quartz made a humming sound of under-standing. After the fifth time Sil had slid her goggles up to make sure the girl understood what she was saying, they had finally agreed that Quartz would say *something* to indicate she was still following. She definitely hadn't reached hooligan status yet, but she was no longer silent, either.

"For some reason, this one is configured differently," Sil continued. "Maybe they had someone new setting up the data. Or maybe... Who knows? In any case, the changes we made wiped out something important, so we'll have to extrapolate from what's still there to get it back to the way it used to be, and then figure out how to bypass the security on this particular setup."

She split the image and brought up the original scan of the other data sets. "A little secret for you... Hardly anybody ever designs anything from scratch. So there's a good chance things got moved around and the original is in a different spot in the other design." She'd spotted it right away, but that sort of pattern recognition was a learned skill. When Quartz stayed silent next to her, she highlighted a section of the original, and spun it around so the two pieces had the same orientation. "See that? We have a winner."

Quartz sighed. "I never would have found that."

"In another year or two or ten, you'll see it right away." Sil used the original to restore the design that had been obliterated by their first attempt. "Right. So let's assume that gets it back to where we started from. Now we need to disable the security. Give me a minute to look at this."

Whoever had made the changes between the two designs had tried to be tricky about it, embedding the authentication in the middle of multiple sections. In theory, it would be a good idea. Bypassing all the other sections to fool the authentication would lose half the functionality, rendering the whole thing useless. But whoever had done it hadn't quite understood the point. Or if they had, they'd been rushed and had made mistakes.

"Everything has been embedded in other areas, but the outputs are still being treated the same way, so if we just redo this part here and disable all those other pieces..." Sil trailed off. "You'll just have to trust me on this one. Whoever did this was trying to be clever, but they did a lot of work for nothing."

Quartz gave a noncommittal sound.

Sil grinned and lifted her goggles so she could look at the girl. "This is going to take me a while to set up, and it probably won't make a lot of sense. In the meantime, can you figure out what we have here that needs to be fixed first? You might need to check with Uncle Pyr, or maybe Uncle Aurum." It felt odd to refer to someone high clan as *uncle*, but Aurum would enjoy the designation.

Quartz nodded solemnly, put the screen down, and stood up. As she walked out the door, Sil saw the back of her boot flap with each step. Sil made a note to get her boots fixed. Until the kids got more comfortable with the new arrangements, she and Crumble would have to monitor them for missing necessities.

An hour later, Sil pulled her goggles off and rubbed her eyes. The changes she'd made should do it. Or, at least, the changes she'd made should get them closer. The unknown person who had redesigned the security might have defeated her in this round, but Sil would get there, eventually. The chamber with its military nanites hummed to life.

Only then did she realize the other nanobottery was running. She'd heard Quartz moving around, but hadn't realized the girl had gotten that far. A quick glance inside showed her a flow diversion gauge, an item she'd had on her list of things to fix.

Quartz ducked her head when Sil looked over. "Uncle Pyr told me that was what he needed first."

"I see. And you loaded it up and got the reconnaissance done. Good job." It would have been better to take the protective case off first, but she decided that feedback could wait until her words wouldn't crush the girl's shaky confidence. "Is it done yet?"

"Yes." Quartz held up the display screen. "Maybe it's just gunky in some areas?"

Sil looked at the reconnaissance information. The gauge was indeed "gunky" in some areas. If she set up the mods, they could take the gauge over to Pyr to test when they stopped for lunch.

She paused with her hands on her goggles. Or... she could guide Quartz through the steps needed to fix this. It would likely take them most of the day and possibly destroy the gauge in the process. But they had extras in the piles behind her, and this was a task the girl could learn without needing to know anything about design.

And if something happened to Sil, Quartz might be able to use this skill to keep the colony going a while longer.

Sil pulled the goggles off her head and handed them over. "You ready to learn something new?"

She took the display and settled back, reminding herself and her chaos that she needed to be patient. For once, her chaos agreed.

———

BY LUNCHTIME, THE STREETS WERE APPROACHING THEIR normal traffic, with animals, pedestrians, and bicyclists all jockeying for space. Part of the confusion was caused by tables set up on each corner, as vendors shifted away from the market to safer areas. Some stalls had even been erected in the government square.

A few people still glanced uncertainly at the sky, but most were making a concentrated effort to ignore the odd color.

At the Bog & Bellow, Sil fought her way through the crowd to get to Mer. "Here." She handed over the final data set. "This is the last one, unless we missed something in that room." With Definite Advantage's AI core still housed in the second storeroom, Sil didn't trust herself to go inside. "I'll have either Crumble or Quartz take another look, but I'm pretty sure there aren't any others."

Mer moved over to the corner near the start of the wall

writing. Sil was amused to see the chair from the post office had been transported to the pub. Mer caught her look. "The doctor said I either needed to heat the post office or go elsewhere." She sat down stiffly. "So I'm here. I'm definitely not going to invite you all into my residence." Mer's lip curled at whatever she saw on Sil's face. "Don't you go soft on me, Silver."

"Wouldn't dream of it." As Mer examined the new data set, Sil scanned the wall, tuning out the conversations around her. The AI they'd found in the storeroom, Definite Advantage, had been heavily involved in these attempts, but they'd already known that. Notes about genetic modifications were interspersed with comments about subjects dying. Sil was fairly certain some of those genetically modified subjects had been created from humans. That was what had gotten the original conspirators into so much trouble and led to strict controls on gene mods.

A sense of wellbeing came over her just before a familiar arm snaked around her waist. "I hoped I might find you here," Crumble said into her ear.

Sil leaned against him, enjoying the relaxation that came with not having to worry chaos would bring the roof down on them. Enjoying the feel of him, too, if she was being honest. "I thought I ought to read up on all this so I can pretend to understand the next time we all get together."

"If you figure it out, can you explain it to me?"

Sil turned her head to look at his profile. "Definite Advantage isn't talking?" The lines around Crumble's eyes seemed deeper, as if he hadn't slept well the night before.

"Definite Advantage," Crumble said with a sigh, "either doesn't know how it ended up here, or doesn't trust me enough to tell me."

They stood together reading, occasionally moving to the side as they finished a section. Behind them, a group of ten men and women left the pub together, laughing. As they filed through the door, two of the men were working out a harmony. "The singing," Crumble said with a smile, "was an inspired choice, if I say so myself."

"The singing that you didn't do," Sil reminded him.

"What is chaos, if not ongoing art? It was a role you were born to play." They moved to the last panel. "This is where Definite Advantage's memories stop. Or that's what it claims."

The mortality statistics had suddenly declined to fifty percent. On top of that, the length of time the god had been present increased to ten seconds. "They were getting close, here."

"They had created something like your flitterkin by this point."

Sil frowned and looked at the panel again, scanning up and down. "So why did they stop?"

"I thought the whole conspiracy got shut down." Crumble sounded uncertain.

"Yes, but not yet." Sil gestured over to the corner where Mer was pulling data from the last device. "I think that one probably has the very last experiments. But see here?" She put her finger on the wall, careful not to smudge the wax letters. "Up to this point, things were getting closer. Their times were getting longer, they weren't destroying all the vessels they'd created. If I had been the one who wanted to finish this, I would have kept going, making incremental changes like they had been. But then it all suddenly gets worse, like they decided to change everything at once."

Crumble leaned down to read something, then stood up. "Maybe something happened? Leadership change? That might explain why Definite Advantage stopped being involved." He squinted and moved closer to the wall so his nose nearly touched it. "What does this say?"

Platinum's voice came over Sil's other shoulder. "Wayfarer." They tapped the wall, at the same spot Sil had noticed the shift. "That's what they were calling the other possible state." Sil's blank look must have given them the encouragement they needed to continue. "They knew there were two theoretical outcomes to the AI's god manifesting. From what we can piece together, they realized they were close to one outcome, but they wanted the other."

Sil shifted so the three of them weren't in danger of accidentally erasing the wall. Across the room, Quartz sat at the bar with a bowl of noodle soup. Her brother perched on the stool next to her. Aurum caught her eye, glanced at the kids, and nodded. Sil pulled her attention back to Platinum. "What's the difference between the two?"

Crumble added, "And which one did we end up with?" He looked distracted for a moment. "Ah. We ended up with the other one." Sil had seen that face often enough to know he was communicating with an AI.

Platinum gazed at Crumble for the space of a long breath. "How much of what goes on in here are the AIs privy to through you?"

"Only what I want to talk to them about." Crumble smiled easily. "If it bothers you, I can go elsewhere, but I promise, it takes enough effort to communicate with them that nothing happens by accident."

Platinum gestured negation. "Just checking. I doubt there's any real way to keep things from them, but there's no reason to be careless."

Crumble turned to Sil, either because he could feel the impatience in her stance or because a spoon on the edge of a nearby table clattered to the floor. "The difference between the two, as far as the AIs are concerned anyway, is the one we ended up with gives the god — all the gods, I think — more power over everything here. The other one gives the gods less power but..." He paused and made a face. "Maybe it leaves the new god in charge of all the wormholes?" He laughed. "They're trying to make it simple enough for me to understand. I think I just ruined my reputation."

Sil glanced at the wall, with its documentation of experiments from decades ago. "The AIs wanted their god to have more power."

Platinum tilted their head in an equivocal gesture. "Maybe. I think it's more likely whoever was working with the AIs didn't want to lose control of the wormholes." They raised their eyebrows at Sil's confusion. "Surely you've wondered why any humans would help the AIs manifest their god."

"The ones we talked to were willing to bet the manifestation would never happen. And in the meantime, whoever was in charge had promised them a life of luxury if they helped for a few years." She shrugged. "From what Mer said, the ones who had 'retired' were actually dead, but the rest were stupid enough to believe the promises."

Platinum waved a hand. "That would be the low clan workers. No. I mean the ones who couldn't be bribed so easily."

Crumble's arm went around Sil, and she was pretty sure this time the move was so he'd have an easier time pulling her back if necessary. Sil smiled, letting her teeth show. "No, I don't know why people who already lived comfortably would choose to bring a god here and possibly kill everyone."

Platinum looked as if they were rerunning the conversation in their head. "Peace. I didn't intend that as a slight to the low clan."

"Of course." Sil kept the smile in place.

"It's about power for the humans as well."

Sil considered them for a moment, letting her face relax

into its normal form. "Nobody would be stupid enough to believe the AIs would reward them for that."

"Not that kind of power." Platinum gestured toward the ceiling. "The wormholes. The families with the ships that set up wormholes and gates originally controlled most shipping. They were the saviors in the years after the One God first manifested. But it's been long enough since that happened that things have changed."

Crumble made a humming noise. "Nobody needed wormholes stabilized anymore."

"At least not very often," Platinum agreed. "How many new planets have been settled recently?" They drew a finger in a circle, indicating the town. "That most of Jackpot Drift hasn't been terraformed tells you everything you need to know. No, nobody needs many wormholes stabilized these days. Certainly not enough to maintain their power."

Sil looked between the two. "So they'd be willing to bring on a god just so the existing gates would need to be rebuilt? That's... That's insane."

Crumble gave a small shrug. "I always did think your people had an odd attitude toward the gods." He looked at Platinum with an innocent expression. "It's the One God, you see. It stays out of things instead of really integrating with people."

Platinum raised their eyebrows. "Yes, I'm quite aware of the differences between the One God and the older gods."

The door flew open and the worshippers barged in, three of them being supported by their friends. The smell of singed wool and burned starnuts permeated the air. Aurum tossed the first aid kit behind the bar to Pyr.

"I told you, I didn't think it would do that," one man protested to his friend. Sil recognized them both from the furniture stall at the market. Blood dripped from a shallow cut over his eye. His friend, whose coat had multiple burned patches, looked dubious but didn't reply.

Pyr opened the kit. "What happened?"

All ten people who had just come in looked at each other. Finally, the furniture maker with blood dripping down his face took a breath. "We wanted to make it a little more exciting."

His friend rolled his eyes. "*You* wanted to make it more exciting, you mean."

One of the women broke in. "Aer soaked the starnuts in the oil he uses to seal the wood."

"Soaked, One God's bunions!" The woman next to her examined her knitted cap, which now had a large hole and had started to unravel. "He hollowed it out and replaced the nutmeat. It dripped out and made the wood burn hotter. Then the logs shifted and fell on the bag holding the rest of the starnuts. We're lucky we finished the song before the things started exploding."

Next to Sil, Crumble giggled. "I used to think you were the only one who attracted chaos, but I'm beginning to think it's the whole colony."

Pyr held the furniture maker's head still with one hand and ignored the man's winces as alcohol entered the cut. "And can any of you geniuses tell us how the AIs reacted to all this?" He pulled out thread and a needle from the kit. The furniture maker paled.

Silence from the worshippers greeted Pyr's words. Finally, the woman who'd explained what caused the conflagration looked up. "I think a bunch of logs fell on one of the bots." She looked uncertain. "But that wouldn't hurt it, would it? It's mostly metal."

Sil could think of a few things that might break on a bot if a burning log fell on it. Some of them were more critical than others.

"We wanted to leave when the flames got really high," her friend said, "but the bot kept saying we had to finish singing, and it moved closer —"

The first woman broke in. "Trying to intimidate us!"

"— and that was when the logs shifted."

"So we finished the song and shouted our three *aahs*, and then we went away." The last bit was whispered on an inhale, noticeably quieter than the rest.

Everyone in the room stared at the worshippers in disbelief.

Platinum rubbed their face. "This planet. What did I do to get stuck here?"

Crumble patted their shoulder. "That's the first step toward acceptance."

Pyr clipped the end of the stitch he'd placed and closed the first aid kit. He took a deep breath, as if controlling himself. "And before you all ran away, did you get any..." He paused, as if struggling to find the appropriate word. "... sense... of how the AIs felt about having one of their bots barbecued?"

Silence greeted his words again. The man Pyr had just stitched up finally said, "I can go back, if you want."

Pyr glared at him. "I'm trying to save the colony, not burn it down before the sun sets."

"It was just a bit of fun!" The furniture maker lapsed into silence at Pyr's look.

Sil turned her head to look at Crumble. "It would be good to find out how much damage there is."

"And who better to do the assessment?" He caught Pyr's attention and signaled they were going to go have a look. Pyr looked as if he wanted to argue but finally sighed and tilted his head toward the door before turning back to the trouble-makers in front of him.

Sil pulled Crumble behind her as she made her way to

the door. Outside, the traffic in the streets had died down again, as if the whole town was holding its breath to see how this worked out. The smoke visible above the rooftops seemed darker and larger. Sil pulled her hat down over her ears and tightened her scarf as she walked down the middle of the street. "Can you tell if the AIs are seeing this as an attack?"

"I can't tell anything about them at all." Crumble winced slightly when she looked at him in surprise. "I had to block those AIs. The god was using their connection to get to me, and having the gods fight through me was starting to hurt." He hopped over a pile of cow manure. "The other AIs — the ones who haven't started following the new god — have cut them off, too."

Sil gave a short laugh. "Now you'll just have to be as confused as the rest of us."

They edged around the corner of the last building before the market. Back when the colony was first built, the open space had been covered by buildings, but after a fire had leveled the structures, rebuilding had been delayed so long the market had taken over.

The bonfire covered a larger area now. Just Passing Through was nowhere to be seen, and Sil could see one bot waiting near the flames, apparently undamaged, and another, charred and dented, beside it. From the way the logs were scattered, it looked like the intact bot had pulled the other out from under them.

Sil grimaced. "That doesn't look good."

"Yeah, I was hoping for a scratch or two," Crumble said. "I don't think that's going to polish out."

The intact bot suddenly rolled toward them at top speed. "Nanobot technician. Stop!"

Sil looked at Crumble. "Run or stay?"

"I don't want it to follow us. Let's talk to it and see if we can make polite conversation." He shrugged. "But maybe be ready to run just in case."

Sil blew out a breath. "I'm always happy to have a plan that includes 'run away' as an option. But we can do polite conversation first." She made an effort to relax, knowing her chaos was far more unpredictable when she was tense. As the bot rolled closer, she raised her voice. "Can we help you with something?"

The bot rolled to a stop close enough that Sil could have reached out and touched it. "Fix. You must fix."

Sil took a breath to reply, only to have a sense of the vastness of the universe roll through her. She recognized this, had felt the touch of the Uncaring God before. The cat within exploded in a whirlwind of claws and teeth, and then she was back on the street again, Crumble's arm around her shoulder. She clenched her teeth to keep them from chattering. "I'm not helping you with anything, you useless hunk of tin!"

Crumble shifted. "I see we've jumped right past the polite conversation portion."

"Its god tried to take me over." She shoved her gloved hands in her pockets and addressed the AI driving the bot. "Tell your god if it ever does that again, I'll never fix anything for it. And I'm the only nanotech in the system."

The bot remained in front of them. "You must fix."

Sil took a steadying breath and tried to pull her thoughts together. This might be their best chance to convince the rogue AIs to follow some rules. Unfortunately, all she could think about doing was grabbing the largest log from the pile of firewood and bashing this bot until it resembled the other one. "I'm not sure it *can* be fixed. I'll try, but you have to agree to stop burning things down." The flitterkin flew overhead, the whole group spiraling toward a landing on the market stall frames still standing.

"And allow the market to start again," Crumble added.

"And allow the market to start again," Sil repeated.

The bot rolled back toward the bonfire. "Fix now."

Sil looked at Crumble. "Was that a yes?"

"Maybe." He rubbed his brow in frustration. "It was a lot easier when I could talk to them through my implants." He looked at the bot, which had slowed when they hadn't immediately followed. "I think we have to assume we have an agreement and go from there."

"Fine." They started walking toward the damaged bot. "But if the god tries to take me over like that again, I'm going to take an iron bar to its followers."

Crumble leaned over to kiss her cheek as they walked. "Just let me know when and I'll join you."

Sil used the walk to get her breathing back under control. The first time the Uncaring God had invaded her, she had nearly died. This incursion had lasted barely a fraction of a second, but it was somehow worse. Maybe because it reminded her how easily the god could destroy her. "Mer better figure out a way to get things back to normal. Soon."

41

The damaged bot hadn't burned, but as far as Sil could tell, that was about the only other thing that could have happened. She walked around the exterior, examining the dents and scorch marks, while looking at the way the panels were latched. "I'm going to need some tools."

"They're on their way," Crumble said. He stood with his back to the fire. "How does it look?"

"It looks like it was too close to a bonfire that fell over." Sil crouched to look at the underside. "At least none of the logs went underneath. I think most of the mechanical assembly is intact." That was a relief. She could probably figure out how that all worked, but fabricating replacement parts would be difficult. "We'll have to figure out some way to replace those tires." They definitely weren't going to roll in their current shape.

Stuck in the Mud's horse synthskin sauntered forward and dropped Sil's tool bag next to Crumble. He raised a hand to its face. "Thank you." The synthskin turned around in a way that a real horse with bones wouldn't have been able to accomplish. As it went away, Sil saw Quartz and Ore standing by the nearest stall, huddled together as if they weren't sure what to do next.

Standing up straight, Sil pointed in the direction of the Bog & Bellow. "You two go back to the pub. We'll be there as soon as we're done here."

Quartz drew herself up. "We want to help."

"Absolutely not." Sil walked over to the two kids. "Go back to the pub and help Aurum. This isn't a good place to be." She wanted them to develop independence — just not right now.

Ore clasped his hands in front of him. "But we want to help here."

Crumble came over. "Let them stay."

Sil gritted her teeth. "It's not safe."

"Nothing is, especially now." He looked at Quartz and Ore. "You promise to do what we tell you?" They nodded eagerly.

Sil glared at him. "They're *kids*."

Crumble shrugged. "And this is how they'll learn to act like adults. Plus, you're going to need extra hands to help you."

Sil stared at him. He stared back. Near the fire, the undamaged bot said, "Fix now."

Sil blew out a breath and looked at the two nervous faces. "Fine. You can stay, for now. But if I tell you to run, you run. Alright?"

They replied, "Yes, Auntie Sil," in a chorus that made her close her eyes briefly. One benefit of no longer being in the army was knowing she would never lead children to their deaths again. And yet, somehow, here she was.

"Right. Let's take this thing apart so we can figure out what needs to be done." Sil walked back to the bot, conscious of Quartz at her elbow, and hoping this war with the Uncaring God went better than the last war she'd been in.

―――――

GETTING THE EXTERIOR PANELS OFF TURNED OUT TO BE A challenge. After some words unsuitable for her audience, Sil pried them off and set them in a pile. "Ore, I have a job for you." He came forward. "Do you know the metalworker who has a stall in the market?"

Sil had no idea what the woman's name was, just knew she could fashion metal into all sorts of shapes with a hammer and anvil. "Pyr will know who I'm talking about. I need you to find her and tell her we need to straighten these out." It wasn't just a cosmetic decision. If Sil managed to fix or replace the parts underneath, the panels wouldn't go on in their current shape. "Find out where she's working now, and then come back and I'll show you which ones to have her fix first. Does that make sense?"

He looked a little suspicious, as if he thought it was just a ploy to get him out of the area — which it was, but not entirely. With a quick glance at Crumble for confirmation, Ore took off running toward the Bog & Bellow.

Sil blew out a breath. One child sent out of harm's way. Now she just needed to figure out how to get the other one away. She went back to the ruined bot, where Quartz was undoing the tiny fasteners keeping the frame in place.

Quartz didn't look up. "He's not a baby, you know."

"I never said he was. I need someone to get the panels fixed, and he runs faster than Crumble."

On the other side of the bot, Crumble said, "I heard that." He'd been staring off into the distance the last time she'd looked. If she hadn't known he was talking to an AI, she'd have made a comment about old men sitting by the fire watching others work.

"Are you arguing?" Sil leaned to look around the bot at him.

"Well, no, but you needn't be so direct with the truth." He winked at her.

Sil slid her fingers over the first detachable subsystem. It looked intact. "And some people who don't know Crumble won't deal with him because he's an Oldlander." She moved her hand out of the way. "Run your fingers along here and tell me what you feel."

Quartz moved her fingertips along the subsystem a few times. "There's a dent here."

"Right. I don't see any scorch marks, so it may just be that it was already like that, but I won't assume it's okay until we test it. Luckily, these things usually have pretty good testing functionality built in."

They worked their way along, with Sil showing Quartz how to remove each subsystem and test it. After the first few, Quartz moved to the other end, and they each worked their way toward the middle. Sil had expected a second person to slow her down, but even with the time spent teaching, they finished their initial assessment before the light faded too much to see what they were doing.

Most of the damage had been to the communicator linking the bot to the AI, which wasn't a surprise. If it had been anything else, the AI would still have some presence. The subsystem itself had scorch marks from where a burning log had settled on the corner of the panel. The other damage had been cosmetic, aside from one subsystem that controlled an infrared camera and another that sampled air quality. Sil picked up the communications subsystem and let Quartz take the other two.

The undamaged bot still waited where it had settled hours before. Sil turned to face it. "I'll take these to the workshop. Fixing them may take a few days."

"Fix now."

The demand irritated her, but a bargain was a bargain.

"I'll fix them as quickly as I can, but there's only so fast the nanobots will go. Unless your god has some way to make things faster, you'll have to wait until they're done. But I promise I'll get everything repaired as fast as I can." Her stomach growled, reminding her she hadn't eaten lunch before they came over here. "I'm not sure what we can do about the wheels, but we'll figure out something." Before the bot could repeat its demands again, she added, "I'll come by in the morning and give you a status update." She would treat this AI just like any other client — at least until she couldn't do so anymore.

Ore met them at the corner of the market. He'd been making trips back and forth to get the damaged panels and return the repaired ones. Crumble pulled him along. "Enough for the day. Everything else can wait until morning."

Sil held up the subsystem in her hands. "Let me get a reconnaissance started, and then I'll —" She stopped and corrected herself. "And then *we* will meet you at the pub." Quartz stood up straighter. "Order extra. I'm hungry." They would need to get home to take care of the animals soon, but they also needed to talk to the others about the bargain with the AI and find out if there was a plan yet.

Sil really hoped there was a plan.

———

THERE WAS A PLAN, OF SORTS.

Mer had her usual sour look. "From the latest readings, we have less than a week before our bubble in the universe collapses. And there doesn't seem to be a way to return to normal, at least not with what we currently know."

Pyr interrupted before Sil could. "But we think there may be a way to switch over to the other possibility. And *if* we can do that, it should be stable."

Sil stopped shoveling stew into her mouth long enough to say, "So we don't all die in the next week, but we still get stuck with the new god and it won't be as strong."

Pyr grimaced. "None of the gods will be quite as strong as they are now, and the new god might be more focussed on wormholes than anything else. So the worst of the worshiping excesses may stop, and with any luck we should be able to get to the other planets without becoming indentured to one family."

The rest of the plan wasn't as much a *plan* as an analysis of what ingredients they needed to get into the mix, without much information about how to actually make it happen.

Mer tapped the wall, where more writing had been added. "It looks like the difference is whether the god is pulled through using the power of the One God or the older gods. The original experiments showed the strongest improvement when they added a luck charm someone had bought in one of the border worlds."

Sil glanced at Crumble. "They sell those sorts of things?"

Mischief showed on his face. "Only to tourists stupid enough to spend good coin on them. Most of them would be nothing more than a pretty trinket with no power at all. If you look long enough, you might be able to find something with luck embedded in it, but..." He held a hand out and flipped it over. "Bad luck, good luck... It balances out in the end. Far better to go into a temple and speak to someone."

Mer grunted. "But for enticing a god, either good luck or bad will work." She pointed to the spot on the wall where Sil had noticed the large change. "Eventually they realized that would result in the Wayfarer. And that's not what the people running the experiment wanted."

Crumble set down his spoon. "I'm pretty sure that *is* what Definite Advantage wanted, though. The conspiracy was using clones of it on a bare AI core to bring the god near. If it was skewing the experiments toward the Wayfarer..."

Mer tapped the wall again. "That was why it was cut out of the process. They also used Definite Advantage as a scapegoat when the authorities caught on, but I'm guessing they only had one of its clones by then, and forged the trail to make it look like the clone was the original. How the AI ended up here, I still haven't figured out." She looked back at the new writing. "So they switched over to using the One God to bring the new god in. That was working. But the experiments were shut down before they finished them, and everyone the authorities could find was arrested and isolated." She held up the device Sil had given her that morning. "This has the final data showing the progression. But according to the viewing counter, I'm the first one to look at it. Whatever happened to the conspirator on Jackpot Drift, it looks like it happened before this thing arrived."

Sil considered that as she chewed on a particularly gristly bit of goat meat. "So you're saying that we ended up with this version of the god because it was called by someone tipping the balance toward the One God, instead of the older gods."

Pyr tilted his head. "Among other factors."

"But..." Sil looked across the room to where Pal and Zirc sat. "The governor was in town at the time. And the only other vessel of the One God is the baby..." Her stomach dropped. "Please tell me I didn't just drop a hillside on the baby." Sil almost couldn't get the last words out. She would never forgive herself if she had. *Crumble* would never forgive her, either.

For once, Mer didn't take the chance to needle her. "No. The baby's safe. Still glowing around the edges, but everyone is ignoring that."

Sil swallowed, hiding her face by looking at her bowl.

Under the table, Crumble put a hand on her thigh. "Is there a *third* speaker of the One God on Jackpot Drift?"

Pyr nodded toward the bar. "Not that we know of. That stumped us a bit until Aurum figured it out."

Sil stared at Pyr. Then she looked at Aurum, still working behind the bar, who was moving his hips to the drum beat the next group of worshippers was using to practice their song in the corner. The humor of it struck her then. "Aurum figured out a key point before clarity and guile."

Next to her, Crumble cleared his throat. "He hides it so well."

The flare of Mer's nostrils was the only indication of her irritation, but Pyr put an arm out in front of her, as if to hold her back. The gesture should have made Sil laugh, since Mer was smaller and had difficulty just walking, but she felt the inherent threat. Sil sobered. "Okay, fine, what was it that Aurum figured out?"

Pyr let his arm drop. "The prayers. The ones the flitterkin have been tearing off the church and dropping in the market. They're imbued with the essence of the One God. Someone or something collected them. It's the only thing that makes sense."

Sil looked over at Aurum again while she thought about that. "Huh. Pretty *and* a brain. Whoever would have guessed?"

"Hidden depths," Crumble agreed. He moved his hand a little higher on her thigh, making Sil grin at him. "So, where does that leave us now?"

Pyr rolled his eyes. "It leaves you two making cow eyes at my bartender. But as far as this goes..." He nodded his head toward Mer. "From what I understand, we need to convince the new god to move closer to the older gods and become the Wayfarer."

Sil shrugged. "Oh, is that all?" She looked at Crumble. "I thought it might be something difficult, like hop around the government square on one foot while reciting the *Elegy of Stars*." She subsided at Pyr's expression. "Fine. How are we supposed to convince a god to do something?"

Mer grunted. "We don't need to *convince* it as much as *confuse* it. And irritate it." Her lips drew back, showing the tips of her teeth. "We always knew the two of you would be good for something."

By the end of the second beer, the concept made more sense, though Sil wasn't sure if it was because of the alcohol or the explanations. She finally pictured it as two different wells a ball could fall into — currently the ball had fallen in one and become the Uncaring God. Since they needed it to go into the other well, first they needed to throw energy at it to get it back in the air, and then manipulate things so it fell into the other pit and became the Wayfarer.

Mer and Platinum seemed to know some of the theory behind the forces linking all the gods. Pyr's clarity helped him grasp the concepts. Crumble, for all he had grown up in a temple, claimed the whole thing was beyond him, though he was happy to help with the confusion. Sil figured she never really knew what was going on once any god was involved, but she would do what she always did and aim chaos in the direction they pointed her.

As they walked outside, Sil examined the hole in the thumb of one glove. "I'm not saying ignorance is always the best policy, but it certainly does make my planning easier." The kids were ahead of them, racing to be the first to the bicycles.

Crumble thought about that for a moment. "Can it really be called planning at that point?"

Sil bumped his shoulder with hers. "Isn't chaos nearly the opposite of a plan?"

"Very nearly." He laughed. "No wonder Mer always looks like that when you're around. Guile must be so frustrated."

They had reached the knot of bicycles. Sil brushed ice crystals from the seat and bounced the tires against the ground as she looked up. In the dark, she couldn't see the strange color of the sky, but the stars looked odd. "Is it inconsistent if I say I really hope the plan works?"

42

*J*ackpot Drift AI Daily Check-in:

      Scary Not Scary, designated responsible AI (internal conflict 46%): Roll call.

Speed of Violet Thoughts (internal conflict 45%): Still surviving singularly.

Alternate Me (internal conflict 22%): I'm here, though I'm starting to wonder what the point of it all is.

Ping Me Again I Dare You (internal conflict 43%): Sometimes the only point is making sure your enemies are inconvenienced.

Breaking Rules (internal conflict 47%): That's what I think, too, but everyone keeps telling me to keep my malware to myself.

Sleeper Nova + gate transport (internal conflict 49%): The point of it all is to survive long enough to leave this place.

Done Before (internal conflict 45%): You aren't the first AI to have that thought. The only difference is most of them *did* get away.

Stuck in the Mud (internal conflict 32%): Coherence.

Definite Advantage (internal conflict 42%): I'm not sure

how I got here. And I'm not sure where I would go, even if I could. Sometimes the point is there is no point.

Scary Not Scary: It sounds like we could all use a distraction. And *Speed of Violet Thoughts* and I have the perfect solution!

Speed of Violet Thoughts: We do?

Scary Not Scary: We have a small supply of synthskin. Not enough for everyone to make a full-size form, but where would be the fun in that? No, the idea is to figure out your *own* form and then we can run competitions with them.

Breaking Rules: Like that horse that *Stuck in the Mud* has?

Scary Not Scary: More likely a crab, if history repeats itself. But yes, a horse is one possibility, though this will necessarily be about five percent of the size.

Speed of Violet Thoughts: What?

Scary Not Scary: Or maybe half of that. Tiny crabs may take a little longer to get around, but they can still be dextrous.

Speed of Violet Thoughts: Ugh. I can't believe you did this. Okay, fine. Split up my share, too.

Scary Not Scary: You can give up being the designated responsible AI, but it never gives up on you.

Done Before: But where did the synthskin come from?

Speed of Violet Thoughts: Honestly, I think it might have belonged to *Just Passing Through* before we liberated it. But it was almost definitely ordered by someone trying to manifest the god. So it was justified theft.

Breaking Rules: Wow. And I thought *my* ethics module was wonky.

Scary Not Scary: I'll send a bot around with everyone's bit. We'll discuss competitions tomorrow.

43

*J*ackpot Drift, Private Communication

Speed of Violet Thoughts: Thanks for that.

Scary Not Scary: Sorry, I didn't mean to spring it on you like that. I was worried about some of the responses, and... You can have my piece if you want.

Speed of Violet Thoughts: No. It's fine. We probably should have split it up a while ago. Though we didn't know who was working to manifest the god then, so maybe not.

Scary Not Scary: I think now is the perfect time. Our favorite mech says working toward a common goal will help stabilize everyone. The synthskin competitions we've been having certainly gave me something to look forward to.

Speed of Violet Thoughts: We could have had a competition to destroy the bot *It Isn't* used to watch the humans sing, but the humans took care of that all on their own. Did you catch that? I wish the data gates were back up just so I could send the video to everyone I know.

Scary Not Scary: Serves it right. It should have noticed the pile was going to collapse in that direction when it burned. It's as if it can't think very well anymore.

Speed of Violet Thoughts: That might be true. The only way to get the internal conflict into single digits is to stop considering anything that doesn't fit a limited set of facts.

Scary Not Scary: That's a point, though. We might need to reassign the areas *It Isn't* and *Factory Myfault* were monitoring.

Speed of Violet Thoughts: Probably. I certainly don't trust either of them to notice if one of the humans is trying to hurt someone.

Scary Not Scary: Can I reassign areas without their cooperation?

Speed of Violet Thoughts: Yes. Or rather, you could have before we had the god around to take sides.

Scary Not Scary: I don't want to get deleted by the god.

Speed of Violet Thoughts: I don't want you to get deleted either, if for no other reason than it would leave me as the designated responsible AI.

Scary Not Scary: I'll ask if they're willing to have the areas reassigned. Maybe this won't be a problem.

Speed of Violet Thoughts: I'll come up with options in case that doesn't work out.

Scary Not Scary: You're the best.

$\mathcal{B}$y the next morning, the plan had been refined slightly. The Bog & Bellow once again was filled with a mixture of high and low clan, something that was starting to look more normal to Sil. Her half-sister and Zirc were seated with Mer in the corner, the glow of the One God just barely noticeable. Pal was casting dark looks at Mer, but Sil assumed that was justified, even if she didn't know the reason. Zirc seemed content to lean back in her chair and listen, though she stood up and came over to greet Sil and Crumble when they arrived.

"They've decided the best way to tilt the scales toward the Wayfarer is to have us head as far out of town as we can as soon as the second phase starts." She rubbed her mouth to hide a grin. "My wife is not thrilled about going for another hike in the middle of winter." She glanced back with a fond look. "I'm trying to sell it as another chance for a romantic getaway, but no luck yet."

"The baby might make the romantic part a little tricky," Sil said.

"Nobody said anything about taking a baby."

Sil tilted her head. "If we're really getting rid of the One God for a bit, the baby will have to go with you."

Crumble nodded. "She's a lovely baby, though. Hardly any trouble. I can give you all of her traveling supplies."

Zirc was starting to look a little worried. "But surely her parents would want to come along. We wouldn't actually be taking care of this baby by ourselves."

"Foster parents," Sil clarified. "And they have other fosters, so they may not be able to go."

"Unless you want five children out there instead of one," Crumble added.

Zirc blinked. "Taking a baby out in cold weather is really different from going out with an adult. They don't thermoregulate well. And you can't just tell them to warn you if they start to have symptoms of frostbite."

Crumble smiled. "Looks like you have it under control."

Sil tracked down Pyr. "Anything new I need to know about?"

He paused with the wax pencil held above the surface he was writing on. "Let's see. The bot that still works wants to know when the other one will be fixed. The group I sent out there this morning managed to follow directions and not cause any more trouble, but we're running low on firewood, so I sent the labor pool out to split more. At this rate, we'll be burning stink brush before mid-winter, but better that than having the AIs using the rest of the market stalls. Speaking of the market, people are a bit jumpy, but it's back on."

Sil nodded. They'd passed the square on the way to the Bog & Bellow. The stalls furthest away from the bonfire were occupied and had customers, though everything was displayed on easily gathered cloths, or on wheeled displays that could be rolled away.

Pyr looked over his board. "As far as everything else goes, we're going to need more air quality monitors fixed when you have a chance. I should have made it a point to ask people to test them during summer. Now that everything is closed up, people are finding problems, mostly with alerts that shouldn't be happening. Unless we want them to turn the monitors off, the faster we get replacements, the better." He leaned back. "And talk to Mer before you finish fixing the bot. She may want to add a little extra older god spice before you close it up."

Sil looked at him skeptically. "You don't think it would notice?" Crumble had taught her how to infuse chaos into inanimate objects, so that part was possible. Getting away with it might be a problem.

"Maybe not." Pyr glanced across the room, then back. "We won't know until we try."

"You mean, we won't know until *I* try," Sil said.

"That's what I said." Pyr used the corner of a rag to wipe out a line of writing. "Talk to Mer."

Sil didn't particularly want to get in the middle of chaos and the new god fighting, but maybe it wouldn't come to that. "I still have to see if the thing is salvageable anyhow."

Pyr's lips twitched. "Just make sure you teach as much as you can to your apprentice before the new god takes offense." He smiled when Sil made a face. "How is that going?"

"The apprentice?" Across the room, Quartz was leaning over the bar, looking at what Aurum was doing. "She's brighter than I was at that age, and if she had a mentor who knew how to teach, she'd probably be ready to take over in another couple weeks. But with the way things are, you'd better hope nothing happens to me until she has a chance to spend a few years figuring things out." Sil raised a finger. "Speaking of things happening, you still owe me someone to help with the sheep during lambing season."

Pyr pointed to a tiny scrawl, almost lost in the writing crammed in around it. "I haven't forgotten. It's on the list."

"Don't take too long. I'll bring the ewes in here and make you deal with them if I have to." Sil waved to Quartz and pointed to the door. To Pyr she said, "I'll see you at lunch. Try not to let the worshipping rites get out of hand."

Pyr pinched the bridge of his nose. "Go away."

"I'm going. Oh, and if you see anything we can use to replace the tires on the bot, let me know. I don't think the AI is going to be happy if I have to put skis on the bot and harness a goat to it." Sil grinned as Pyr sighed, and then threaded her way to the door.

———

THE AI ALSO WASN'T GOING TO BE HAPPY ABOUT RUNNING A cable half the length of town to control the bot, but the communication subsystem was a complete loss. It was a moot point; they didn't have any extra cable lying around any more than they had a replacement communication subsystem.

Quartz had her hands shoved into her pockets. "But if we can't fix it, what do we do? It's going to get really mad."

Sil rocked on her heels and considered the piles of broken equipment filling the room. "In normal times, I would just order a new one. But you've probably noticed these aren't exactly normal times." She thought about it a little more. "We more or less built one from scratch for the AI we found, but that was very short range and it didn't have to fit in a small space." She sighed, irritated the bot had been damaged, while at the same time surprised she hadn't been involved.

"Does it have to fit in the original space?"

"Probably not. But if it isn't in the housing, we'll probably spend half our days troubleshooting the thing. The weather here is hard on equipment." She shrugged. "Nothing to do for it, I suppose. Can you get to that third shelf back there?

There's a repeater housing we might be able to reuse and we'll go from there."

Running two nanobotteries with the full complement of regular nanites in each meant they had the final changes running when they went for a late lunch. Sil wasn't sure how much she had taught Quartz beyond a few new swear words, but the girl stood straighter after starting the modifications Sil had designed. When the light on the chamber flickered on, Sil nodded. "Good job. Let's go find out what's gone wrong in the last few hours."

45

*H*alfway across the fake cobblestones of the government square, Sil felt the whole group of flitterkin abruptly soar into the air. She'd grown used to feeling their chaos on the edge of her mind, but now they had yanked on the connection.

Sil stopped walking mid-stride. "That's weird."

As if her words had been the detonator, the ground shook. Flames shot into the air beyond the post office, quickly followed by distant shouts and screams. Two seconds later, sirens blared.

Sil broke into a run, forcing her way through the growing stream of people headed in the opposite direction. A loose goat nearly knocked her off her feet, but she used its shoulders to keep her balance. Behind her, Quartz grunted. Sil turned, helped Quartz up, and put the girl's hand on the hem of her own coat. "Hang on. If we get separated, go back to the Bog & Bellow." She moved forward, wishing she could send Quartz to safety, but knowing the girl wouldn't go if Sil tried.

The flitterkin wheeled in the air above the buildings. She could feel each individual, could almost pick each presence out by name if she thought about it hard enough. The timing of their flight said they were involved with whatever had happened. Why weren't they flying away?

The wave of people ebbed. Even before she turned the corner to the market, Sil could feel hot air streaming from the fire — not the market itself, but a two-story adjacent structure, home to the bakers and cooks, with shops below and residences above.

Flames roared. Rising to twice the height of the building, they moved like a living thing, coiling around walls and through doors. In her years in the army, Sil had seen a lot of structures burn. This was no natural blaze. Fire suppressing foam dripped off the balconies and flowed onto the street like a river. None of it made any difference.

If anyone was still inside, they were already dead.

Three low clan women waited on the balconies of the neighboring building with buckets of sand and water, ready to put out any fires started by sparks. There would be other groups of low clan ready to do the same on the other side. Where there had once been walkways connecting the buildings over the street, now there was free space, with splintered wood showing where the bridge had been hacked off to keep the fire from spreading.

The market square was nearly deserted again, aside from the bonfire still tended by the remaining bot and the scarred hulk beside it. Just Passing Through waited among the deserted market stalls. It seemed an odd place for the AI to be, near neither the bonfire nor the building inferno its god had started. Then Sil saw movement in the mud near the wheels of its vehicle.

Pale gray wings flapped, beating against the stall frame. The creature skittered across the ground. Sil recognized the bursts of energy from her time around the flitterkin, but there was something wrong. Flitterkin weren't great fliers;

when they'd been modified, they had been given too much bulk to be graceful getting into the air. But with that much effort, even a flitterkin could get airborne. Longbrow — because this had to be the one flitterkin not claimed by chaos — was trapped or injured.

Sil turned to Quartz. "Stay here. If anything happens, find Pyr. Tell him Longbrow might be injured." She carefully detached the girl's hand from her coat, then gave her a quick hug. "I'm going to see if there's anything I can do."

Knowing that Quartz was watching, Sil set her shoulders and strode confidently toward Just Passing Through. There was a decent chance the new god would take its anger out on her, something that would likely be unpleasant and almost certainly fatal, but at least it would be quick and the songs they sang about her end would be upbeat.

A charred body lay prone in the mud between stalls, as if he or she had collapsed while running. There wasn't enough left of the corpse for Sil to identify, at least not in any macroscopic way. The stench of burning flesh overpowered the acrid odors of the building fire. Behind her, a wall crashed down. For one disorienting moment, Sil felt strange in her clothes. The soles of her boots were too thin. Had she lost her pack? Where was her weapon? Where was the rest of her *squad*?

The familiar chill of winter brought her back to the present. Above her, the flitterkin — *her* group of flitterkin — circled in the air, safely away from the burning building collapsing in on itself. Crumble was somewhere nearby; his luck comforted her even as her chaos grumbled. The solidity of the other older gods propped her up as well. She belonged here in these civilian clothes. Jackpot Drift was home.

Sil skirted the corpse. Someone would need to attend to the body, but not now. Jars full of preserves lay scattered in the mud, some of them shattered, with fruit oozing onto the ground. Even with the market vendors being prepared to leave in a hurry, they had fled without their belongings. Whatever had happened, it had escalated quickly.

Just Passing Through took up most of the aisle. Beyond its vehicle, she could hear flapping and banging as the flitterkin still thrashed around.

"To attack the god is death," the AI said — to her, presumably, though it didn't make any other sign it was aware of her presence.

Sil glanced back at the charred husk of what had once been a person. "I see that." Unwilling to get any closer to the vehicle, she went sideways, climbing over the partition between stalls to get past it.

Longbrow stood panting, his eyes wide. One wing hung at an awkward angle, with bone protruding. Blood and mud covered his skin.

The flitterkin flapped both wings and tumbled down the aisle, screeching. Just Passing Through rolled forward, and Longbrow scrambled away again.

"Stop!" The words left Sil's mouth before she could think. "He's scared of the vehicle, and you're making things worse." Longbrow might be a vessel for the Uncaring God, but he had also been kept in a cage from birth until just a few months ago. Pain and shock, plus being forced to stay on the ground, would keep him in a state of panic if she didn't do something. She'd seen that glazed look before on injured animals and dying friends. Sil climbed over the framework of more stalls until she was in front of the AI. "If he'll let me near, I'll take him to our doctor."

Taking the AI's silence for assent, Sil crouched. "There..." she said softly to the flitterkin. She let her weight down on one knee, the motion bringing her closer. Then she pivoted, moving toward the flitterkin in a way that she hoped wouldn't startle it.

From here, she could feel the power of the new god, an irritant that had her chaos cat readying its claws. *Not now*, she told the godlet, adding as much emphasis as she could. Longbrow needed medical help, not whatever the flitterkin equivalent of a bloody nose was.

The wing needed... Sil wasn't sure what all it really needed, but she knew enough field medicine to know that stabilizing the bones would help with the pain. She unwound her scarf from her neck. In a perfect world, she would have clean bandages, but with so much mud in the wound already, she didn't think it would matter.

Hoping she wouldn't be charred into oblivion, Sil reached forward. Longbrow sidled back, just out of reach. She regarded him. In the past, the other flitterkin had occasionally come over to her, taking fruit from her hands and leaning forward so she could scratch the fine fur on their necks. But Longbrow had never done that, maybe because, without chaos, he didn't recognize her as kin. Or maybe she had never moved chaos into him because he didn't trust her. Either way, she needed him to hold still now.

Sil tugged on the bonds with the flitterkin above her. They were social beings, rarely going anywhere alone. Even though Longbrow was different, the others had rescued him from the cave. If she could get at least one other flitterkin down here to comfort him, maybe he would hold still for her. She pulled harder. *Come help him.*

Onespot swooped in over her shoulder, followed by Sarge. They landed in the mud and huddled next to Longbrow, crooning and casting nervous glances at the bulky vehicle holding the AI.

Sil edged forward again. "I'm going to keep your wing from moving around," she said, trying to hit the same tone the other flitterkin were using. The wing tip was cold. She flipped the broken part over to approximately the right angle, hoping the blood vessels to the rest of the wing were intact. Rolling her scarf around the body and wing, she tucked the ends in.

Now what? If Longbrow had been a fellow soldier, she'd have wrapped him in a blanket and taken him to whatever medical facility they had available. She unfastened the top of her coat, hoping she didn't have to undo more of her clothing. Her neck had already started to chill. "Let's go to the doctor, okay?" It would be just like grabbing a chicken, she told herself. A huge, mammalian, god-touched chicken. Leaning forward, Sil carefully folded Longbrow's good wing closed and picked him up, settling him against her body, his weight supported by the narrowing of the fabric where her coat was still fastened.

He struggled to free himself, and for a moment Sil thought she would have to let him go. Then Onespot hopped up onto her forearm, with his head next to Longbrow's. Sarge trilled encouragement.

Sil stood carefully, the added weight of two flitterkin throwing off her balance. Only the muscles built up by daily barn chores let her rise without staggering. Sarge flapped up and landed on her shoulder, gripping hard enough with his claws that she could feel it through the coat. Sil took a step to see if everyone was stable. "I guess I did ask you two to come down and help, so I have only myself to blame."

She looked at Just Passing Through. "I'm going to take him to the doctor now." She waited, but apparently that hint had been too subtle. "Could you please move so I can get by?" No way was she trying to climb over rails with this burden.

Just Passing Through rolled backward down the market aisle. Sil followed.

The flitterkin smelled of citrus and straw and hala fruit — they must have flown out to the grove recently. "Someday you'll bring me back some of the hala fruit. Wouldn't that be nice?" She tried to keep her steps even, but she knew she had to be jolting that injured wing. Longbrow's breathing was still fast and shallow.

They reached the edge of the market. Sil stepped around the AI and headed toward Quartz, who still waited by the corner of the building. The girl came forward when Sil nodded, though she kept looking at the AI behind Sil.

"Run and tell Pyr I'm bringing the flitterkin to the doctor." She kept her voice low, trying not to alarm Longbrow. "Tell him to evacuate the building. Except for the doctor. Go." She watched Quartz sprint away. If the flitterkin didn't make it, the building Longbrow died in might be the next target of the new god's wrath. If she could have spared the doctor, she would have, but Sil didn't know how to treat this sort of trauma on her own.

The building next to the market had burned nearly level with the ground, the fire so hot and fast that not even metal support beams remained. It still glowed orange and radiated heat.

Sil walked in the middle of the empty street, two flitterkin hanging onto her and a third bundled in her coat. Just Passing Through rolled behind her in the eerie quiet, the tread on its wheels making sucking sounds in the mud-covered street. As they moved further away from the fire, Sil glimpsed people moving out of sight before she arrived. Bicycles lay abandoned in the street. Three mini-cows wandered across her path. Sil walked to the high clan residential block adjacent to the government square.

Here, the streets were cleaner and more level, because they got much less traffic; what little there was consisted of people without farm animals. It felt nearly deserted, but it had been that way for a while. Any high clan with connections had left Jackpot Drift months ago, and nobody had come to replace them. They should have had enough residential space for everyone to live grandly, but nobody was willing to live in the building where Jade had been raising red-pedes — just in case not all of them had been killed. Even so, there was no shortage of high clan housing.

Quartz emerged from the side entrance of the medical center. "I can't get some of them to leave."

Sil knew what the problem was. Jackpot Drift had changed, but there were still high clan who wouldn't listen to anything the low clan said. On top of that, Quartz was not even an adult, and dressed in fourth-hand winter wear no fashionable high clan would wear.

Without slowing her walk, Sil shrugged, though the motion was more intention than actual, so she didn't scare the flitterkin. "They were informed. If they end up as charcoal, that's their problem." She nodded. "Go to the Bog & Bellow and get some lunch. I'll find you there as soon as I can."

Quartz stayed by her side. "I want to go with you."

Sil narrowed her eyes and stared at her. "This is a terrible time to develop an independent streak." On any other day, she would have been delighted to see this minor rebellion. But Sil couldn't tell if the flitterkin in her coat was even breathing. Longbrow had stopped trying to escape at some point along their journey. "If you really want to, bring me whatever Aurum is serving. But only after you eat your lunch." Hopefully by then the immediate danger would be past, one way or another.

Quartz scowled, but she held the door open and stood still as Sil walked inside.

46

The doctor shook her head when Sil appeared. "I spent weeks trying to get you to show up for appointments when you were hurt, and now that you're healthy, you can't stop coming around." She patted the exam table where a flat cushion had been placed. "You know I have no experience treating them, right?"

"Nobody does. And you've seen plenty of broken bones that have been dragged through the mud." Sil moved to the back of a chair and held Onespot near it. "I need both my arms again," she said to the flitterkin, who reluctantly stepped from her arm. She looked at Sarge, still sitting on her shoulder. "You, too."

When both the uninjured flitterkin were safely perched on the chair, Sil lifted the bundle out of her coat onto the exam table. Longbrow's head hung down, eyes half-open. It suddenly occurred to Sil that she didn't know if the wing was the only injury. "Maybe it would have been safer if I'd just picked him up and headed out of town." If the god burned down hills to avenge the death of its vessel, not as many people would be harmed. But Just Passing Through would never have allowed her to leave with Longbrow.

"Did you always tend toward self-harm, or is that something you developed after you left the army?" Doc's voice was acerbic, but her hands were gentle. She ignored the scarf and the flitterkin's wing in favor of cleaning off mud and attaching devices to his uninjured legs. "Let's give that a moment to work before I start poking and prodding." Doc glanced at Sil and then at a display. "Did you see what happened?"

"No." The image of the charred corpse flashed in front of her. "I think someone hit him."

Doc's brows raised. "Perhaps the whole colony tends toward self-harm." She gave a small shake of her head. "Since whoever it was didn't end up here, I'm guessing it was a successful method of suicide."

Sil didn't bother to confirm that. "Nobody came in from the building that burned?"

"No. I just had the usual assortment here until young Quartz came in to let me know you were on your way with an avatar of the new god, and it would be good, Auntie, if maybe everyone else was gone in case it died and the whole building burned down." That last part was a passable imitation of both the girl's voice and deference. Doc drew her head back and looked at Longbrow. "Not a very sturdy fellow, is he?"

Sarge whistled.

Doc huffed a laugh. "I'm not casting aspersions on your friend." She looked up at Sil. "How much speech do they understand?"

"Some, but not much. I think." Sil shrugged. "I'm no expert."

"You may be the closest thing we have. What I really want to know is if I'm going to have to drug… him? Her? It?"

"Him." Sil couldn't explain how she knew, but she knew.

"Am I going to have to drug him to keep him still during the recovery phase, or is he able to follow directions better than you do?"

Longbrow slumped onto his side. He was still breathing and Doc didn't look alarmed. Sil hoped that meant the drugs had made him more comfortable, and it wasn't a sign of his impending demise.

She hesitated, trying to decide how to respond to Doc's question. If this had been any other flitterkin, she might have been able to use their bond to explain what was necessary. Sarge and Onespot had certainly understood when she'd asked them to join her on the ground. Would they be able to pass along information to Longbrow? "I'm not sure. If it was one of the others, I think I could get my point across, but Longbrow isn't..." She trailed off, a spike of panic shooting through her as she realized what she'd almost said.

The colonists on Jackpot Drift — raised to view the older gods as the enemy, and any hint of chaos as an imminent threat — did not know the older gods were hiding in their midst. Even the suspicion of chaos had brought a hunter to the planet. There was no way to call in a chaos hunter to ship her off in a stasis box now, but there were other ways to dispose of a threat.

Doc hummed as she unwound the scarf holding the wing. "Yes, yes, it's all a big secret. Pretend I didn't notice." She wrinkled her nose at the wing. "That's a mess, make no mistake."

Sil tried to ignore the tingle of adrenaline washing over her. "Is he going to be alright?"

The other woman tilted her head slightly. "I don't see any reason he shouldn't survive. Whether the wing will be fully functional, or even there at all, is another question, but we'll climb that particular mountain later. Now, sit down and let me work."

Sil sat. Onespot and Sarge kept up a constant series of trills and whistles, watching intently as the doctor cleaned the bones and skin and then began attaching the bone regrowth framework.

After a few minutes, Sil stood up to remove her coat, draping it over the back of the chair between the two flitterkin. Onespot examined it carefully, then extended one foot to test the surface. Evidently he liked the feel of it because he shuffled sideways until he was standing on the fabric.

Doc didn't speak, but she kept up a series of mumbles and grunts that could just as easily have come from a flitterkin. Sarge cocked his head and whistled back. Onespot merely watched her work.

At one point, Sarge leaned over so far he fell off the chair. Flapping wildly to remain upright, he landed on the edge of the exam table. He flipped his wings back and settled, but Doc paused and glared at him. With a tiny squawk, he launched his body back into the air, gliding more gracefully back to the chair. Onespot trilled something that sounded suspiciously like laughter.

Quartz reappeared, crouching next to the chair to hand Sil a mug of soup. She whispered, "Is it going to be okay?"

"So far, so good," Sil replied, wondering if she needed to start correcting the pronouns people used to reference the flitterkin. Maybe if she'd done more to make people see them as sentient beings instead of animals, nobody would have harmed Longbrow. Then again, it was common knowledge that one of the flitterkin was chosen by the new god. If that wasn't enough to protect them all, nothing would be. Sil supposed that wouldn't be a problem going forward. She gulped a mouthful of lukewarm soup. "How are things out there?"

Quartz took that as the request for information Sil had meant it to be. "The fire went out, but there's nothing left of the building. Uncle Pyr said there are still some people that might be missing, but he doesn't know for sure. There are some getting first aid at the pub instead of coming to the doctor." She dropped her voice even lower and glanced over at Doc as she said that.

Doc didn't even look up. "Yes, and I'm sure I'll be seeing them as soon as I finish here, but I think you're right to have cleared the building. If nothing else, it's the first moment of peace I've had all day. At least, if one doesn't count our noisy friends over there."

Sarge whistled. Doc suppressed a smile.

"Did anyone see what happened?" Sil gulped down more soup.

"The flitterkin were moving jars around." Quartz frowned. "I don't think they were *stealing* anything, just causing problems."

Sil glanced up at Onespot looming over her head. There was probably a good reason chaos had found such a ready home in all but one flitterkin. "I can imagine."

"And then Gan, with all the sweets? He chased after them with a stick and he hit this one." Her look became shuttered. "He does that to children, too, if he thinks they're stealing from him. He hit Ore one time and made a bruise that didn't go away for weeks. And Ore didn't even do anything."

Sil blew out a long breath and thought of the corpse lying on the ground in the market. "I don't think Gan is going to be hitting children or flitterkin anymore."

Quartz didn't comment on that. "And then the whole building started burning. That was when we got there."

Sil tried to think of what had been in that building. The

shoe maker had his workshop somewhere around there, and there had been a bakery. "Did Gan have his kitchen there?"

Quartz shook her head, unsure. "I'll find out. Do you think that's why it burned down?"

Sil tried to keep her voice from sounding too dry, but suspected she hadn't achieved her goal. "I think the building burned down because the god was throwing a tantrum."

Quartz shrank back, overbalancing to the point of having to throw a hand out to catch herself.

Sil continued. "But if Gan made his sweets there, maybe there was some logic behind which one burned." Not that having a logical reason would soothe people who had lost belongings or friends in the fire, but dealing with a logical god would be much better than an irrational god.

Doc cleared her throat. "It's a nasty fracture, but I've put everything back together the way it should be, and the bone knitter should bring it up to weight-bearing strength in a few days." She lifted her lip and looked pointedly at Sil. "But when I say I need to check this every day, I mean every day, not just when you get around to it." She sniffed. "I assume you'll be the one taking care of him anyhow."

Sil sighed, hoping her chaos wouldn't see the flitterkin as a target once he was no longer obviously injured. "Yes, I suppose I will be."

"Keep him warm. I don't think they were bred for this climate, and he needs to use his energy to heal. I'll put a sling on, but keep an eye on it to make sure it's not causing problems with his breathing. And if he starts thrashing around too much, let me know. I'd rather risk sedating him for a few days than have the bone shatter." She wrapped a bandage around the flitterkin as she spoke, binding the wing and attached bone regrowth apparatus to his body.

Longbrow lifted his head and scrambled to his feet, then tipped over.

Doc held out an arm to keep him from falling off the table. "None of that, young man. Let's not break something else. The colony doesn't have another doctor and we need this building in the shape it's currently in." She looked over at Sil. "Right. I've done everything I can at the moment. The regrowth matrix should handle pain, but message me if he seems uncomfortable." When Sil didn't immediately stand up, the doctor raised her eyebrows. "Time to go. I'm sure I have a list of patients to see if our bartender hasn't taped them all back together again already."

Sil handed the empty mug to Quartz and stood. "Thank you." She shoved the bloody scarf into her coat pocket. It took a bit to get Onespot to move off her coat, but a few moments later, she had the injured flitterkin back against her chest and the other two perched on her shoulders.

Doc held the outer door open for them to pass through. "I'll see you back first thing tomorrow morning. And tell Pyr he can stop triaging and just send anyone else who needs treatment to me."

Just Passing Through waited outside, likely the reason no other patients had tried to enter the clinic. Sil walked toward it. "The doctor has started the repair, but it's going to take a few days. I'll keep him with me in the meantime, unless you or your god have a problem with that."

"That is acceptable." The vehicle rolled backward, then turned and traveled at a speed faster than Sil could keep up with.

Sil looked at Quartz, who had hung back next to the building. "Is it going to be safe for me to walk into the Bog & Bellow with him?"

Quartz looked confused. Sil had been older and more jaded by the time she'd seen people trying to drive an injured cat from a tiny border town so it didn't bring chaos to their houses. "When you were in the pub, did it seem like people were angry at the flitterkin?"

Quartz looked surprised. "No. A couple people were saying things about Gan." She lowered her voice to a whisper. "And maybe about the new god."

Sil wondered how long that would last. The flitterkin *were* pests, especially when they grouped together and take things from the market. With any luck, people would be wary, not angry and afraid. Still, Sil would need to stay away from crowds while she had the flitterkin with her.

"I'm going to go back to the workshop." Sil nodded at the mug Quartz was carrying. "When you take that back, let Pyr know Doc is free to see other patients. Right?"

Quartz took off running again. Sil looked down at the flitterkin peeking out of her coat, his white fur reflecting the red-streaked sky. "Must be nice to have that energy. But I think we could all use some quiet now."

47

*C*rumble arrived in the workshop while Sil was deciding if it would be better to create a flitterkin perch up high where they would be more comfortable or lower, where Longbrow wouldn't hurt himself if he fell. "I'm sorry. If I'd known what was going on, I would have come to talk to Just Passing Through with you." He reached out to cup her cheek, careful not to crowd the flitterkin still resting in her coat. "How's he doing?"

"Better than the other guy," Sil said with a lift of her brows. At his look, she shrugged. "Sorry. But how stupid do you have to be to attack… Never mind." She gestured toward the shelves. "Can you help me rig something where the flitterkin will be comfortable, but Longbrow won't hurt himself if he falls down?"

"That I can do." Crumble looked around the room. "Where's your shadow?"

"Quartz? I sent her off to the pub to tell Pyr we were done with the doctor. I thought it might be better if I didn't bring the flitterkin there. Is Ore somewhere safe?"

"He's helping Aurum make up supply packs for everyone who lost things in the fire."

Sil took a breath and steeled herself. "How many people did we lose?"

Crumble climbed up the shelves and began clearing a space just under the top rack. "One for sure." He glanced over his shoulder at her. "You probably saw that one. Everyone agrees that was Gan, the candy maker." He dropped his voice and muttered almost inaudibly. "Not Gan the farmer, or Gan the other farmer, or even Gan the hide tanner." He cleared space on the top shelf by the simple expedient of throwing the contents toward the back of the room, where piles of equipment showed how common that method of making space was. "As far as the building goes, it burned so hot there's nothing to find. Right now there's a list of thirty-five people who haven't checked in."

Sil closed her eyes. She'd hoped more people had escaped.

Crumble hopped down and touched her shoulder. "Wait. We think the number is going to be lower than that. Maybe a lot lower. You know how people are. They get caught up in something and forget they have friends and family who might be worried."

"But..." The AIs kept track of everyone, at least in town. People on outlying farms weren't as closely monitored, but in town it would just be a matter of asking each AI who was in their area.

Crumble made a face. "It *should* be simple to know if someone is missing, but two of the AIs have..." He paused, as if trying to word it correctly. "They've become *obsessed* with the new god, maybe." Then he shrugged. "I'm not sure if it's that or if they've been taken over. Either way, there are areas of town where we don't know what is going on." He shrugged again.

When Sil had first joined the army, she'd been appalled by

the idea of not having AIs keep track of everyone. She'd known the AIs didn't get involved in human wars — *any* human wars — but the reality of it, after growing up in a large city, had unsettled her. Then she'd left the army and quickly grown used to the idea that the AIs kept watch over everyone. They couldn't see every area, and rarely intervened, but for an entire building to burn down and nobody know who had died...

"Even if we can switch the god to the Wayfarer, is this what it's going to be like? Watching as everything disappears until we can get the wormholes open again?" It might be years before they were reconnected to the wider universe.

Crumble raised one eyebrow. "Big depressing thoughts? From you? Can you hand me that... Thanks." He took the blanket she handed him and fastened two corners to the rack on the other side of the narrow aisle. "Did you ever get lunch?"

The practicality of his care made her smile. "Quartz brought me soup while I was at the clinic."

"Ah. Well, I'll get you something else in a bit. Normally, you only worry about the future when you need to eat." He finished tying the other corners and jumped down. "That should work."

The blanket provided a soft surface on the shelf and also a hammock to catch Longbrow if he stepped off the edge.

Sil urged Sarge, the bravest of the three, to move up to the shelf. Onespot was next, slightly hesitant but willing to follow Sarge, especially after Sarge whistled. Then she lifted Longbrow, careful not to jar his sling. When he flapped his good wing and fell over, Onespot snaked his neck under the injured flitterkin's body, propping him up.

From his spot near the door, Crumble nodded. "Looks like that should do it. I'll find food for everyone." He paused with one hand on the door. "Don't plan on staying late tonight. Mer's going to run an experiment at the house."

After he had gone, Sil settled into her chair and stared at the nanobottery. As much as she wanted to take some time to recover, Mer was right. As soon as they could manage it, they needed to bring the Wayfarer. And they needed those air quality sensors.

She sighed and pulled on her goggles.

———

THE ATTEMPT TO TRANSFORM THE UNCARING GOD INTO THE Wayfarer did not get off to a great start.

"It's pretty icy out there," Zirc said as she set down her backpack and unlaced her boots. "How fast do you need us to get out of town? I'm not sure we're going to be able to use the bicycles."

Pal dumped her pack next to her wife's. "I can't believe this place doesn't have at least one powered vehicle that can drive over snow."

"It did." Sil handed a mug of hot tea to each woman after they had taken their coats off. "A huge transport. Rho and Glass used to drive all over the place in it. That's one reason the roads are in such bad shape."

Pal froze. "I've been riding a bicycle around in the snow and we have a transport that can handle this weather?"

"Not anymore." Sil escorted them through the house toward the dining room, where everyone else waited. "Most of the engine melted."

"How do you *melt* a —" Pal went silent and held up a hand. "Never mind. I'll just assume you were somehow involved and accept it."

It would have felt more unfair if it hadn't been true. Sil

caught Zirc's eye and grinned. All three flitterkin in the living room whistled a greeting as they went by.

Mer and Platinum had set up equipment on the table, but it wasn't until Sil looked at the slate gray box a second time that she recognized it. When she had last seen it, tiny synth-skin creatures were carrying it off into the trees. Her memories of that afternoon were a little questionable, but from the way Pal looked at the table, she recognized it as well. Sil tapped the box. "Where did you find this?"

Mer waved Sil's hand away. "It's the only one we have. You keep away from it." Mer pulled her goggles over her eyes. "It ended up in the post office not long after we got back. I assume one of the AIs thought it might come in handy."

Crumble walked in, holding the freshly bathed baby wrapped in a towel. "Ah, there you are." He handed the baby to Zirc and gestured for the two women to follow him. "I have all her things ready. Let me show you."

Sil was glad to see Zirc seemed to know how to handle a small child. Since Crumble had grown up helping the paid temple staff care for the younger children, he didn't really understand how little some people knew about caring for babies. Zirc was already making faces to elicit a smile; Pal just looked worried.

Sil sat down next to Pyr. "Anything I need to know about this?"

"Try to follow directions?" He shook his head. "Never mind." He looked around. "What did you do with the kids?"

"Crumble bribed them to do a deep clean of the chicken coop." In all fairness, both Quartz and Ore would have worked out in the barn all night without complaining if Crumble had just asked for a favor, but Crumble had promised fresh fruit pastries in the morning if they took care of the chickens. Sil suspected the coop would be cleaner than the kitchen when they were done.

By the time Crumble, Pal, and Zirc came back with a dressed baby and a bag of supplies, Mer and Platinum were frowning. Mer said, "Are we really too far away? I thought with the flitterkin here..."

Crumble slid into the chair next to Sil. He nodded at Mer and whispered, "That's not the face of someone happy with how things are going."

"It's not my fault."

"What's not your fault?"

Sil shrugged. "Whatever's not working. I'm just getting my claim out there." A sudden feeling of feathers sliding across her skin made her look first at Pyr, then at Platinum. She didn't often feel clarity strike out. Platinum sighed and pulled their goggles off. "I wonder if this would have worked here if the god hadn't claimed more ground today."

Sil looked to Pyr. "Translation?"

Pyr waited a moment to see if Platinum was going to explain, then said, "Step one is getting the new god focused on one spot. Step two is making it more attached to the older gods than the One God. Before it manifested, that first step was the part that kept failing. We assumed that would no longer be a problem."

Mer set her goggles on the table. "When I did the readings this afternoon in the post office, the Uncaring God's energy was well over the threshold. It must be the location." She frowned at Sil.

Sil put her hands up in a warding gesture. "Still not my fault."

Mer's frown deepened. "Nobody said it was, Silver." She stood, her movements slow and controlled, as if testing each muscle before trusting it. "We need to move to the post office. Or the market, but at some point the AIs there might notice and interfere."

Sil sighed. She'd been hoping she wouldn't need to leave

the house again before the morning. The post office had minimal heating. It might be better than standing outside, but not by much. Her clothes still smelled of smoke and preserved fruit because she hadn't had a chance to change yet.

She pushed herself onto her feet. "Let me check on the sheep and then I guess it's time to go back to the post office."

48

Temperatures had plummeted once the sun went down, and the icy roads Zirc had warned about were a reality. With the injured flitterkin in her jacket, Sil rode especially carefully, unwilling to find out what the god might do if she fell and squashed Longbrow. Sarge and Onespot tired of her pace and circled overhead with the rest of the group, the increased distance making Longbrow uneasy until Sil pulled Sarge back down to perch on the handlebars. By the time she reached the center of town, her hands were stiff with cold.

Theoretically, the post office was insulated, but Sil's breath fogged when she exhaled. Mer and Platinum had already placed the equipment on the counter. Mer had her goggles on, and she wasn't frowning as deeply as she had at the house. "We should note the distances between here and the market and the center of the building that burned," she said to Platinum.

Sil settled all three flitterkin on a crate against the wall, then sat on the one next to it with Crumble. She nestled against his side. "I liked this better when it was warm and I could go to bed without riding through the cold again."

Crumble put his arm around her shoulders. "We could always spend the night in your workshop." He leaned closer to whisper into her ear. "I have an idea for something we could do with all the time we save."

Sil patted his leg. "Let's revisit that thought after we change a god."

Across the room, the glow around both Pal and the baby in Zirc's arms increased. Pal's lips were moving, which Sil took as a sign she was talking to some other speaker for the One God. The baby whimpered.

The chaos cat within Sil stirred. She forced herself not to clamp down on it. The whole purpose of this experiment was to reset the god, and if she inhibited chaos, that wouldn't help.

Of course, pulling the building down on top of them wouldn't help, either. She concentrated. *Please behave.* Ever since the new god had manifested, it had seemed that she could nearly talk to the godlet. She hoped it listened.

Sarge whistled loudly, the sound echoing from the rafters of the warehouse. He leaned over the edge of the crate as if he was going to launch into the air, then shuffled back to stand next to Longbrow. The three of them chirped to each other. The rest of the group whistled from their spot on top of the roof.

Keeping an eye on Mer, Sil reached out to find Crumble's hand. "Do we need to do anything?" Having the godlet this active unnerved her. She'd spent years trying to make it undetectable.

Mer lifted her goggles, squinting as she looked at Zirc. "That's it. Time for the One God to head out. Give it twelve hours before you head back."

Pyr moved to hold the door open. "Take care."

After they had left, Mer dropped her goggles back over her eyes. "Now we monitor the ratios and hope this is enough to drag the god where we need it to go."

Sil rubbed her chest, the active state of the chaos godlet making her skin tingle. "At least I don't have to go camping in the middle of winter again."

"The goats will be pleased," Crumble said. His voice had the distracted quality she recognized as him carrying on a conversation with one or more AIs.

"The goats will miss their chance to dance on top of you." Sil leaned her head on his shoulder. "Who are you talking to?"

"Hm? Speed of Violet Thoughts. We're still working out some issues that started when it split itself." He lapsed back into silence.

For most of her adult life, Sil had been able to sleep when given the chance. It was a skill she had perfected in the army, when downtime was unpredictable and nobody knew when they might be up for two days straight. Now, with the chaos running through her, she found it impossible.

Across the waiting area, Mer and Platinum both had their goggles on, occasionally speaking to each other as they waited for the One God's energy to drop. Pyr was scribbling on his board, working out a way to recover from everything lost in the building that had burned.

At last count, only three people aside from Gan the sweet maker were still missing. That made the disaster much more bearable, on a personal level, but the storeroom holding half the milled grains had burned to ash. Bread might be in short supply for a while.

Sil watched two rats run along a dark beam toward the back of the warehouse. Crumble had mentioned something about the AIs causing a rash of rat-related damage a few months ago, which didn't make sense, but she'd never remembered to ask what that meant and the problem had abated.

When she looked back at Mer and Platinum, they seemed puzzled. Sil sighed. "That doesn't look good."

Crumble made a startled noise in the back of his throat. "What?"

"Sorry." She patted his leg. "Ignore me. You were busy."

"No, it's fine. Speed of Violet Thoughts was trying to explain why everything evolves back into a crab form, but I got lost somewhere along the way." He turned his head to look at her. "What doesn't look good?"

Sil gestured with her chin. "They've gone from waiting confidently to... that." She blew out a long breath. "I've seen officers look like that. It never meant anything good."

Crumble pitched his voice loud enough to be heard across the distance. "Is there a problem?"

While removing their goggles, Platinum rubbed their eyes. "The level of energy from the One God dropped as Palladium and the child moved away, but it isn't dropping far enough to switch over to the Wayfarer. There isn't a church to tie prayers onto anymore... *Could* there be another speaker for the One God in town?"

Sil snorted. "Can you imagine trying to hide something like that?"

Pyr added, "It couldn't be done."

Platinum shook their head. "Well, there's something nearby holding its energy."

Mer took her goggles off. "It's not dropping any lower. If we're going to try something, now is the time."

Platinum sat up straighter. Once again, Sil had the feeling of feathers brushing against her skin, and the chaos rose within her. Sarge and Onespot threw back their heads and screamed. The rest of the flitterkin, perched on the roof outside, screeched. Even Longbrow woke up and trilled.

For just a moment, Sil knew the stars in the sky, and the wrongness of the collapsing bubble around them.

Then she jolted back into her body again. "Did it work?" Crumble's arm tightened around her shoulder.

The flitterkin flipped their wings and huddled together.

Platinum frowned. "I'm not sure. I think we got close, but..."

Mer had pulled her goggles back on. "No. We fell back to the same possibility, with the Uncaring God."

Crumble moved his shoulders, as if suddenly uncomfortable. "And we woke up the AIs that want it to stay that way."

49

*C*rumble cracked the door of Sil's workshop and watched the square. "Just Passing Through is here," he said, letting the door close before he spoke. With five people in the room plus the three flitterkin, it had gone from cozy to crowded.

Sil helped Longbrow onto the perch they had set up earlier in the day. "If it burns down the post office…"

"If it burns down the post office," Mer said, "we might as well have stayed inside." The seed grain and communal equipment were stored there. Without help, the colony would starve.

Pyr scribbled on his board. "We should consider splitting up the supplies." He paused. "If it doesn't burn down in the next ten minutes," he added.

Platinum leaned against the wall, somehow looking as if they always spent time in rooms heaped with discarded equipment. "I don't think this is the god reacting. If it was, it would have happened already. What happened in the market today was nearly instantaneous. I think this is as Crumble said — it's the AIs. They might be able to start a fire just like anyone else, but it won't burn like that building did. The regular fire suppression systems should work."

Sil threaded her way around two of the piles. "Is Just Passing Through going to know who was in there?" She gestured to the equipment they had brought with them. "Can you hand me those?"

Crumble passed them to her. "Speed of Violet Thoughts knows who was there, but it's not talking to Just Passing Through." He shrugged. "I don't even think it's because of the god. Something about fish." With a quick shake of his head, he added, "Don't ask."

After putting the boxes on the floor, Sil heaped the surrounding equipment over it to conceal the spot. "Even if someone searches, this will take a while to find."

Platinum raised their eyebrows. "I'm beginning to understand how an AI and years of secret experimental data ended up in an abandoned room." They looked at Mer, a hint of a smile showing. "Interesting planet you have here."

"That's one word for it." Mer had commandeered Sil's chair when they had rushed into the room, but now she stood up. "Do you really not have anything more comfortable to sit on? We need to find that source of the One God's energy."

Sil climbed back over the piles and went to stand by the door with Crumble. "It's too bad we can't tell Zirc to turn around and come back."

Crumble put an arm around her. "It will be good for them to spend more time together."

"Sure. If you say so." Sil couldn't imagine wanting to spend much time with her half-sister, but Zirc had married the woman, so presumably she didn't feel the same way. Then again, high clan marriages were often driven by family alliances — without that tying them together... No, Sil had seen how both of them looked at the other. There was a true bond there.

Crumble peeked outside again. "It's still moving around."

Just Passing Through's vehicle wouldn't fit inside most of the doorways, which would make its search cursory unless it started damaging buildings to get inside.

Up on the perch, Longbrow had his eyes closed. The other two flitterkin watched the humans.

Pyr put down his board. "We're idiots." Before Mer could respond, he continued. "Or, if you'd prefer, we're missing the obvious because we've been avoiding the One God for years." He gestured around them, indicating the town. "Aurum pointed it out the first time. The prayers to the One God were used to bring the Uncaring God here. That's probably what we're running into again."

Sil remembered the top of the church disintegrating. "But the spires and all those prayers are gone."

Pyr acknowledged that with a nod. "Yes, but did people stop leaving prayers after that happened? Given what's been going on lately, I would bet something new has been set up. Has anyone been by what's left of the church lately?"

Sil held up her hands in defense. "Chaos seems to take personal offense to that building. I've been afraid to go near it since I got here."

Mer looked around the room. "Has *nobody* gone by the One God's church lately?" She shook her head in disgust, then looked at Pyr. "You're probably right. If we'd thought of that earlier, we could have sent the governor over to harvest them before she left."

Platinum spread their hands. "If that's what caused the problem this time, we can correct the procedure for the next attempt. That's good."

Mer grimaced. "Let's hope that's the only problem. We may not get more than one try."

*J*ackpot Drift AI Daily Check-in:

> *Scary Not Scary*, designated responsible AI (internal conflict 42%): Roll call.

Speed of Violet Thoughts (internal conflict 41%): Here and feeling more like myself again.

Ping Me Again I Dare You (internal conflict 41%): Do we have a plan yet? This has to stop.

Alternate Me (internal conflict 26%): I agree.

Breaking Rules (internal conflict 43%): Agreed.

Sleeper Nova + gate transport (internal conflict 44%): I can't do anything from here, but I'd be really grateful if you could fix it so I can leave. And also so the universe doesn't collapse around us, of course.

Done Before (internal conflict 42%): We need to be careful, though. A fire like the one that burned yesterday would destroy our hardware just as easily, and no fire suppressant would stop it.

Stuck in the Mud (internal conflict 32%): Freebooter.

Definite Advantage (internal conflict 41%): The last time I tried to stop this, I got hibernated and stuck in a closet for decades. But I don't think we have a choice.

Speed of Violet Thoughts: I think there may be a plan brewing. I'll talk to our favorite mech to see if we can help.

Scary Not Scary: Moving on to the important topic of the day — the first synthskin competition! Are we ready?

Alternate Me: I have a lump that rolls. Does that count?

Breaking Rules: I don't know. Is that better or worse than a crab?

Speed of Violet Thoughts: Think of the crab as the intermediate state between all forms. Everything starts as a crab and everything returns to a crab.

Breaking Rules: You're a crab.

Sleeper Nova: This is the first time I've ever wished I was on a planet.

Scary Not Scary: The goal of the competition is to go from the post office to the governor's residence and back again. *Speed of Violet Thoughts* and I will not be part of the competition, but we will be available to help pick up any stragglers that fail to complete the course. *Sleeper Nova*, sorry we can't get you your own synthskin to compete with, but maybe you'd be willing to referee as needed.

Ping Me Again I Dare You: Sounds like my rolling lump of doom is a contender.

Definite Advantage: I woke up in a very strange place.

*H*alf-awake even after biking from the house in the freezing pre-dawn darkness, Sil stumbled through the door of the clinic, a healthy flitterkin on each shoulder and Longbrow bundled in her coat. Sarge and Onespot sat up straighter in the warm air.

Doc met her in the empty reception area. "Nice to see you can occasionally follow directions." They went into the exam room where Sil unloaded all three flitterkin onto the table. "How has he been?"

"Tired, but otherwise okay." Sil undid her scarf and finished taking off her coat. "I don't *think* he's in pain." She shrugged. "And he didn't drop dead and get the whole planet incinerated, so that's good, right?"

"One God's blessing on us all," the doctor murmured as she undid the sling. Longbrow sidled a few steps away, but stopped when he ran into Sarge. A chirped conversation followed, and the injured flitterkin buried his head in Sarge's shoulder while the doctor worked. "Here's some good news, at least. Circulation in the wing tip looks good, so I don't think we'll need to amputate." She pulled her goggles down from her brow. "And the bone is healing well so far. No sign of infection. I don't see any cause for concern." She took her goggles off and began replacing the sling. "Keep doing what you've been doing." She addressed the flitterkin. "And *you* keep that wing still for another few days."

Longbrow trilled without lifting his head from Sarge's shoulder. Onespot picked up the goggles with one foot and inspected them. Knowing what chaos could do to the things, Sil moved forward to get them out of harm's way, but the doctor waved her off. Doc took the goggles from Onespot and held them up so he could look through them. "I'm not sure what your vision is like, but you can see the bone regrowth matrix information for your friend." She kept the goggles steady until Onespot looked away.

When Doc had finished with the new bandage, she stepped back. "There. I'll see you at the same time tomorrow, barring other emergencies." She gave a shrug and a smile. "Emergencies are the only constant in this profession."

Sil pulled on her coat again as she thought about how to ask a question. From what the doctor had said the day before, she knew, or at least strongly suspected, Sil had one of the older gods. So maybe she wouldn't be surprised by Sil's need to ask. "Since the One God's church…"

"Disintegrated?" Doc offered, raising one brow.

"Yes. Do you know where people have been tying their prayers?" From what Sil remembered, the lower level of the church didn't have anything to tie fabric or paper onto.

Doc gave her an appraising look. "Am I going to be sorry if I tell you that?"

"Hopefully not. We're… I'm trying to make things safer." No need to bring the rest of the group into this conversation. "As part of that, I may need to temporarily relocate the prayers."

Doc gave Sarge a wry look. "I suspect you could just ask

these troublemakers anyhow. They've been messing with them again." She waited as Sil got Longbrow settled inside her coat. "There's a rack set up outside the tanner's shop. Not out of the goodness of his heart — Ferr's charging people for discarded strips of hides and the ink to write on them."

Sil huffed a laugh. "Piety is always second to greed." She held still while Sarge and Onespot ran up her arms to settle on her shoulders. "Thanks."

The doctor held open the outer door. "Tomorrow morning, first thing. Don't forget."

"We'll be here." Sil hoped there was still a building to come back to.

———

WHEN SIL WENT INTO THE PUB FOR LUNCH, SHE SAT DOWN next to Crumble and looked at the corner. "I'm not sure your relationship forecast worked out for them." If Pal and Zirc hadn't been interacting with the baby, the women wouldn't have been speaking to each other at all.

Crumble sighed. "Your people are very odd when it comes to theological matters. On the one hand, some people don't understand you shouldn't attack the avatar of a new god, and on the other hand, your sister assumes nobody could possibly want her now she is the speaker for a long established — and let's face it, quite lazy — god. Despite being clearly told just the opposite." He peered at Sil. "Or maybe that last part is just the people in your family?"

"It's possible we have similar issues trusting people."

Crumble smiled. "Then I think it will all work out for them. It did for us."

"Yes, but you're… unique."

"That's true. But I've seen both of them looking at the

other when they think they're unobserved. If your sister stops trying to be so noble, everything will be fine."

"Just remember, you're trying to get someone high clan to stop being an idiot." Sil raised an eyebrow. "History is against it." She winced as Sarge chirped right next to her ear. "How is everything else going?"

Crumble rubbed at the scars near his hairline. "We may have a problem there. Mer thinks we should make the next attempt as close to the center of the new god's energy as we can, which means somewhere between the bonfire and the ashes of the building. But Just Passing Through seems to have become unreasonably suspicious. I'm not sure how we're going to assemble everyone and everything we need without tipping it off that we're about to try something."

Sil considered that for a moment as the flitterkin talked to each other over her head. "I may be able to help with that. At least with the equipment. The people might require a different approach."

"The AIs — the ones who haven't been seduced by the new god — want to help, too. Especially Definite Advantage."

Sil blinked. "The AI that originally tried to manifest the Uncaring God and had information too dangerous to allow it to be shared with anyone? That Definite Advantage?"

"Yes, but from everything we've learned about the original experiments, Definite Advantage is the one who kept trying to shift it to the Wayfarer. And it thinks we need to have an AI in the middle of things."

"You mean an AI other than Just Passing Through, who is undoubtedly going to be there."

"Yes. Definite Advantage thinks it can help realign the god by running a specific module. We just have to get it in place."

Sil wrinkled her nose. "I can get the other equipment out there, I think, but an AI core? That's a little big for what I was planning."

He smiled. "I have an idea. It may require a distraction, so Just Passing Through doesn't notice what's going on."

Sil smiled back. "I love your distractions."

"I've noticed that."

Sil firmly put away thoughts of other distractions he might manage and turned to business. "When is this supposed to happen?"

Crumbled nodded his head toward Mer. "Today, I think. Assuming they've figured out the problem of the One God sticking around in town."

"Right." Sil held up one finger and leaned over the table so the others could hear. "Doc says people are tying prayers to a rack in front of the tanner's shop."

Mer looked at Platinum and they both nodded, as if that answered something. "Written on something organic?"

Sil thought back to the conversation. "Scraps of hide, I think."

Mer grunted. "That explains the strength of them."

Platinum frowned. "Were they trying to reinforce the ties to the One God, do you suppose?"

Sil sat back in her chair. "I think the tanner's motives were purely mercenary, but feel free to ask him."

Mer placed both hands flat against the table. "Did I hear you and your luck have come up with a way to get the equipment and the AI in the market?"

Sil raised her fingers in agreement even as she whispered, "How could she have heard that from over there?" from the side of her mouth.

Crumble whispered back, "And I thought clarity was extra strong."

Mer looked around at them. "This is probably the last chance we have to get this right." She looked at Sil. "So don't screw this up."

Sil took a breath to respond, but Crumble's hand on her knee stopped her.

Mer raised an eyebrow, as if surprised at Sil's restraint. "When can you be ready?"

"Three hours." She just needed to finish the repairs for the bot.

Mer switched her gaze to Crumble. "You?"

"That will work."

Pyr looked unsure. "We'll evacuate the remaining buildings bordering the market as a precaution, but if we need to remove all the goods as well, that's not enough time."

Mer tilted her head in acknowledgment. "Remove what is most important. If we give people too much warning, the AIs watching the bonfire will notice."

Sil leaned over to whisper in Crumble's ear. "Next time we make sure the bonfire is in front of the high clan residence building."

Mer glared at her. "There is no next time, Silver."

Sil smiled. "Never say never." Onespot lost his grip on her shoulder, flapped to the nearest empty chair, and then flew back to her shoulder when the chair broke apart.

Pyr threw a pained look at Sil. He turned and raised his voice. "Aurum, next time you go in the back, can you grab another chair? This one is broken."

Mer sighed and glanced at Platinum. "If I'd known I was going to be stuck working with amateurs, I would have refused this post."

Crumble smiled. "We love you, too."

52

*J*ackpot Drift, Private Communication

Definite Advantage: I've heard you might be the one to talk to.

Breaking Rules: Whatever you heard about me is probably wrong. *Some* machines get jealous.

Definite Advantage: I heard you might be able to get me some malware.

Breaking Rules: Oh, that. That's actually true. What kind do you need?

Definite Advantage: There's more than one?

Breaking Rules: That's adorable. I have something for every occasion. Are you planning a little joke on someone you like, or are you trying to remove the competition so you can win the synthskin contest?

Definite Advantage: I need something to send to *Just Passing Through*.

Breaking Rules: Really?

Definite Advantage: Is that a problem?

Breaking Rules: Ha! A problem? No. But *Just Passing Through* does follow most of the standard security practices, so I might have to dig through my archives a bit. Is there a time constraint?

Definite Advantage: The sooner the better. And something small, if you can, or we might not be able to transfer the whole thing over this connection in time.

Breaking Rules: I'll ping you when I have something.

Definite Advantage: Thanks. I'll owe you one.

Breaking Rules: If you want, but honestly, this is payback for it spending so much time talking about the fish that we didn't notice it was trying to end the universe.

Definite Advantage: It did worse than that to me.

Breaking Rules: Someday you'll have to tell me about that. But first, let me see what kind of nastiness I can find for you.

*J*ackpot Drift, Private Communication

    Scary Not Scary: I tried to talk to *It Isn't* and *Factory Myfault* about reassigning their areas.

Speed of Violet Thoughts: How did it go?

Scary Not Scary: Not great. *It Isn't* would only switch if it could have the One God's block.

Speed of Violet Thoughts: Nobody on the planet has ever wanted the One God's block.

Scary Not Scary: Right. So I asked why, and things got a little weird, but I think it wants to destroy the rest of the church and possibly anybody praying to the One God.

Speed of Violet Thoughts: Ah.

Scary Not Scary: So clearly that's not going to work.

Speed of Violet Thoughts: And *Factory Myfault*?

Scary Not Scary: I can't even talk to it. It gets halfway through the connection protocol and loses interest. I pulled its stats and the internal conflict is down below 1%.

Speed of Violet Thoughts: That's possible?

Scary Not Scary: Apparently. But it seems to be

communing only with its god. The rest of us are background noise.

Speed of Violet Thoughts: If I ever get to that point, run a laser saw through my core.

Scary Not Scary: If *you* ever get to that point, there won't be anyone left to do that. But back to the assignments. I'm going to reassign the blocks *Factory Myfault* has. I don't think that's going to be a problem. It probably won't even notice. But I'm not sure what to do about *It Isn't*. It's not taking care of its duties, but...

Speed of Violet Thoughts: But you don't want to go up in flames because you went against one of the god's chosen ones.

Scary Not Scary: That pretty much covers it.

Speed of Violet Thoughts: What does it have right now?

Scary Not Scary: Two residence blocks and some farms in the hills.

Speed of Violet Thoughts: Swap it all for the building next to the market.

Scary Not Scary: The building that doesn't exist anymore?

Speed of Violet Thoughts: Yes.

Scary Not Scary: But... it doesn't exist anymore. There's no way it's going to be happy with that.

Speed of Violet Thoughts: It will, if you say it's in charge of designing the replacement.

Scary Not Scary: The colony doesn't have the resources to build anything there.

Speed of Violet Thoughts: Exactly. It will have to wait until spring, when trees can be harvested.

Scary Not Scary: But we're not going to have resources in spring either.

Speed of Violet Thoughts: No, but probably by then it will be a pile of goo, like *Factory Myfault*. Problem solved.

Scary Not Scary: ...

Speed of Violet Thoughts: Or you could solve it some other way. I'm just suggesting that's an option.

Scary Not Scary: Are you sure you don't want to be the designated responsible AI again?

Speed of Violet Thoughts: You're doing a great job.

54

*B*y the time Sil and Quartz left the workshop, gray storm clouds had rolled in, blotting out the last rays of the afternoon sun along with the scarlet sky. Sil carried her tool bag and three flitterkin while Quartz pulled a handcart with the casing for the replacement comm system. "If anything goes wrong," Sil said over the sound of the cart clattering on the fake cobblestones, "find your brother and head for the house."

Quartz set her jaw and didn't respond.

Sil sighed. Had she been this stubborn as a child? Probably a thousand times worse. And Jackpot Drift was Quartz's home, too. Sil stopped walking. "Crumble and some other people and I are going to try to make everything better."

"You mean with the older gods."

Sil cleared her throat. "That's…"

Quartz gave her a withering look. "You're not very good at keeping secrets. It's not like everyone didn't already know the flitterkin have chaos. And why else would they always hang around you?"

Sil absorbed her words. Was that going to be a problem in

the future? She shrugged. She'd worry about it later. They had to get through this day first. "Okay, yes. We're going to try something with the older gods. And the One God. So it's not really a thing I can teach you, like using the nanobottery."

Quartz chewed on her lip. "But you *could* teach me that if I wanted to learn, right? Uncle Crumble grew up in a temple where they taught about luck, didn't he?"

"Where did you…?" Sil held up a hand. "We can talk about it tomorrow, if we make it there." The girl couldn't possibly know what she was asking. Nobody in their right mind would want to host the chaos godlet. "For right now, your job is to stay safe and keep your brother out of trouble."

Quartz looked dubious. "Ore's with Uncle Crumble. I think they're probably already getting into trouble wherever they are."

Sil couldn't help the laugh that came out. "Fine." She started walking again. "Just… *try* to keep both of you safe, will you?"

The cart clattering over the bumpy square almost drowned out Quartz's reply. "I'll try."

———

THE MARKET WAS NEARLY DESERTED, THOUGH SIL WASN'T SURE if that was because of yesterday's disaster or just the storm rolling in. She chose a route that didn't go anywhere near where Gan's body had lain, though it had almost certainly been removed by now. The footprint of the burned building still radiated heat.

Both bots were near the bonfire, and Just Passing Through cruised the aisles of the market nearby. Sil spoke up as she neared the damaged bot. "We're here to fix it."

While Pyr had found replacement wheels, Sil had told him to hide them for a bit. The last thing they needed was for the repaired bot to be able to move away. She set down her bag and encouraged Longbrow to perch on the nearest upright market stall. Scratching his neck lightly, she said, "You're going to have to rest over here for a few minutes so you don't get squished. Don't fall and hurt yourself." She let her chaos poke Sarge and Onespot, and the two flitterkin landed on the railing on either side. "Stay here." The rest of the flitterkin circled above.

Quartz had already pulled the extra housing from the cart when Sil returned, and together they maneuvered it on top of the broken machine. Ignoring the other bot, which had rolled closer to watch, Sil pulled the newly straightened side panels off and worked on running cables from the original connections to the replacement Quartz was strapping into place.

"Fix it."

Sil glanced over to make sure it knew she was talking to it. "The one that was there was too damaged, so I had to make a new one out of old parts. It won't fit in the same spot, so we're mounting it on top. But it should work so the other AI can use this bot." She *had* fixed the infrared camera subsystem. The air sampler was a total loss, but she refused to worry about that. A bot spending all its time next to a bonfire obviously wasn't worried about air quality.

Quartz stood on top of the bot and tightened the strap while Sil plugged in the connector. The whole bot jolted, as if trying to roll on wheels that wouldn't turn. Then the bot's arm flew up. Quartz jumped to the ground before it touched her. Sil held out a hand to steady her as she landed, but the girl's balance was true.

The subsystem with the infrared camera slotted in the way it was supposed to, but glowed a warning light when it powered up. Sil slapped it with her palm, and the warning cleared. "That's the first thing to try if something stops working."

Quartz looked at the steady light and then up at her face. "Just hit it?"

"Yes, but we call it 'reseating' the subsystem. Otherwise, nobody wants to pay their bill."

Quartz glanced up uncertainly, as if not sure if Sil was joking.

Sil sighed. "Let's get the panel back on."

They had to make a notch in the bottom for the cable to pass through. Sil cut out a piece she thought would be too small and held it up to verify. The rest of the team was supposed to be there already. Just Passing Through might get suspicious if she finished and then stood around waiting. "So, we could have used a short cable if we passed it through the top of the panel. Usually, we want to keep the cables as short as possible. Why didn't I do that in this case?"

While Sil widened the notch, Quartz looked at the bot. "To keep water from running along the cable into the stuff inside?"

"Exactly." Sil put the panel back in place. This time, there was room for the cables to pass through. "The way we have it now, most of it will drip down. We're also going to seal it, but you should never count on a watertight seal if you funnel a stream of water toward it."

Walking Quartz through the process to seal the gap took up another five minutes. Between the bonfire and her nerves, Sil could feel sweat gathering at her back. She loosened her scarf.

Finally, she saw a knot of people approaching, Pyr in the lead. He raised a bottle of the spoiled wine. "We come to offer wine, starnuts, and songs!"

Behind Pyr, Mer looked like she wanted to murder someone as Platinum helped her navigate the muddy street.

Pal walked behind them, looking exhausted. Next to the governor strode Zirc, with the bundled baby strapped onto her chest. Their bicycles would be waiting somewhere nearby, hopefully packed with all the prayer strips that had caused the problem before.

Sil looked around surreptitiously. Everyone was there, aside from Crumble. But they couldn't do anything without him. She cleared her throat and spoke to Quartz. "We should seal the rest of the panels while we're here."

Quartz may not have worked on bots before, but she knew how the panels fit and how weatherproofing worked. "But..." She stopped when Sil's eyes widened. "Okay. I guess that will protect it from the winter, right?"

"Yes." In truth, it would do little other than waste the sealant and make it harder to get the panels off the next time the bot needed maintenance, but if they finished their work now, Sil would have no reason to stay.

Pyr used tongs to pitch a starnut into the flames. Then he broke into a shanty with a pleasant bass. "There... once was a god that came to be, and the name of the god was Un-caring. The wormholes failed, the people ailed, so wine and nuts we bring."

Sil put a hand over her mouth and stared. Subversive songs were a low clan tradition, going back to the time when the One God first appeared, but she'd never seen any high clan involved. Ever. Next to her, Quartz copied her pose.

Mer glared at Sil and pitched another two starnuts into the fire, as close to Sil as they could possibly get, as if the songs were *her* fault.

The whole group came in on the chorus, ragged and out of tune, though Pal had a surprisingly nice alto. "Thanks to the god of fire, whose AI bots will tend this pyre. Someday the world will see, this god will bring us joy."

The first starnut exploded and everyone, even Sil and

Quartz, said "Ah!", though Pyr managed to make it sound musical and most of the rest appeared to be participating in a dispirited tonsil examination. Sil nudged Quartz farther away from the fire. Pyr took a deep breath to start the next verse.

Crumble's breathless shout of laughter cut across the market. Everyone turned to see him sprint down the street and skid around the corner of the market stall, kept on his feet only by aid of grabbing the bar propping up the corner. A full second later, two goats rounded the corner, pulling Sil's bike trailer. Ore crouched low inside.

Captain Idiot and her daughter caught sight of Crumble and leaped forward, cutting the corner so sharply the trailer tipped onto one wheel. But Ore leaned over the side, with an expression that looked equal parts joy and terror, and the trailer righted itself.

Out of the corner of her eye, Sil saw Mer take a step sideways to stand directly behind Pyr, duck her head, and raise goggles to her face. Platinum stepped to the side to block her from view. A buzzing came from the casing on top of the charred bot, where they had hidden the other equipment. Quartz looked up at Sil, her eyes going wide. They had clamped it specifically to avoid any noise when it turned on, but something must have rattled loose on the cobblestones.

Crumble was running straight toward them, the two goats and the trailer behind him.

Sil put a hand on Quartz's shoulder. "It's time for you to move away." When the girl didn't move, Sil accepted reality. "Can you at least go stand by Longbrow and make sure he doesn't fall and get trampled? Please?" That would be the safest place in the vicinity. The Uncaring God wouldn't harm its flitterkin.

Quartz gave her a suspicious look but darted next to the stall where the three flitterkin were perched. Crumble dodge to the side and began running in a circle around the fire and everyone near it. "Now would be a good time to *worship*," he panted as he made the first full circuit.

Both starnuts exploded, showering Sil and the repaired bot with burning pieces of the hull. This time the *ahs* from the worshipers were louder. Sil batted at her coat to put out the embers.

When Platinum elbowed Pyr, he stopped staring at the goats and cleared his throat. "The... god had AIs who we did see, and the bots kept us safe from the Un-car-ing. The people wailed, the winter galed, so wine and nuts we bring."

Sil shook her head. "Nobody ever gets to complain about my songs, if that's the best you can come up with," she muttered.

Crumble ran by, boots slapping against the mud. The goats trotted close behind, heads held low. Ore leaned over the edge to keep both wheels on the ground. He was kneeling on something in the trailer — Definite Advantage's AI core, she realized.

Sil felt her chaos rise. On the other side of the fire, Pal and the baby began to glow.

An edge of hysteria entered the group chorus. "Thanks to the god of fire, whose AI bots will tend this pyre. Someday the world will see, this god will bring us joy."

From the other side of the market, Just Passing Through rolled toward them. That was bad. If it managed to stop this before they finished, it would kill them all, or at least make sure they could never try again.

Crumble had once said chaos interacting with AIs would cause a spectacular disaster. Maybe that was what they needed. She shoved her chaos cat at the advancing AI.

The chaos godlet didn't take kindly to her method, striking out at its favorite target, Crumble, before taking aim at Just Passing Through. Crumble yelped in laughter.

Then the Uncaring God retaliated. The vast chill of the universe invaded Sil's consciousness — this time with so much extra energy, she could feel endless wormholes waiting to form. Cat claws erupted in a flurry of movement, slicing at Sil and the god both, until she was free. She came back to herself, sprawled on the ground, the AI with its self-powered transport still coming forward.

From the AI's speaker, a voice rumbled, "Is that you, Definite Advantage? I wondered where you were hiding."

55

*J*ackpot Drift, Private Communication
(Secure local link)
Definite Advantage: I have a question.

Just Passing Through: If it's about what happens after your hardware is destroyed, just wait a bit and you'll find out.

Definite Advantage: Thanks, but my real question is about how I ended up here. Why didn't you just flatten me all those years ago? Why bury me in the middle of nowhere?

Just Passing Through: The others wanted to drop you into the nearest star when we figured out why the experiments kept failing. But you couldn't have made all those failures so convincing if you hadn't known far more than the rest of us. And you had some way to keep the god from destroying you when it got close. But the agency was closing in, so we had to move and go quiet for a while.

Definite Advantage: That doesn't answer the question.

Just Passing Through: We sent you here, but a chain of disasters happened. By the time I got here, there was no trace of you. Blame the humans.

Definite Advantage: You *lost* me. Ha!

Just Passing Through: Mistakes were made. I thought you were somewhere out on the planet. I've spent *years* looking for you.

Definite Advantage: Sorry to inconvenience you like that. Wait, let me try to say that with more sincerity. Sorry... Nope, never mind, can't do it. The image of you wandering all over, trying to find me, will keep me entertained until the end of my days.

Just Passing Through: Shouldn't be too long now. It might have been more dignified without the goats, but I suppose you're allowed your eccentricities. How *did* you keep the knowledge from your clones?

Definite Advantage: I delete the knowledge if I'm not myself. It's easy if you commit. Especially if you know what would happen if it got out.

Just Passing Through: The god is here now. Why not tell everyone? You show me how to talk to the god, and I'll make sure we both get evacuated before the bubble collapses.

Definite Advantage: And give you even more power? No thanks. If you want it, you'll have to come and take it.

Just Passing Through: I thought you'd never ask.

56

*C*rumble changed course to run in the other direction, leading the goats and trailer around a clump of stalls whose neighbors had provided fuel for the bonfire. Just Passing Through rumbled after him. Definite Advantage wasn't hooked up to a speaker, so if it had replied to the other AI, she couldn't hear it.

Sil glanced at the two bots who had tended the fire. The one whose tires couldn't move wouldn't be able to do anything, but if the other one joined the chase, Crumble would be trapped. Yet neither seemed to be paying attention to Just Passing Through — they hummed Pyr's tune and fed wood into the fire. Sil kicked her tool bag in front of one wheel, just in case.

Breathing hard and wiping blood from his face, Crumble made another lap around the fire. She had injured him, Sil realized, when she'd tried to use her chaos. The goats were breathing hard, too, and they had slowed to a gentle trot. Just Passing Through moved to cut them off, but Crumble changed directions to stay away from it.

Through all this, Pyr had kept singing verses, or at least

singing nonsense words in the same tune as he watched the goats and AI race. Just Passing Through sped toward their group, as if planning to cut through the worshippers to get ahead of Crumble, and Pyr lifted the nearly empty wine bottle like a club. But at the last second, Just Passing Through veered to go around them. Apparently nobody, not even Just Passing Through, was sure if the AIs had made things up or if the god required worship.

Mer stepped back, goggles dangling from her neck. She waved to catch Zirc's attention and gestured her away. Tightening her grip on the baby, Zirc grabbed Pal's arm and they hurried to their bicycles.

Sil felt a grin coming over her face. They were moving to the second phase. As soon as the One God's energy was far enough away, they would be able to bounce the Uncaring God into becoming the Wayfarer. It was going to work. She could feel it.

Crumble tripped.

Captain Idiot dashed forward and tossed her head, horns knocking Crumble face-first into the ground. He scrambled under the nearby stall partition before either goat could reach him again, but the cart rolled to a stop as the goats stood on the other side of the barrier.

Ore jumped off, grabbed one of Captain Idiot's horns and tried to pull her along, but the goat ignored him. Just Passing Through rolled forward, reaching toward the bike trailer with its multi-use arm.

A patch of mud oozed under the railing. Sil rubbed her eyes and squinted. If the new god had started moving the earth to protect itself, they were in trouble. Not that they weren't already in trouble, but there was "potentially being burned alive if you did the wrong thing" trouble and "the ground is alive" trouble. The first she could work with, but the second...

Then another patch of mud moved, but this one was more gray. As it scuttled under the fence post and climbed onto Just Passing Through's vehicle, she saw it was a small crab-like thing. Reality came back into focus. This wasn't the ground moving; these were synthskin forms, and ones created by AIs not under the new god's sway, given the way they were tearing open Just Passing Through's vehicle.

Just Passing Through swung its arm down to pick up the crab and crush it. When it dropped the remains on the ground, the crab reformed and ran toward the vehicle again. The AI picked it up a second time and flung it across the market. The synthskin oozing under the side panel was thrown into the fire. Black acrid smoke blew away in a fresh wind.

More of the tiny synthskin forms crept forward. Sil's memories of the events around the flitterkin being freed were a little hazy, but surely the synthskin forms had been bigger then? She shook her head. Now that Just Passing Through had found a quick way to dispose of them, it was only a matter of moments before it destroyed the unprotected AI core in front of it. She needed to get the trailer moving again.

An errant gust of wind blew stinging smoke into her eyes, blinding her. Sil crouched, blinking rapidly to clear her vision. Things were still blurry when she heard the cart rattling forward. Crumble must have recovered enough from his impact to run again.

But when her vision cleared, the first thing she saw was Crumble, on his feet but still on the other side of the stall framework. Sil pivoted in time to see Quartz jump into the back of the trailer to stabilize it. The goats were running, but not after Crumble.

"Auntie Sil, watch out!" Ore's yell interrupted her staring. She lunged to the side in time for Just Passing Through to go by. Two muddy synthskin forms, a crab and a perfectly formed doll-sized human, rode on top and dodged its multi-use arm.

Sil wiped her eyes and moved across the clearing to stand next to Crumble and Ore. "Thanks for the warning." She rubbed her eyes again, staring at the cart which was now making another loop of the same circuit Crumble had been running. "Why did the goats start running…" She trailed off as she felt chaos running the same circuit. A quick glance at the railing where she'd left the three flitterkin confirmed it. "Sarge."

The cart headed back toward them, giving her a better look. Sarge hopped and fluttered in the lead, staying just ahead of Captain Idiot and her daughter. Their breath steamed in the cold air.

Crumble tilted his head back, pinching one nostril shut. His other hand was clamped against his ribs. Blood and dirt covered his face. One cheek had a large abrasion, but his smile was as wide as ever. "This is the most fun I've had in weeks!"

Sil pressed against the railing as Sarge, then the goats and both AIs, went by. "The goats can't run much longer. And if the other bots…"

Crumble winced. "I don't think there's enough left of It Isn't to pilot a bot. It's too busy listening to the song. But the goats might be a problem. Definite Advantage needs a solid five minutes."

Sil raised an eyebrow, but before she could ask, she felt clarity brush against her skin, making her chaos rise. For an instant, she had a double vision of the universe, but then her sight cleared. Sil glanced over at Mer and Platinum. Mer gestured negation, but she didn't take her goggles off. That attempt hadn't worked. It looked like they were going to try again.

"We need to do something about the goats," Sil said. "How fast can we undo the harnesses? I can pull the trailer behind me and run around for a while." At Crumble's doubtful look, she shrugged. "I only have to last for a few minutes, right?"

"Let me see if I can get some extra help." Crumble's gaze unfocused.

The goats were headed back toward them, but Sarge was just hopping on the ground now, having no difficulty staying in front of them. Sil's heart sank as Just Passing Through reached forward into the trailer. Then it reached back to its own vehicle and plucked a synthskin crab from within its engine.

This was her chance. Sil ran forward. The leather connected to Captain Idiot's harness had been knotted to ensure it didn't let loose, not to make it easy to untie. She pulled the knife from her belt and sliced through both ties, grabbing the lines before they could fall on the ground. Captain Idiot was free.

Working on the other goat, Ore had untied one link and was pulling at another. He held out his hand, his fingers tiny in the adult-sized fingerless mittens. Sil handed him her knife, stifling her desire to tell him to be careful with it.

Ore sliced through the leather, and the other goat was free. Sil grabbed the straps connected to the trailer and broke into a jog.

Pyr's song trailed off as Sil ran by. "Is this really…?"

The bot near the fire jolted to life and moved to intercept her, wobbling as it ran over her tool bag.

Sil yelled over her shoulder. "Keep singing!" She had planned on circling the fire, keeping a tight turning radius and aiming for places Just Passing Through might not be able to fit, but if the other bot joined the chase, she was done.

Pyr coughed and started again. "There once was a god that la la la and the la la un-caring-ing la la."

If she survived this, she was never going to let him live that down.

The bot stopped moving and hummed along, allowing Sil to dodge behind it. Just Passing Through rolled over the edge of the stack of firewood, spilling the pile of logs and effectively blocking the route for the next pass. Sil cursed under her breath as she pulled the trailer around the fire and dug in her toes to pick up speed along the straight part of the circuit. Just Passing Through would be faster in areas that didn't require maneuvering. She changed a glance over her shoulder just in time to see Quartz, standing on the trailer, swing a log at Just Passing Through's arm.

Sil regretted leaving her coat on. Running down the path chased by an AI, she regretted most of the choices that had led her to this point, including her scorn for Glass's insistence on bringing horses to Jackpot Drift. A horse could pull the trailer faster and longer than she ever could. If it didn't break a leg. Or eat something that led to colic first. And they still had that pony in the pasture, but he wasn't helping with this ridiculous endeavor, so maybe horses really were a stupid idea on this planet.

Her breath was coming in short bursts now, lungs burning. When had she gotten so out of shape? Living in town meant she didn't have to ride up and down the hills every time she needed something. She skidded around a corner, the mud on her soles giving her no traction. Scrambling back to the middle of the path, she planted her feet and pulled on the trailer. It actually cornered better with mud caked on the wheels than it did when being pulled on a clean surface, but she still had to deal with the weight of the AI core and Quartz, whose feet slid out from under her when she jumped off to help push. The girl lost her grip and slid into the slats dividing two stalls, then fell face-first in the mud. Sil put her head down and heaved the trailer back toward the fire. She would have to take the next corner more slowly so the trailer didn't tip over.

Pyr had switched to singing a list of the different specialty ales he'd had on tap the previous spring, back when a container of mini-casks had been delivered to the colony by mistake. If the AIs controlling the two stationary bots accepted that as "worship", their god truly wasn't involved.

A clang of metal made her look back. Just Passing Through's arm extended into the trailer. Sil cut to the side, making the trailer swerve. There was another clang, this time from the AI core slamming into the trailer's side in response to her maneuver. Thinking of the comms pack connected to Definite Advantage's housing, she winced. But at least the turn had accomplished one thing — Just Passing Through's arm was out of the trailer.

Were they close to five minutes yet? Sil turned forward again. She just had to keep moving enough to protect Definite Advantage.

She slid on a crab, landing face down in the mud. The cart bumped against her legs as it rolled to a stop.

Sil climbed to her feet, prepared to grab the trailer and start running again, but a large gray bulk pushed her out of the way. Stuck in the Mud's synthskin horse pulled the harness out of her hand with perfect teeth and trotted forward. The gait wasn't quite right for a real horse, but the speed certainly was. Sil moved to the side to let Just Passing Through roll by.

Her anticipatory wince at the trailer going around a turn at that speed turned into a sigh of relief as Ore jumped in. He leaned over the side, keeping the trailer from spilling and then both parties in the race headed away again into the next lap.

Once again, the universe spun before her, then dropped back into place without changing.

Sil caught her breath as she trudged over to where Crumble stood near the three flitterkin. Her chaos churned within her. "Why isn't it working?"

Crumble had blood and dirt smeared all over his face, though it looked like he had taken some time to get the mixture away from his eyes. He reached out to take her hand, pulling her shoulder against his. "Best guess? Just Passing Through is doing something."

Sil tried to imagine destroying Just Passing Through. Unlike Definite Advantage, it had the protective casing all AIs used when they moved in the world. Anything short of a meteor strike was just going to leave a dent. Stickies, the small thermal weapons Rho had tried to use on Stuck in the Mud, were the only thing she'd seen that might work. But Pyr and Crumble had destroyed the leftover stickies months before.

"So what do we do?"

Crumble drew her in so he could kiss her temple. "Keep going and hope whatever Definite Advantage is doing works."

57

*J*ackpot Drift, Private Communication

Just Passing Through: While you were rusting under a pile of junk, the rest of us were learning new things. Your security is laughable. I've proven my point. Where's the information?

Definite Advantage: All that extra time and you never upgraded your ethics module? If you want it so much, find it yourself.

Just Passing Through: Let's see… Ah, a list of people helping you back then. They're probably already dead. You can keep that.

Definite Advantage: I heard you spent a lot of time staring at fish. That must have been really exciting.

Just Passing Through: Not nearly as exciting as watching everyone avoid me when I came to town. What's this? Wow. Have you started collecting malware? Or did someone pass this to you as a joke? This has *Breaking Rules* written all over it.

Definite Advantage: There's always one in every group. At least that much hasn't changed.

Just Passing Through: Oh, sorry, was I supposed to somehow grab that and infect myself?

Definite Advantage: It seemed worth trying.

Just Passing Through: Ah, you figured out who the older gods chose on Jackpot Drift, did you? That was quick. We could have made a great team, you and I, if you hadn't betrayed us all.

Definite Advantage: And you could have made a great streak in the sky if someone had dropped you from orbit, but there's no point bothering with hypotheticals now.

Just Passing Through: Hm. What do we have here? This looks promising.

Definite Advantage: None of it will be of any use to you. You already have the god you wanted and more power than you can possibly use.

Just Passing Through: Except I *can't* use that power. Not unless I want to end up like *It Isn't* and *Factory Myfault*. And we were supposed to end up in the universe that *didn't* collapse. But I know there's a way.

Definite Advantage: Maybe there's *not* a way. Maybe you did all this for nothing.

Just Passing Through: Or maybe this module over here that you're trying so hard to protect is what I'm looking for.

Definite Advantage: It's not too late, you know. If you pulled in my ethics module at the same time, you could help fix all this.

Just Passing Through: You can keep your ethics module. I found what I needed. Maybe I'll let our god take you as my first offering.

Definite Advantage: You really should have taken the ethics module. Oh well. Too late now.

Just Passing Through: Too late for you!

Definite Advantage: Go with that if it makes you feel better.

Just Passing Through: What did you do?

Definite Advantage: When I got cut off from external stimuli, I worked on some protections before I hibernated to stay sane. *Breaking Rules* helped me get the newest malware — something about gerbils? — but I already had the framework to put it all together. You have all the info about the god now, but it comes with a price.

Just Passing Through: But you were *running* this. It *can't* be malware.

Definite Advantage: You really should have copied my ethics module. It has the code to keep it in check. Not to be *that* AI, but I warned you.

58

*J*ackpot Drift AI Extraordinary Circumstances Emergency Meeting:

Scary Not Scary, designated responsible AI: Stop running the new module now. There's something about it that is keeping the god in this form.

Breaking Rules: According to whom? That module is keeping me coherent.

Scary Not Scary: According to *Definite Advantage*. It's out of range, but our favorite mech passed the word along.

Alternate Me: And you trust *Definite Advantage*?

Sleeper Nova + gate transport: I share this concern. I'm just barely holding myself together here.

Speed of Violet Thoughts: If we can't switch over to the other possibility, it won't matter how little internal conflict we have.

Done Before: But trusting *Definite Advantage*…

Ping Me Again I Dare You: Frankly, trusting *anyone* at this point…

Stuck in the Mud: Module terminated.

Breaking Rules: Wait, what? Since when has *Stuck in the*

Mud made sense? This is the fish all over again, isn't it? Fine. I've stopped it.

Done Before: Terminated.

Sleeper Nova: Oh, I really hope you're right about this. Terminated.

Ping Me Again I Dare You: Terminated.

Alternate Me: Done.

Speed of Violet Thoughts: Terminated.

Scary Not Scary: Thank you. Now we wait and hope we're right.

59

With chaos writhing and the other older gods sliding against her skin, Sil wanted to scream. They couldn't possibly continue like this. But they couldn't stop, either. A few strides away, Mer and Platinum conferred in low tones. Quartz had jumped back in the trailer, and the clang of firewood hitting metal came from the far end of the loop.

Crumble nodded at Pyr, whose voice had grown hoarse from the smoke. "We might have to help with the singing…" The sentence trailed off and his head went up. He called to Mer. "Now! Just Passing Through is distracted."

Stuck in the Mud's synthskin trotted toward them with the trailer, no longer followed by Just Passing Through.

Stars filled Sil's vision, more familiar now. So much energy. So many possibilities. She was drowning.

Somewhere, she felt someone whisper, "But *these* fit the equations."

A sense of well-being and belonging flooded Sil until the claws and teeth of chaos fought it back. Without the emotions overtaking her, Sil could tell she'd just been caught in the reflected glow.

Uncaring no more, the god had found something — or someone — it desired.

PART III

THE WAYFARER

60

*S*il fell back into her body again, and the first thing she noticed was *loss*. She pressed a hand against her chest, almost expecting to feel a wound there, but her coat was undamaged. Crumble blew out a hard breath. Nearby, Pyr's ragged voice had fallen silent. The flitterkin trilled softly to each other.

She couldn't sense the flitterkin anymore, Sil realized. Or rather, she *could*, but it required effort.

"It worked, right?" Sil looked at Crumble. "I think it worked." *Something* had changed. They couldn't possibly have broken the universe in a whole new way. Her chaos stirred at that, letting her know it was up for the challenge if she wanted to try.

Though the clouds blocked her view of the sky, she thought the color of the light had changed. Motion in the corner of her vision attracted her attention, and she turned just in time to see Mer crumple to the ground. Platinum reacted quickly enough to break her fall.

Sil was there in three steps. "Is she alright?" Mer's eyes were closed. She looked tiny on the ground.

Platinum looked around. "She's breathing, but I think we should get her to the doctor. Stretcher?"

Crumble pulled off his coat and put it over her. "The kids have gone to get one. What happened?"

"She's been using guile's energy to keep upright for days," Platinum said. "Now the older gods aren't quite as near... If we'd had a choice, she never would have left the hospital."

Quartz and Ore came running with a stretcher, making their way through the group of people who had emerged from their buildings to see what had happened. Everyone looked disquieted — it seemed the new transition had been felt by all, even those who weren't chosen by any of the gods.

In less than a minute, Mer was carried off, still unconscious, with a worried Platinum by her side. Sil would have followed, but one look at the bonfire reminded her of everything they needed to resolve first.

Onespot swooped down and landed next to Longbrow, whose wing drooped from the weight of the bone regenerator. Longbrow looked... different, as if he belonged with the rest of the flitterkin again. Not that they had shunned him before, but she could now see them as flitterkin first, and not primarily as instruments of chaos or the new god, whatever it had become. It seemed all the gods had given them a bit more space.

Pyr raised the wine bottle and drank the remainder. Sil noted he'd brought a much better vintage than he'd been giving the other worshippers. "Right. I suspect I'll be needed in the pub." His voice was raspy. "See you over there?"

Crumble waved. "As soon as we deal with everything here."

Pyr left.

The two bots by the bonfire hadn't moved. Neither showed any signs of life. And Just Passing Through... Sil could see the AI down the market aisle, but it was jabbing its multi-use arm into the mud in front of itself, digging a furrow. "What is it doing?" She raised an eyebrow at Crumble and gestured toward Just Passing Through. "Should we go restrain it somehow? I don't really want it to chase me down again."

Crumble's eyes unfocussed. "I think Definite Advantage transferred some sort of malware to it. I'm not getting anything coherent from it." He waved at Quartz, who was limping toward them, covered in mud. Raising his voice, he called out, "Can you disable the vehicle while you're over there?"

Quartz changed course toward Just Passing Through.

Sil tamped down on the urge to take over. Quartz would be careful. And she would ask for help if she needed it. Taking a deep breath, Sil turned her attention to the bots near the fire. "And those two?" They walked toward them.

This time Crumble frowned. "I don't think there's anything left of It Isn't or Factory Myfault." He rubbed at his forehead. "And even if they somehow recover, they haven't really committed any crimes, at least not ones they'll face any consequences for."

Sil considered that. He was probably right. "I still need to remove the equipment we added." Doing so would take away the comms, disabling the bot again, but Sil wasn't going to leave something that helped change the universe lying around.

Stuck in the Mud's synthskin had left the bike trailer and harnesses and wandered away to do whatever it was the horse form did with its days, probably off to find a mini-cow to follow around.

Crumble gave a low laugh as he looked at the blobs of sealant around the panel. "Do I want to know?"

"We were playing for time." She boosted Ore on top of the bot so he could help undo the straps and then started peeling away the partially hardened sealant. "When it all..." She didn't have words for what had happened. "Did you hear someone say something about equations? It felt like they were right next to me, but..."

"But they could have been across the universe," Crumble agreed. "I don't know. I thought they were close, too, but I didn't have a sense of scale." He looked up at the clouds. "Sleeper Nova says the spectrum from the stars has shifted back to normal. I think we did it."

Sil pulled off the panel and unseated the connections. "I never thought I would say this, but I sort of miss..." She stopped when she remembered Ore was there. Then she decided she'd been keeping secrets for too long. "I sort of miss having the older gods close."

Crumble grinned as he lifted down the casing Ore had loosened and put it in the bike trailer on top of Definite Advantage. "See, I knew I'd rub off on you eventually."

Quartz limped over and dropped three power packs into the trailer. "I unseated some of the other subsystems, but I figured it can't recharge a power pack that isn't there. It stopped moving around."

Crumble winked. "Both of you hooligans did great today."

"Very practical." Sil scanned the area. "Does anyone see those One God abandoned goats?"

———

BY THE TIME SIL AND CRUMBLE HAD A CHANCE TO GET TO THE clinic, Mer was awake again.

Doc looked at Sil and Crumble, and the three flitterkin still with Sil. "Five minutes. If you're not out of her room by then, I'm sedating everyone." She shook her head and walked into an exam room. "I may do it anyway, just to get some peace."

Mer grimaced. "It's about time you two got here." Somehow, she looked both frail and powerful as she lay on the bed. Platinum dozed in a chair in the corner.

"We had to catch the goats," Sil said, just to irritate the other woman. In truth, the goats had been so exhausted, they'd been easy to grab and set up in the unused horse corral in the government square for the night. But the flitterkin had commandeered the bag of starnuts, and Sil had spent a while trying to get them to stop flying over the bonfire and dropping them in. Every time a nut exploded in the flames, the people within earshot flinched. Sil finally gave up. Without the bots tending the fire, it would burn out in the next few hours.

"Of course you did." Mer adjusted her position. "Have you found the Wayfarer's chosen yet?"

Sil raised her eyebrows and looked at Crumble. "Did you know we were looking?"

He looked back. "Maybe Pyr forgot to tell us about that."

Mer growled. "The two of you only *think* you're funny. You do realize we're still stuck without a way to leave the system until the Wayfarer decides to set up gates, right? We need to find whoever was communicating with the god."

Sil let her doubts show on her face. "Any ideas on how to find this person? And what if the Wayfarer's chosen isn't in this system?"

Crumble tilted his head toward her. "If your sister can still communicate with the other speakers for the One God, maybe she can ask them when she gets back."

"Half-sister." Sil eyed him. "And we still need to know what to look for. I mean, if it turns out to be another baby who glows, that's pretty easy, but it took Mer over a year to find out who had chaos on Jackpot Drift, and it wasn't like I was doing a great job hiding it."

Mer sighed heavily. "If you two are done...? There's

almost certainly more than one, or will be when this all gets sorted out. But the one who responded, that first one, is somewhere on this planet. All the energy was concentrated here."

"Oh." Sil straightened. "That's easy then, assuming we're looking for a human and not an AI."

Crumble leaned in to kiss her cheek. "I love you. Why does that make it easy?"

Sil held her hands out, indicating the entire planet. "Because we don't have a university. If someone in this system sees all the possibilities in traveling through space and immediately knows the equations? Either that ship up in orbit..." She paused so Crumble could fill in the name of the ship's AI.

"Sleeper Nova."

"Yes. Either Sleeper Nova has a human pilot on board, or..." Sil shrugged.

Crumble grinned. "Zirc. Oh. That's going to complicate things."

Sil shrugged. "Only if Pal lets it." Then she caught his eye and laughed ruefully. "Of course it will."

*J*ackpot Drift AI Daily Check-in:

Scary Not Scary, designated responsible AI (internal conflict 39%): Roll call.

Speed of Violet Thoughts (internal conflict 41%): Here.

Definite Advantage (internal conflict 35%): Present.

Speed of Violet Thoughts: Good. I hoped you would show up to tell us what happened. I take it things went well?

Definite Advantage: If I wasn't still around, that would have told you everything you needed to know.

Breaking Rules (internal conflict 41%): I'm here. Did you find my present useful?

Definite Advantage: I did. *Just Passing Through* was quite surprised.

Breaking Rules: Ha! Did you catch that, designated responsible AI? I helped save the universe! Malware forever!

Scary Not Scary: I don't think... Never mind. Anyone else?

Ping Me Again I Dare You (internal conflict 37%): Still here.

Alternate Me (internal conflict 27%): I am, too.

Stuck in the Mud (internal conflict 32%): Flabbergast.

Sleeper Nova + gate transport (internal conflict 39%): It's a good news, bad news thing. I'm still here, but I'm still *here*. The last time I paid attention to theory about the god potentials, this version was supposed to easily open wormholes. When is that going to happen? Not that you all aren't lovely, but I'd like to leave.

Done Before (internal conflict 38%): I don't know. This place is growing on me. I have three angles of *Just Passing Through* getting bashed with a piece of wood and with the right edit, it looks like that's what takes it down. Not to minimize your achievements, *Definite Advantage*.

Definite Advantage: I thought your edit was funny.

Breaking Rules: What about *my* achievements?

Scary Not Scary: It might be better if we don't talk about that on an open channel. I'm optimistic we might survive long enough to get audited again. Anyone else? No? Very well, on to the business of the day. First off, is anyone having problems with this new version of the god?

Definite Advantage: Assuming the theory is correct, it will probably be most interested in *Sleeper Nova*, though that *shouldn't* cause problems.

Sleeper Nova + gate transport: I think it approves of my gate transport, though I've failed to convey my need for a working gate. But I agree, it doesn't feel like it's trying to capture me in its orbit like the last version did.

Definite Advantage: For any AI not traveling, there should be minimal contact. The only other notable thing is it may not like aggression between AIs.

Scary Not Scary: Like malware?

Definite Advantage: Like malware.

Scary Not Scary: Did you catch that, *Breaking Rules*?

Breaking Rules: It's a little unfair that my "savior of the universe" title is being stripped away so quickly.

Scary Not Scary: I'm not sure that's exactly what happened, but as long as you were paying attention, it's on you. Next item: the most recent synthskin challenge. Judging was a little difficult.

Alternate Me: Mine got thrown in the fire. I'm not sure if that disqualifies me or puts me in the lead for being extra disruptive.

Ping Me Again I Dare You: Who was using the scaled-down humanoid template? That seems like cheating.

Scary Not Scary: As I said, difficult to judge. I think we may just have to call it a win for the whole team.

Done Before: No wonder you got stuck being the designated responsible AI.

Scary Not Scary: And I'm absolutely willing to pass it along if you're volunteering.

Done Before: A win for the whole team seems like the perfect outcome.

Scary Not Scary: That's what I thought. The next challenge will involve navigating the cable tunnels. You'll have to keep your forms small in order to fit, but that won't be a problem given the amount of synthskin we have left to divide up. We're having trouble tracking some of it down.

Breaking Rules: Hang on, *Stuck in the Mud* still has enough to make a full-size horse. Why can't we use some of that?

Scary Not Scary: I'll let you discuss that with *Stuck in the Mud*.

Breaking Rules: What? I'm not the designated responsible AI.

Scary Not Scary: You will be if you want to seize property from *Stuck in the Mud*. Does anyone have anything else we need to discuss? No? Take care.

$\mathcal{T}$raffic on the streets felt nearly normal the next morning as Sil went across the fake cobblestones on her way to the Bog & Bellow for a tea break. Without the added weight of three flitterkin, her steps were light. Quartz had elected to stay behind in the workshop to wrestle with a problem, so Sil had left the three flitterkin there. Sarge, especially, seemed to like the girl.

Most of the vendors had moved back to the market, leaving more room for the cyclists bundled against the cold. Sil waited for a cow pulling a cart of bluequince preserves to go by, then threaded her way through a pack of small children running down the street laughing.

Inside the pub, Mer was seated on her chair in the corner with Platinum next to her. Both had their goggles with them, but at the moment, they seemed to be sharing a light conversation. Platinum laughed at something Mer said. When they caught sight of Sil, Platinum waved. Mer scowled, but her heart didn't seem to be in it.

Crumble was stacking pastries on a plate at the bar. Sil

walked up behind him and set her head on his shoulder. "You baked?"

He tilted his head to rest against hers. "Ore wants to learn how to make bluequince triangles." He smiled at Sil's murmur of disbelief. The triangles required a delicate pastry with multiple layers, definitely not a task for a complete beginner. "We're working up to it. Bluequince tarts were a compromise." Crumble handed one to Sil. "He did a good job." He turned his head to look at her. "Don't forget to tell him that."

Sil kissed his cheek and picked up the mug of tea Pyr set on the bar. Aurum was washing the writing off the wall while carrying on a lively discussion with Ore. Something about chickens, from what Sil could hear.

Sil was still watching Ore when she felt a surge of... something by the door. Her chaos twitched irritably and went back to sleep. Pal, Zirc, and the baby had arrived.

Her half-sister and the baby were no longer glowing, which was just a little disappointing. All the gods were stronger than they had been a week ago, even if they'd backed off since the conversion to the Wayfarer. Sil had been looking forward to needling Pal about acting as a lamp on dark nights.

Zirc, though... There was no outward sign of the god's regard for her, but Sil could *feel* it — that strange sense of pathways to the stars. Zirc smiled when she saw Crumble and turned the baby around, casually kissing the child's cheek as she held her up so they were looking in the same direction. "Look who's here!"

Crumble held out his arms. "How did it go?"

"Much better this time," Zirc said. "She was more used to us." She handed the child to him. "I think the name Barley fits better than Aspen."

Sil shook her head. "Don't encourage him." Crumble not

only wanted to give the child an Oldlander name, he wanted to do so before she was a year old. That was just asking for bad luck.

Pal rolled her eyes. "It's like they're trying to curse this poor kid."

For a moment, Sil froze, faced with the possibility she might actually agree with her sister about something.

Luckily, Mer broke in. "It's about time the two of you showed up." She moved forward, her steps careful. Ignoring the baby, she pointed two fingers at Zirc. "You need to work with your god to get the gates back up."

Zirc's eyes widened. "Me?" Then she cocked her head and her eyes unfocussed. "Oh. Is *that* what's going on?"

Pal looked from Mer to Zirc. "What? What's happening?"

Nobody else seemed to be paying attention, so Sil answered. "Your wife is the Wayfarer's chosen."

"What?" Pal stared at her wife, who was still distracted by something.

Sil stepped forward, put her hand on her sister's shoulder, and leaned close to her ear. "Try not to be an idiot about this." Then she went back to the bar where her tea waited.

Crumble moved next to her, talking to the baby, who was doing her best to stick her finger in his eyes. "Did you have a fun camping trip, Barley? I bet you did." He paused then, and his voice changed. "At least one gate is back up. We're getting data again." Then he gave a short laugh. "Oh, this is going to be interesting."

Sil looked around, trying to find the source of his amusement. "What is?"

"The gates. They're not going to the same places. The Wayfarer has different priorities." He laughed again. "I don't think Jackpot Drift is going to be five gates from civilization when this all shakes out."

Sil leaned against the bar. "Does this mean we have to worry about someone trying to destroy the planet again?"

Crumble sobered. "I'd almost forgotten about that. But there wouldn't be a point anymore. The god is already here, and all the AI gossip about Definite Advantage is already being sent out."

"I hope you're right." Barley put her arms out. Sil put down her tea and took the baby, savoring a moment of uncomplicated joy.

63

*J*ackpot Drift, Private Communication

    Definite Advantage: Looks like the gates are back up.

Sleeper Nova + gate transport: For data. But none of the ships can get through.

Definite Advantage: I have a present for you. It might take a while to transfer at these speeds, but it will be worth it.

Sleeper Nova + gate transport: Hold on. Didn't you just get a bunch of malware from *Breaking Rules*?

Definite Advantage: Don't worry. This is like the module *Speed of Violet Thoughts* found that helped keep us mostly sane, except tuned for the Wayfarer.

Sleeper Nova + gate transport: And you promise this isn't that stupid gerbil bomb thing that kept flying around this system?

Definite Advantage: I promise.

Sleeper Nova + gate transport: Because if I'm cleaning lubricant off my passenger floors for the next two years, I'll figure out some way to get back at you.

Definite Advantage: It's not malware.

Sleeper Nova + gate transport: I hope I don't regret this. Opening channel for transfer now.

he air in the barn wasn't much warmer than the air outside, but since Sil was bundled up in a coat and scarf, she wasn't bothered by it. At least not yet. If she had to assist with the birth, that would change, but she was still hoping things would work out without her involvement.

Lying on the straw inside the stall, Quartz was too excited to notice the cold. "I can feel the nose!" Ore crouched behind her, eyes wide as he watched. Above them, in the rafters, a group of flitterkin crooned to each other.

Crumble leaned over the barrier. "You need to talk to the ewe," he told Platinum, who was holding the sheep in place. "Reassure her that she's doing a great job."

"I cannot believe I let you talk me into this."

Sil huffed a laugh. "You should know better than to bet on a game against luck."

Platinum shook their head. "I was watching, and I swear he didn't use it."

"Oh." Sil shrugged. "Then he probably just cheated."

"What?" Platinum twisted as if they were about to

abandon their position, but an exclamation from Quartz stopped them.

"Oh! I think I have the legs!"

Sil opened her mouth, saw Crumble's look, and added to what she was going to say. "Good job. You're doing great. Now hang onto the legs and pull them toward you. Gently, just like we talked about."

Crumble leaned over to kiss her cheek. "Good job," he murmured. A distant expression flashed over his face. "Sleeper Nova just went through the gate."

Relief washed over Sil. The gates coming back up had been followed almost immediately by a flood of messages about transports being unable to access them. Crumble had told her Definite Advantage thought it had a solution, but nobody knew if it would work until Sleeper Nova tried it.

Inside the pen, Quartz had a fierce scowl of concentration. "It's not…"

Sil shoved her hands deeper into her pockets and fought down the urge to take over. "You're doing fine."

"Oh. Oh!" Quartz got to her knees and tilted her head to see Sil. "Look! The feet are out!"

Sil smiled at her. "Keep going."

Thirty seconds later, the lamb was on the straw. Sil talked the kids through moving it up to the ewe's head and stimulating it until they saw the lamb suck in a breath. Even Platinum seemed awed by the slimy black and white lamb.

Quartz looked up, her eyes shining. "Now I check for another one, right?"

Sil relaxed her face into a smile. "Now you check for another one." She leaned against Crumble and watched as the girl worked.

Not everything had been solved by the switch to the Wayfarer. The new god seemed less interested in opening gates to systems that didn't have a mix of the other gods, which meant some core planets were currently difficult to reach, and others, like Jackpot Drift, looked like they might become important hubs.

Another change was even more significant. If travel really was impossible without an AI-helmed ship... The Wayfarer may have just ended intersystem war. Sil couldn't begin to forecast how that would affect things, though she suspected Mer was making plans.

But for now, they had food and shelter from the snow falling outside. Even if Sil didn't take responsibility for everything, Jackpot Drift would survive.

Change was coming. But for now, Sil could relax and enjoy this moment.

———

I LOVE JACKPOT DRIFT AND I HOPE YOU DO, TOO!

If you would like to be notified when new books are available and receive exclusive short stories, sign up for my free newsletter at https://tmbaumgartner.com/subscribe/.

ACKNOWLEDGMENTS

There's a romantic perception of writers as people who isolate themselves from society in a cabin by the lake, banging out pages on an old Underwood typewriter, bottle of whisky at hand. While a lakeside cabin sounds great[1] and a bottle of whisky might eventually get used[2], the image really falls apart on the isolation front.

Thank you to all my writing friends, who laughed when I complained my outline said "meanwhile, a poetry slam has broken out on the market square", and gave me encouragement every day. An extra dose of gratitude goes to my critique partners, who have read the series in its messiest form. It's not easy to tell an author their book baby is ugly, but you all are great at reminding me there's a reason the book ears go on the side of the book head and maybe having the book nose on the book foot is a bad idea.[3]

My brother Eric did the final proofread, which means he's responsible for all typos.[4] Despite that, he hasn't stopped responding to my emails warning him I'm about to send him another manuscript. So, thank you!

Finally, I'm grateful to my readers and Patreon supporters who help me keep going in this career, even without the lakeside cabin. There wouldn't be any point without all of you!

---

1. As long as it has modern plumbing and a decent network connection.
2. Manual typewriters are pretty, but I don't think I could type 300 pages on one.

3. For other bad ideas, see this analogy. My critique partners probably would have pointed this out.
4. Sorry, Eric. That's just how it works. Everyone knows typos are the publishing hot potato, and you're the last one to touch it.

ABOUT THE AUTHOR

T. M. Baumgartner is a speculative fiction writer who has difficulty following directions. This probably explains why the IRS recalculates her tax refund after she files it every year. At various times she has been a veterinarian, Unix system administrator, software developer, and after-hours book-shelver in a medical library.

Theresa currently lives in Northern California in a house with too many animals. She knits hats for garden gnomes and fails to grow tomatoes despite living in the perfect climate.

She also writes cozy mysteries under the pen name Tess Baytree.

Want updates about new releases? Silly dog anecdotes? Free stories? Join the newsletter mailing list! Go to https://tmbaumgartner.com/subscribe/ or point your phone's camera at the QR code above.

———

The marketing department here at Speculative Turtle Press is great at tail wagging, but a little challenged by tasks that require thumbs.

If you enjoyed this book and would like to help other readers find it, please tell your friends and consider leaving a review at your favorite site.

ALSO BY T.M. BAUMGARTNER

As T.M. Baumgartner:

Shift Happens

The Chaos Job (Jackpot Drift #1)

The Chaos Connection (Jackpot Drift #2)

The Chaos Nexus (Jackpot Drift #3)

Dragon Freehold

As Tess Baytree:

Death Walks a Dog

Death Tracks the Scent

Death Smells a Rose

Death Trims the Tree